DESTINATION MAISIE

MEL FRANCES

mb books

Copyright © 2023 by – Mel Frances – All Rights Reserved.
It is not legal to reproduce, duplicate, or transmit any part of this document in either electronic means or printed format. Recording of this publication is strictly prohibited.

Destination Maisie is a work of fiction, although inspired by real events, the characterisation and narrative are entirely fictitious and purely a product of the author's imagination.

This book is dedicated to the memory of Florence, my lovely Mam. Thank you for showing me the ways of compassion and acceptance. Miss you x

'I am her child, and that is better than being the child of anyone else in the world.' Maya Angelou.

CHAPTER 1

April 1976

Dance classes and music lessons were fine, but deportment and elocution sessions bored Maisie to tears. She offered up a luxurious yawn as she lay on her bed practicing vowel sounds. Mid-yawn, she burped loudly then giggled, her foster brothers would be proud of that. A fortnight ago, on the second of April 1976, Maisie turned sixteen, and was growing into a stunning young woman. Her skin glowed a deep golden brown following a recent Mediterranean holiday, and her long, sleek brunette hair perfectly framed her dark brown eyes. Maisie heard her foster mother, Lizzie Blossom's voice from downstairs.

'Are you ready, Maisie?' Lizzie said excitedly at the foot of the curved stairway, which led into a large hallway.

Maisie rolled her eyes, as she rolled off the bed, and reluctantly padded downstairs, humming the tune to *Dancing Queen*, she loved that song, it sounded exciting and exotic. ABBA was her favourite band, she longed to sing like Agnetha or Anni-Frid, she didn't mind which.

'Come now, let's see that lovely smile, shoulders back.' Lizzie flounced away, and Maisie followed, distraught at the thought of parading around the department store fashion salon, in a variety of outfits. The middle-aged women would *hum* and *hah*, whilst manipulating clothing around her body during their, Club Couture

1

sessions. Often Maisie would be left in her underwear, shivering, not necessarily with cold, but embarrassment, as garments were slipped on and off her body by the women who proceeded to fuss and cluck about colour, shape, fabric, and so on.

Maisie darted back upstairs. 'Wait! I need my robe.'

A kindly store assistant in attendance at a recent fashion session, bought the robe from the lingerie department and gave it to Maisie, so she could at least shield herself from the shame of exposure. Their eyes met on the occasion the assistant handed the pale lemon, lace-edged satin robe to Maisie, with a mutual understanding of their useful, but superficial placement within this upmarket feminine society. Maisie never forgot to take her robe with her, the comfort blanket she could hide behind.

Maisie reached the foot of the stairs and soon they set off for the thirty-minute drive south into the city of London. As the car left the lengthy driveway, Maisie gazed back at the house, the diamond shaped leaded windows with their dark wooden frames disappeared into the distance. She wished with all her heart she could return to the house and spend the afternoon playing board games with her foster brother, in the small summerhouse where they'd stay all afternoon.

She put her hand inside the pocket of her rust-coloured dungaree pinafore dress, and scratched gently but rhythmically at the ribbed corduroy material. On this cool April day, Maisie insisted upon wearing this favourite mini-dress, coupled with a polo-neck top and tights. She was concealed in this outfit. She convinced Lizzie she hadn't time to change, with the intention of avoiding the floral ensemble her foster mother had suggested. Lizzie often commented about her tom-boyish looks whenever she appeared in jeans.

'Walk tall Maisie, that's it, head high, chin up, we don't want to see droopy shoulders do we?' Lizzie said as Maisie paraded in front of the women, having changed into a mint green flouncy peasant-style maxi dress with huge puffed sleeves. It restricted her chest, now that she had begun to take on her womanly form. Maisie felt as though she couldn't breathe; she was stifled by the dress, and the women.

'She's so beautiful, Lizzie,' declared one woman, 'you must be so proud of the way she has … blossomed.' The women inevitably chuckled at the play on words.

The praise was all about Lizzie Blossom, and her altruistic motivation to present this beautiful object she had created and moulded, living vicariously through Maisie's life. None of the women knew Maisie, or even really saw her, only her looks and potential future fame.

Maisie kept her gaze lowered until she was instructed again to, *'look up, smile, shoulders back.'* She believed if any of the women could make eye contact, they would see her truth inside, which would reveal her deepest insecurities and vulnerability. Maisie was increasingly less enamoured with her privileged life. Her two eldest foster brothers were working in London, and foster dad, Bertie was abroad; they were home only for sporadic periods. Maisie adored Christmas, birthdays, and their family holiday when they were all together, but it was a long time in between these fun annual events.

Every six months, a welfare worker arrived to assess her progress in care. Maisie was tiptoeing along the upstairs hallway and overheard part of a conversation emanating from the unclosed door. She halted, crept forward, then crouched down at the top of the stairs behind the balustrade spindles and listened intently.

'I don't think we can accommodate that. It wouldn't be fair on her,' said Lizzie.

'Well …' the young welfare worker hesitated, 'we often find it can be positive for young people to know their birth mother has made contact.'

Maisie was stunned; hearing anything that may reveal her past was thrilling, as Lizzie would only offer vague information about the circumstances.

'Really? I'm not so sure it would work for Maisie. She's settled now, and doing so well. She's getting good academic results, and her music lessons are coming along a treat.'

'Does she ever ask about her birth mother, Ellen? Or … perhaps show any curiosity about why she lives here?'

'Hm, she used to, as I think she was confused at first, but no … no, she's never mentioned anything for years.'

Maisie flinched at the top of the stairs; she was incensed, she had kept asking but was always rebuffed. She had gleaned a little from Bertie, but guessed he was under strict instruction not to reveal anything identifying, and would skillfully distract her. She was furious at these adults making life decisions she had no possession of, or influence over.

'We met her birth mother Ellen years ago; you know that don't you?'

The welfare worker replied, 'yes, I saw in the notes you agreed to a meeting with Ellen a year after Maisie came here, when she was seven.'

'It went pretty well, we felt it was the least we could do to let the woman know Maisie was healthy. She played in the park whilst we chatted.'

'Ellen must've found that quite difficult, not to communicate with her daughter, or have a hug. It can be very heal—'

'The woman gave her up don't forget!' retorted Lizzie. 'We've done everything possible for the girl, and now *she* wants to come back and take credit, I don't think so.'

'Mrs Blossom we totally appreciate everything you're doing for Maisie, truly we do. Anyway, here is the letter from Ellen. Please keep it safe, and if you feel you can share it with Maisie at any point, I will be glad to visit and help her understand what happened in her early years. There must be times she is confused.'

Maisie, still crouching at the top of the stairs, assumed her foster mum reluctantly snatched whatever correspondence was being handed to her.

Lizzie became conciliatory. 'I've booked a screen test with a theatrical and cinema agent next week. It's all so exciting, Maisie is thrilled she can't wait,' Lizzie said with a flourish of her hand,

DESTINATION MAISIE

'the professional photographic portfolio I arranged has certainly paid off.'

If only Maisie could have witnessed the welfare worker's shoulders slump as she acquiesced, she was getting nowhere with Lizzie; Bertie had always been gentle and easier to converse with. Maisie was not at all thrilled, the screen test was her worst nightmare.

The door opened, 'Maisie darling where are you? Your welfare worker is here.'

Maisie recoiled, then stood and composed herself immediately with a nonchalant air, controlling the internal tremors of anger, and frustration at the gatekeepers of her life history. The poise she learnt during deportment lessons had come in handy on this occasion. Maisie couldn't concentrate during the session with the worker. Her eyes betrayed the smile, darting around the room; she tried to use laser vision to look into Lizzie's handbag resting beside her, and behind cushions, vainly searching for a hint of an envelope; maybe she'd hidden it between books on the bookcase. Where was Ellen's letter?!

Maisie was fearful Lizzie might destroy it, not knowing where the letter was made her ill. She hoped Lizzie would keep it for Bertie to read, they usually shared what was happening in their lives, but he was abroad. Lizzie may even post the letter overseas to him, and it could get lost. Maisie was anxious, yet vigilant whenever they went to the post office; she kept her radar engaged, and had peeped inside Lizzie's handbag when it had been safe to do so. It was driving her crazy; there was a letter, in her mother's handwriting, maybe asking questions about her, or giving information about herself and her life. It was torture not knowing.

On her best behaviour for days afterwards, Maisie giving no hint she had heard the conversation. She was, *as good as gold*. All Maisie had of her mother Ellen was a blurry photo; she looked about twenty, with her name Ellen Simpson written on the reverse. It must have been taken when she met with the Blossoms, but she had no other identifying details and didn't know how to find her.

Maisie racked her brain and recalled details from the clandestine conversation she overheard. Lizzie had asked if she, presumably Ellen, still lived in Manchester. A place called Sinton, Maisie thought she heard the welfare worker state. She preserved these memories clearly. She had an idea and dashed into the study, she looked for Sinton as she scoured Bertie's huge yellow A to Z road atlas. This wouldn't seem unusual to Lizzie as it had been a regular activity for Maisie and her brothers to look for funny, and rude-sounding streets and places when they were younger. They would roar with laughter when they spotted them; Backside Lane in Doncaster, Fanny Avenue in Sheffield, Great Cockup in the Lake District, and Happy Bottom in Dorset being a few of her brothers' favourites. Maisie couldn't help but find them herself in the well-thumbed atlas, with a satisfying smirk on her face.

Maisie determined Ellen's location must be Swinton, as Sinton didn't exist. It tore her apart, why didn't they tell her? She vowed to find Ellen. She asked her foster parents about Ellen a few weeks after the welfare visit when Bertie had returned home, attempting to be blasé. Lizzie was taken aback, and Bertie replied they had no more information about her mother. Maisie never knew whether Bertie was privy to Ellen's letter or not and could hardly ask. If he did know, she would try to glean the information when they were alone, but they rarely were these days. Then he'd be gone again.

Maisie feigned illness with menstrual stomach cramps one afternoon, saying she couldn't possibly go to dance classes, predicting Lizzie would still meet up with her friends for afternoon tea. As soon as the front door closed, Maisie leapt downstairs and began riffling through papers in the dark wood-panelled study drawers; in the large kitchen, skirting around the deep square earthenware basins to look in all the cupboards and the pantry. But no, she thought, this wouldn't be a good hiding place. She was becoming frantic; only one and a half hours to scour the huge dwelling. She pulled dining room cupboards open, and searched the living room library bookcase, but nothing.

Tentatively, Maisie crept upstairs and went into the master bedroom, nervously and meticulously replacing every object as she looked in drawers, cupboards, wardrobes, everywhere. She spied several hat boxes on top of Lizzie's vast wardrobe. She grabbed the chair from Lizzie's dresser, reached up, and gently lifted each box into her arms, cautiously lifting the lid and peering inside. She had a feeling; she somehow knew the letter would be in one of the boxes.

Some had hats in them, though Lizzie rarely wore hats these days; one box had photographs inside, and another had official documents. Maisie calmed her anxiety, resisting the temptation to drag everything from the top of the wardrobe and fling the contents around the room until she found the letter. She came upon a summer bonnet printed with bright multicoloured fruits, adorned with a lavish red ribbon, which she popped on her head.

'What on earth is she keeping this monstrosity for? Like wearing a fruit salad … it's gross.' She replaced the box in its place and continued searching.

In the smallest penultimate box, amongst other papers, she saw a small cream envelope, with neat blue ink writing. With hands trembling, she read Ellen's words, sitting cross-legged on the floor, tears rolling down her cheeks. She discovered Ellen did indeed live in Swinton. She was married with three daughters and was sending her love to Maisie Florence, writing both her names, hoping she was happy, and asked meekly if she could please see her again. Ellen wrote about the enclosed photograph, showing her sisters' names and ages. There was no photograph; Maisie was devastated. Had Lizzie destroyed it? She scrabbled around in the box in case it had fallen out of the envelope, but no joy. She settled to read the letter over again.

The only sound in the room, was the regular soft tick of the oscillating torsion pendulum, inside the glass-domed gold anniversary clock on Lizzie's dresser. Maisie jumped as it suddenly chimed, as loud as a church bell clanging! She turned in fright, rigid, staring at the tiny golden globes spinning to and fro. The gentle tick resumed but was amplified in the eerie silence. It was four o'clock, Lizzie would be back within half an hour. Maisie scarpered to her room, grabbed a pencil and pad and copied every last word, comma, and full stop from Ellen's letter, re-checking the address four times. Her hands were shaking uncontrollably as she kissed Mrs Ellen Clarke's signature and carefully placed the envelope back in the box, returning it to the exact position on top of the wardrobe.

Maisie was about to replace the chair in its rightful place at the dresser, then caught sight of herself in the full-length mirror; the fruity bonnet was still on her head. She heard a door open downstairs! Surely it wasn't Lizzie back so soon. Maisie's heart was thumping, and her hands shook as she took off the bonnet, desperately trying to remember which box it was in. Maybe she should hide it in her room, but no, that would not do at all; she couldn't risk it.

'Hello Mrs Blossom, it's only me.'

It was Jane, the housekeeper announcing her arrival downstairs. Maisie heaved a sigh of relief, hearing Jane chuntering her way toward the kitchen. A look at the clock, it was twenty past four, she needed to act quickly. Was it the yellow hat box, Maisie decided yes, a garish box for a garish hat. Once the fruity bonnet was back in its box, she placed the chair in front of the dresser, ensuring the indents the feet had made in the carpet exactly fitted, so nothing looked amiss.

Maisie swept her discerning eyes around the bedroom, and caught sight of Lizzie's fox fur collar. It's limp limbs and ginger bushy tail flopped over the armchair in the corner. It's taxidermied amber and black, glass-beaded eyes stared at her in an accusatory manner; it knew she had been up to no good. It had once been a real live fox; she hated the, vile dead thing. When Lizzie was out, her brothers used to sneak into the bedroom, grab it and chase Maisie around the house and garden with it. At first when she was small, she would cry, cower and run away from their taunts. Later on, she could almost out-run all of them with her long legs and swift pace. She stuck her tongue out at the sinister deceased fox.

Ensuring absolutely nothing looked out of place, she tip-toed out of the room, clicking the bedroom door shut. Maisie went into her room, laid face down on her bed, and cried; she couldn't stop crying with frustration, anxiety, and anger, yet happiness. Maisie had three sisters, and her mother had not forgotten about her; Maisie now knew where she belonged. She didn't find it difficult to act as the obedient, dutiful, happy foster child. The glowing secret she held inside her chest, knowing her birth mother Ellen wanted to meet her, filled her heart with joy. Over the next few months, Maisie hatched a plan.

CHAPTER 2

Summer 1969

Maisie was placed with The Blossoms in 1966 when she was six years old. She had been with them three years when, on a glorious summer day, Bertie Blossom called for her, as he did every summer, to go fishing. 'Are you coming out on the lake?'

'Of course!' replied the olive-skinned, leggy nine-year-old galloping along the hallway. Her tousled dark hair flowing and bouncing, as she leapt down the outside steps and ran with abandon across the lawn.

'Whoa, Flossie! Don't forget the picnic,' Bertie shouted. He sometimes chose the derivative of her middle name as a term of endearment, gently poking fun at her, knowing she would admonish him with her usual retort.

Maisie darted back into the house yelling, 'it's Florence, not Flossie!' and briefly flung her arms around her beloved foster dad, then dashed off to the storeroom for the baskets and rods. She was never interested in preparing the food, and would plead with the housekeeper, Jane, to complete the task; Maisie could wind Jane around her little finger. After a ten-minute drive, they arrived at the lake. On the boat Maisie was grappling with a fly, tying it to the end of her line; she pricked her finger and gazed trance-like at the oozing bright red fluid.

Bertie noticed her disquiet. 'You okay Flossie?' No response.

Maisie stated in monotone, 'I was smacked when this happened when I was learning to sew, because I got blood on the material.' She visibly shrank into herself, holding out her bloodied finger, hand shaking.

'The nuns?'

Maisie nodded submissively. Bertie became used to these moments of her inverted terror, and his heart melted for his bright, breezy, beautiful foster daughter. How could they be so harsh as to physically chastise those little ones. Bertie suffered himself from his time during conflict. The insidious traumatic flashbacks crept upon him whenever they chose, taking all of his resolve to calmly suppress the images. Maisie was only a child and he needed to help her cope with her own dark, frightening memories.

Bertie retrieved the small green first aid box from his fishing bag, and gently wrapped a sticking plaster around Maisie's finger, first wiping it with some yellow strong-smelling iodine. The placebo effect of the scent comforted her, and he knew about keeping injuries free from infection, to prevent the gangrenous mess that could form in wounds if not treated swiftly. He rested his hand on hers momentarily, which was enough reassurance. Maisie had been his solace post conflict; he was one of the unlucky ones, sent to Korea in the early 1950s in support of the USA. Maisie helped him heal with her affection, and abundant free-thinking imagination.

The smell of jasmine floated around as the boat rippled and bobbed on the calm lake in the hot sunshine. As the happy pair waited for a bite, Maisie would create stories of scary deep-water creatures.

'Oh no! The water-dragons are coming for us.' Maisie began.

'We must enlist the help of the brave tree-warriors!' Bertie exclaimed with military intonation.

Maisie thrilled at the adventure they were about to create, imagining the trees on the shoreline uprooting themselves, wading raggedly and steadfastly toward them.

'We'll have to wake the lake-nymphs, we need their magic powers.' She placed her hands elbow deep in the water and stirred frantically, giggling, creating ripples of glinting sunshine reflecting in her face. Bertie looked on enthralled by her creativity. His sons never had the imagination; yes, they inhabited characters of soldiers, cowboys, and pilots, tearing around the garden during play, but they were limited when it came to the plot.

Maisie's initial night terrors shocked both him and Lizzie, with distressed howls, hands firmly placed over her face. *'The Bats! No, please no!'* The black-winged flutterers he knew represented the nuns. Only Bertie could reassure her at first, and would inwardly shudder, wondering how things could have turned out, had she been left vulnerable to unsafe men.

Lizzie, the authoritative matriarch in the family, would admonish Maisie when she returned from playing with the boys, and her clothing was grubby, grass-stained or worse, torn. Maisie observed her brothers receiving sanctions for wrongdoing; mowing the lawn, polishing boots, cleaning the car, or chopping wood. She, however, would be asked to sit quietly and think about what she had done. The black bats would be hanging there, waiting in the dark night to swoop down and punish her for every mistake.

Bertie often intervened, making light of Lizzie's scolding; though his compassion stretched towards his wife too, he understood her need for female companionship, for beauty, for all that was pretty and fragrant. The best times were when Maisie helped Lizzie in the garden, he enjoyed observing the older female educating the enthusiastic younger one. This is when they were at their most content.

Bertie had suggested becoming Maisie's legal guardian, however, there was always a reticence with Lizzie, so it was never mentioned again.

Four years later in the summer of 1973, Elizabeth Blossom was sitting at her Louis Phillipe dressing table, looking at her reflection in the triple mirrors. The spindly table legs seemed to bow under the weight of copious lotions, potions and perfumes placed on mirrored trays; hairbrushes, clips, and other cosmetic paraphernalia filled the table top. Lizzie angled the two-sided mirrors so she could view her profile on each side. No-one knew exactly how old Lizzie was, but she knew she was approaching forty-five, and becoming concerned that age was catching up with her. The face that stared back at her, showed the gathering of loosening skin around her eyes and jowls. Lizzie tilted her head backwards so the light from her tiffany lamp reflected upwards, diminishing the darker circles now showing around her eye sockets. The lighting effect also caught the sparkling silver hairs emerging at her temples. Lizzie was careful not to over-extend the pose, which would look too obvious to the ladies at the salon; they knew the illusion she was trying to create; she needed to perfect this look.

The Blossoms were preparing to celebrate their wedding anniversary. Tapping the back of her hand under her chin, Lizzie exclaimed. 'Good God, Bertram! I'm getting a double chin.'

Her unsuspecting husband was removing his pants and jumped at his wife's raised voice using his full name, believing another admonishment was coming his way. 'Elizabeth, you're as beautiful as the day I met you all those years ago my darling.' He meant it, he was devoted to his wife since the day they met when she was a pretty twenty-year-old receptionist in the office, and he was the handsome army officer who fell deeply in love with her.

Lizzie was indeed a beauty, with classic English rose features; sparkling blue eyes, cupid's bow lips and a clear skin tone. She longed for a daughter, a girl in her image she could shower her affection upon, and raise her to adore everything pretty and feminine. She would take her imaginary daughter to dance classes, and she would become a prima ballerina, or maybe even a movie star. Lizzie longed for the glamour, but a baby girl was not to be, and on the birth of her third son, she hid her disappointment well, knowing her dreams would not come to fruition. The difficult forceps birth and toxaemia in pregnancy almost killed her. She required a blood transfusion and a month's stay in hospital to recover from the trauma of giving birth for the third time. 'How is Maisie doing, she seems out of sorts these days?' pondered Bertie.

'Must be teenage stuff, she's never been the same since she hit thirteen. Won't do this, doesn't like that, she's rather obnoxious. The boys were never like this.'

'She has a lot to be confused about, and her body will be going through changes too; it's not straightforward for her.'

'The only time she's ever happy is tumbling around with the boys, or when you take her fishing, and goodness knows what else. Quite the tomboy, but so beautiful.'

Lizzie gazed at her ageing reflection and again longed for the youth that was denied her because of her own family's military life; moving from town to town; never settling in one place until she married Bertie, who in time took a position based predominantly in England. Lizzie desperately wanted to project her own charm and charisma upon Maisie and lead her to a lucrative career, but Maisie was resistant, to Lizzie's utter frustration. 'Sometimes I feel she's quite ungrateful, after all we've done for her.'

'Do you remember those big, sad brown eyes when we first met her.' Bertie chuckled. 'The nuns had them all lined up and were encouraging her to smile and be pleasant … but she was having none of it.'

'I have never seen such a beautiful child in all my life, she quite took my breath away. I knew immediately we could make something of her. She really stood out amongst the rest, honestly, some of them looked nothing more than street urchins.'

'That's because most of them were,' added Bertie wistfully. 'I hope she's happy here. Losing her adoptive mother must've been such a blow, and to be returned to an orphanage by the adoptive family is quite inexcusable.' Bertie shook his head.

'Maisie won't have remembered her, she died when she was only three. We've done everything for her, good schools, dancing and music lessons, holidays in Europe, and teaching her about the finer things in life. I do wish she had more interest in couture. There's a fashion show at the Palais Ballroom, and the manageress has insisted Maisie attends for deportment lessons before modelling on stage. It's never too young to learn, but she sits there looking completely bored. She wants to stop going to ballet, and to be honest, she is becoming rather too gangly, but perfect for modelling as she's tall and slim; I keep an eye on her weight too.'

Bertie was sheepish. 'I truly don't think she is ready for fashion shows, Lizzie my love. Let her have another year of being a child. Our Maisie still prefers playing with her brothers, but that may change. I find it extraordinary she still joins me out on the lake, but it does calm her down somehow.' Bertie beamed.

Lizzie gave an exasperated snort. 'She needs to calm down alright, when she's leaping about when the boys are playing guitar. Who is it … Zed Neplin or something? Terrible racket! I wish she'd liven-up like that, especially when I take her to deportment and elocution lessons, she looks so fed up.'

Bertie laughed. 'It's Led Zeppelin,' then thoughtfully, 'our eldest needs a haircut soon, they're probably not keen on the hippie look at his university.' He appeased his wife, suggesting, 'Maisie should probably go along to observe at first, we don't want her looking silly if she doesn't get it right.'

He knew exactly how to get around these discussions; Lizzie wouldn't want to feel humiliated if Maisie got it wrong, as it would reflect upon her. Bertie was pleased he won this round; Lizzie conceded Maisie would not be part of the fashion show this year.

The Sunday after the anniversary celebrations, the Blossoms attended church. Bertie felt Maisie's hand tighten around his, and he noticed her stiffen as they approached the ominous building every week. Her imploring eyes cut through him as they left her after the service at Sunday School. Their youngest son had ceased religious lessons, and Maisie would be left there alone, feeling unsafe without the protection of her brothers.

'Do … do I really have to stay for Sunday School?' Maisie asked, nervously.

'Of course, you have another year before you finish,' replied Lizzie, overriding any response from Bertie.

Maisie's shoulders slumped. 'But I can be more useful doing chores around the house. We can get some new plants for the garden, and I'll work hard to make it look beautiful.'

Bertie intervened defying his wife, despite her sharp glance his way. 'You know, I think we can find something you'll enjoy, you *have* grown out of Sunday School.'

Like the six-year-old she was when she joined the family, Maisie skipped alongside Bertie, gripping his hand. A suitable philanthropic activity was found, helping out every Sunday tending the gardens at the nearby Windmill Hills residential home for elderly persons. She threw herself with gusto into the, *Plant-a-Tree in 73,* campaign, a response to a virulent strain of Dutch Elm Disease killing forests in swathes. Several saplings were planted in the grounds, and a healthy silver birch specimen was named the, *Maisie Blossom Birch,* in her honour by the residents.

Maisie had an affinity with nature, at her happiest covered in soil, hair piled up in a ponytail, tending the garden in her brothers' hand-me-down overalls. She was overjoyed when someone's dog would bound up to lick her face when walking in the park. Bertie often caught sight of her gazing at the sky, watching the hurried, fluttering flight of a single tiny bird, or flocks of larger birds floating high on thermals. She was spellbound watching a starling murmuration in the distance beyond the woodland near their home. Bertie sensed her desire for freedom, as did he at times.

Several weeks after Maisie was established as a regular volunteer at Windmill Hills; Lizzie Blossom was grooming in her three-way mirror, scooping up and applying copious amounts of thick night cream from a huge pale pink pot on the dresser.

'Maisie always plays up when the welfare worker comes around to check on her progress,' she said.

'She probably feels nervous in case she's going to be sent away if she doesn't behave, or that we won't want her here any longer. It's like someone swooping into the house every six months to determine whether you stay or go. Must feel awful,' said Bertie.

Lizzie never quite understood the precarious, temporary existence Maisie sensed, that she was disposable and could, at a moment's notice, be packed off elsewhere. She had to be, *as good as gold*. Part of Maisie's inability to trust, was that every mother had abandoned her up to now.

'Why on earth would she think that? Don't be ridiculous Bertie, surely by now, she knows she's here for good.'

Chapter 3

The bi-annual child welfare visits continued until the revelation of Maisie's, mother's letter in 1976. Every Sunday evening thereafter, once she was settled in bed, Maisie read her copy of Ellen's letter. For almost six months, she had secreted her allowance in a box under her bed, as she no longer bought the cosmetics and clothes Lizzie encouraged her to when out shopping. She was meticulously planning her escape. Maisie reconciled that she would miss Bertie and her brothers, but would definitely not miss the next stage of the auditions Lizzie had planned, after the excruciating experience of the first screen test she had endured. Lizzie was determined she could be famous, but Maisie couldn't think of anything worse. She hated exposure.

Christmas, Easter, and Maisie's seventeenth birthday on the second day of April 1977 had come and gone. Bertie and the eldest two boys were working in the city, and were rarely home. The youngest brother had started university, and was living in halls of residence. It was isolating being home alone, but Maisie remained compliant; she was doing well continuing her education at the local secondary school. She had a few friends whom Lizzie approved of, who would call round to watch videos, listen to music, and watch *Top of the Pops*, a weekly treat. The boys who used to call round no longer did since her foster brothers were away; it wasn't encouraged either. Lizzie was over-protective of Maisie, who only had one boyfriend, which didn't last, as he wasn't from a respectable family. She was occasionally allowed to meet a few girls at the Wimpy Burger Bar in town under strict curfew conditions.

Lizzie was meeting with her ladies clubs more often, leaving Maisie alone in the house to complete homework, improve her needlework, read books, and practice piano. For months, Maisie clocked the housekeeper's hours and meticulously timed Lizzie's regular afternoons out. In those three and a half hours, Maisie could be on her way to Manchester.

Leaving day arrived. As soon as Lizzie left the house, Maisie slid the small, solid brown suitcase from under her bed she'd filled with items and clothing she may need. Maisie didn't need to double-check; she had done so every week. She went into the master bedroom, carefully lifted the hatbox containing Ellen's letter, and took it, placing it carefully in her bag.

It was a cool spring day, so she chose to wear her sturdy walking shoes and winter coat. Maisie had acquired lots of cosmetics during her visits to the department stores, and had learnt about making up her face from the ladies who prepped her for those modelling sessions. She gave an extra flick to the black eyeliner, then applied copious cake mascara with the tiny brush dampened with spit, adding pale sugar-pink lipstick to finish the look. She needed to make herself look older than her seventeen years to fend off any questions about her age. Taking one last look at herself in the bedroom mirror; from her sturdy brown shoes, her fitted double-breasted military-style maxi coat with gold buttons, up to her long straight dark hair, and pale face with heavily made-up, dark eyes staring back at her.

Maisie displaced any thoughts of the devastation her leaving may cause her foster family, especially Bertie, he was the only one who could have persuaded her to stay, but he was not here.

'He's never here!' she said angrily, wiping black mascara tears from her face staring into the mirror. She used all of her inner energy, forcing the wail of abandonment not to explode, then crumble inside. Maisie checked; her purse, a pack of tissues, Ellen's letter, and a lipstick were placed in the tan leather saddle-bag that draped diagonally across her body. She picked up the jam-packed small brown suitcase and walked out of her bedroom. Maisie silently walked down the sweeping stairway, out of the front door, locking it behind her, and with swift steps, headed along the back country roads to the village rail station.

In survival mode, Maisie breathed deeply, half running to the station, where she scanned the railway timetable. She had noted routes and times for local trains to London on previous visits. A fractious ten minutes passed, nerve-endings jangling when she heard a man's voice.

'And where are you off to, Miss?' It was the railway guard smiling at her.

Maisie had practiced her response. 'Off to visit my aunt in London, she's meeting me off the train.'

'Ah, I see, going shopping are you, to those fancy big stores?'

'Erm yes that's right.' She tried to smile, hoping he didn't notice her lips quivering, grateful the guard had gifted her an explanation.

Maisie sat huddled in the corner of the shelter on the platform … waiting. She was unsure how she would get to Manchester from London, but she had Ellen's letter, which had the address written on the reverse of the envelope. She quickly checked her purse! Had she remembered to put all of her savings in there? She rummaged around and found the notes neatly folded, sighing in relief. Thoughts of a random encounter with someone the family knew flashed in her mind … how would she explain why she was at the station.

Startled! The loud dual-tone parp of the oncoming diesel train broke her reverie. She checked the seat number on her ticket yet again; she must make this look like she knew what she was doing, confidently, she walked down the carriage, but she was terrified.

Maisie began to enjoy her journey into London, though the underlying trepidation remained. She didn't make eye contact with anyone, but focused on a young mother with a baby sitting across the carriage. The train soon arrived at Paddington Station. She left the platform, looking to make sense of the rows of printed timetables behind large glass frames. She spotted the trains for Manchester among many other towns and cities. The mother and baby had drifted away, and she was isolated in a sea of men in suits, marching briskly to and fro with purpose, as were many women with shopping bags, plus some young and older couples gazing at the timetables.

Maisie consumed the noise around her; echoing voices in the huge domed station, the frantic patter of feet up and down nearby stairs. She heard a news vendor encouraging hurried passengers to make a purchase from his stall. She was accidentally shoved by someone zipping by her; it was all crowding in on her. What on earth was she doing? Her determination failed for a few moments. Maisie felt an underlying sense of uncertainty and kept looking around, expecting a police officer to be following her; or she'd imagine Bertie stepping out in front of her, looking furious, hands-on hips, taking her arm and returning her to their house. Then she remembered that Ellen wanted to see her and rallied.

Maisie tightened the grip on her case, pulled her shoulders back, and approached a pleasant looking elderly guard. She repeated her story about visiting an aunt, in Manchester this time, but had lost the note with the correct train times on it. Fortunately he was a kindly, if exasperated soul and gave her explicit instructions, where to buy her ticket for the train, and directions to the platform. She was pleased she didn't have to embark upon a journey on the scary underground.

Before they parted, he said, 'you be careful, Miss, don't go wandering off anywhere. Stay on the train in your seat, with your belongings close by, until you meet your aunt.' It was spoken with genuine care, because he knew she was lying.

Maisie had quite a while before she needed to go to her required platform, so took time wandering around the station looking at the posters adorning the walls. There was a huge one for Players cigarettes. Another was a fat businessman cartoon wearing pinstriped trousers; a black jacket, a bowler hat, and an umbrella hooked on his arm, not dissimilar to a few men she had seen strutting around the station. He was propped up against a bar, holding a glass of beer. The words, *A Double Diamond Works Wonders,* was printed in red below the image.

She picked up a magazine from outside a newsagent kiosk, and flicked through the pages. She stopped at an advertisement showing a beautiful young woman wearing an almost transparent bra, with delicate embroidered flowers over each cup. Maisie was relieved the floral embellishment covered her nipples. Written in a crescent above the model's head was, *Triumph Has the Bra for the Way You Are.* She had the terrible feeling that could have been her, half naked in a magazine, if Lizzie had her way. Deep down, Maisie knew she would have, at some point, disappointed Elizabeth Blossom.

Maisie was delighted at two movie posters expressing a desire for space sagas. One depicted two robots; one a small dome shape, the other a metallic man, beside a hairy yeti creature. Two men, and a woman with amazing dark brown eyes, with her hair curled around her ears in two buns, were holding some sort of space zapper guns. *Star Wars,* was printed in futuristic letters below. Another showed a vast starlit sky, and an empty road leading toward a blinding light in the distance. The words, *Close Encounters of the Third Kind,* were written above with; *We are not alone,* written beneath.

Maisie was intrigued and hoped her new found freedom would allow her to watch more grown-up movies than she had seen with Lizzie; full of pathetic women in old-fashioned big dresses singing about romance. They reminded her of the stupid dolls with crocheted skirts that covered toilet rolls, always had a daft bonnet on too. Thinking about bonnets reminded Maisie when she discovered Ellen's letter in Lizzie's hat box, and the guilt of absconding from her foster home flooded through her.

She shook off the feeling, headed for the platform, found her window seat on the Manchester train, and squeezed her ankles together, rigid with her suitcase between her feet. Feeling secure in her buttoned-up coat, even though it had turned into a warmer day, she gazed out of the window, feeling somewhere between exhilaration and abject fear. She kept peeping at Ellen's letter, checking it was still there, still real.

There was one station change, and Maisie was in a state of panic until she was secure in her seat on the final leg of the journey, which was largely uneventful, watching blurry towns, villages and countryside stream by. Fifteen minutes before reaching Piccadilly Station in Manchester, a young man was shiftily trying several seats; maybe he didn't have a ticket, Maisie thought. He dropped down in the seat beside her. She remained staring out of the window.

'Want a ciggy?' he rasped, holding out a pack of cigarettes. He was skinny with straggly hair that flopped in rats tails over his shoulders. His pale, watery eyes stood out from sunken eye sockets, with sallow skin. He wore a black bomber jacket over a grubby t-shirt, and his flared jeans were marked and stained. He reeked of a sweet-smelling, sickly aroma mixed with tobacco smoke. He repeated, 'hey, I'm talking to you. Do you want a ciggy?' He bellowed smoke in Maisie's face.

'No thank you.'

'Oh, a posh bird! Come up from London, eh, Lady Muck, to see what us poor northerners get up to.'

For the first time on the journey, Maisie was like a child, she did not know how to manage this. She was used to polite, courteous men and looked around for help, but everyone ignored her. A tinny tannoy announcement told her Piccadilly was the next stop.

'Excuse me, this is my stop,' she said, edging past him.

'Hah! This is everyone's stop, love, mine too.' He swept his legs into the passageway to let her by. 'Where you off to then?'

Maisie stood in the queue waiting to alight, he was right behind her. Too close. Each muscle and sinew tightened. She stepped off the train, gripping her case; he swayed alongside, trying to get her attention. Why wasn't anyone helping her, it was obvious she was being intimidated. She looked for a kindly guard, but there were none, only hordes of people going about their business ignoring her plight. Maisie was visibly shaking, nearing the exit of the station with no clue where to go. He followed, continuing to harass her. She'd had enough, Maisie turned and looked at him with venom in her eyes.

'Ooh what's up darlin'?' Don't be so—'

Maisie punched him hard in the face and ran for her life out of the station. Her foster brothers had shown her some good moves. She was used to playfighting with them; she was strong, tough, and a really fast runner, he'd never catch her. She sprinted away as he held his bloodied nose while onlookers laughed. She heard his fading profanities as he gave up the chase.

Maisie slowed to a brisk walk, turning several street corners, glancing behind every so often. She straightened to her full height and walked into a nearby upmarket department store; comfortable in this environment, she could hold herself correctly, and converse with people much older. She entered the ladies powder room, stifling her cries, sitting on the toilet lid in a cubicle. She opened her small cosmetic bag and patted her face with her powder compact, removing every trace of smeared mascara that had spilled down her face. She reapplied her lipstick and, feeling a little calmer, emerged from the cubicle, hoping no-one would notice her. Maisie sat in one of the compartments where a dozen pink velveteen seats were placed around a horseshoe of mirrors.

'You alright?' A woman asked, leaning back in that concave way a notably, heavily pregnant woman does. Her monochrome, geometric print mini dress was stretched to the limits. Her hair was piled high, revealing large, white daisy earrings, with bright egg-yolk yellow centres. The accent sounded strange, but it was a soothing voice.

'Ye … yes, thank you, but I've lost the note with the correct bus number for my aunt's house in Swinton.' Maisie's similar ruse, 'I need to get to Piccadilly bus station, I think.'

The pregnant woman knew exactly where Maisie was headed in Swinton, recognising the street, and informed her how to get there.

Maisie took the bus, as directed, but suffered anxiety throughout the journey, questioning why she had left her comfortable life. What if Ellen rejected her, after all, she hadn't suggested Maisie should come and live with her. Would Lizzie and Bertie ever forgive her, maybe they wouldn't have her back? Maisie glanced at her watch; Lizzie would know she was missing by now, probably ringing Bertie or even the police! She alighted the bus at the end of the street, stood, and said under her breath, 'oh god, what have I done.'

Maisie walked slowly down the neat, cosy street of Victorian terraced houses. She stopped, frozen in time and space, hearing children's laughter, and in the front garden of one of the modest houses, she saw three little girls playing together. A woman was sitting on the front step wearing a green paisley print dress that sat above her knees, her long limbs stretched down to her feet, encased in block heel strappy sandals.

Maisie stared at the elegant, beautiful woman with pixie-cropped fair hair; she reminded her of the actress Julie Andrews, who she knew from Lizzie's favourite movie, *The Sound of Music*. Maisie was about to turn away when the woman spoke to the children, and Maisie recognised her voice; somehow, it triggered an echo in her brain from a long distant memory. But Maisie didn't recognise her face, and thought she would instantly *know* her mother Ellen, but not understanding why that should be. Rooted to the spot, she couldn't move, holding her heavy winter coat in the crook of her elbow, wiping the beads of sweat from her forehead with the back of her hand.

The woman looked over to her and seemed to recognise her, but remained tentative. They stared at each other. Maisie thought

25

she would usher the children inside, and slam the door shut, but she didn't. The woman walked to the front gate and looked at her with curiosity. Maisie stepped forward a few paces, she couldn't take her eyes off her. The children were vying for their mother's attention, but she calmed them and opened the garden gate. Maisie kept walking toward her, not once looking away.

As Maisie drew closer, the woman asked softly, 'are you lost sweetheart, do you need help?'

There was an awkward few seconds when neither spoke or moved.

Maisie held out the letter.

The woman took the letter from her and recognised it immediately.

She was indeed Ellen Clarke, her birth mother. 'Oh, Maisie. Maisie Florence, is it really you?' Ellen put her hand to her mouth in disbelief.

Maisie offered a weak, 'yes,' with a nod. The suitcase and coat were dropped onto the ground, as they fell into each other's arms.

'I'm so sorry turning up like this, please don't be angry.' Maisie looked down, 'I shouldn't have come, your husband may be angry with me. I'm so sorry.'

Ellen was unable to speak as she sobbed. Her little ones looked up, quite amused, giggling to each other, not realising the emotional trauma they were witnessing. Ellen released Maisie and held her hand tightly; she turned to the three pretty little upturned faces and said, 'this is Maisie, I haven't seen her for such a long time.'

The youngest, petite little girl with blonde pigtails, in a broderie anglaise dress with lemon flowers bordering the hem, looked up, and gently took Maisie's other hand. 'Hello, Maisie, would you like to come and play?'

Chapter 4
March 1960

A turquoise Ford Anglia car was being buffeted along a rainy dual carriageway. Every so often, the spray of a passing vehicle would soak the windscreen. Ellen's father would activate the skinny, squeaky wipers as they furiously tried to clear the opaque vision. The March winds were howling outside. It had been a freezing, snowy winter in the early months of 1960. In the rear seat of the car, Ellen Simpson was trying to concentrate on the streaks of rain running down the window, counting how long each droplet took to reach the bottom.

Ellen's dress was stretched around her middle, she could no longer fasten the large wooden buttons on her coat. Lying across the back seat of the car, eyes tight, faking sleep, she listened to her parents' conversation. The nausea had worn off thankfully, she dared not vomit, putting her parents to any further trouble. They were good, kind people, but this … this had rocked their world.

'How is she doing?' Ellen's father asked in low tone.

'Who knows,' her mother replied.

The stilted conversations over the past few months were excruciating. They had been a content, happy, humdrum family; one of many in the quiet post-war terraced streets in their Manchester suburb. Then Manny arrived, and he certainly rocked everyone's world, at least every girl's world who came within metres of him.

He exploded onto the scene, when his foreign family came to live in the neighbourhood. He was super cool, movie-star handsome, and tall with broad shoulders. He oozed charm and sexuality. No-one had ever seen anyone like him before in their sleepy town.

Ellen thought about Manny's deep brown eyes, his warm breath on her face, the dark hairs on his olive-skinned forearms and chest that spread down his torso; her body couldn't resist him. He smelled of exotic, faraway beaches and sunshine. Even now, thoughts of his deep accented voice evoked a longing she knew she would never feel again. His touch thrilled her and awoke every sensuous nerve and fibre in her fifteen-year-old body, which was ripe for the picking. Manny's eighteen-year-old potent maleness was irresistible that evening, and the many evenings afterwards when she visited his home. His mother and sister were at work, and Ellen couldn't believe they were left unchaperoned to do as they pleased. Her parents knew nothing of their forbidden love, and believed their well-behaved dutiful daughter was visiting friends, with no reason to think otherwise.

Ellen discovered she wasn't the only one Manny romanced, but by the time she realised this heart-breaking detail, it was too late, he was never going to stay with her. It wasn't long after she told him of the pregnancy, his family immediately packed up and moved on.

Manny, Ellen mouthed his name, as his child writhed inside her. She stroked her stomach to quell the queasy feeling, and calm the undulating movement of her baby on this long journey. She tried to focus on keeping as still and silent as possible. She would think about Manny now, and after she had the baby, she would never speak his name again, and would try to forget him.

Ellen was terrified; tears squeezed out of the corners of her tightly closed eyes, and dampened the cushion her mother had laid on the back seat for her to rest on. She couldn't conceive what it would be like to push a baby out of her body. Her mother tried to explain, but embarrassment prevented her from giving any sound advice. Ellen had virtually lived inside the house since the rumours around the locality were found to be true. Some neighbours offered sympathetic smiles, others disdainful frowns.

Arriving at the mother and baby hospital was traumatic. Ellen had no idea where she was, but knew her parents would be back to pick her up and take her home, minus baby. After her first sleep-deprived night in the strange echoing dormitory, Ellen wearily unpacked her belongings. She glanced at the neat handkerchiefs, pristinely laundered clothing and underwear, soaps, and other basic toiletries, plus a notelet stationery set her mother had placed in her bag.

Ellen wrote about Manny. She recalled his family arrived in London from Greece, she couldn't remember if it was Crete or Corfu, somewhere beginning with, C. Something terrible happened to his father in London, he wouldn't say, so his mother moved the family North. This was all she knew.

Ellen wrote about living in the hospital for unmarried mothers when she had a few minutes of reflection in the evenings, lying in the uncomfortable bed on the ward, filled with the other, *fallen women,* as she heard them being referred to, and worse. They completed domestic tasks, mostly laundry taken in from wealthy families and hotels, in return for their sanctuary.

On the second of April 1960, she gave birth to a healthy baby girl. A few days after she had recovered from the birth, Ellen wrote at length about the pain of childbirth and being left alone whilst in labour. She wrote that she had looked around the assorted medicine bottles on shelves in the stark, bare delivery room, and if she could have got up, she would have taken all of the medicines so it would kill her and she could end the torture and torment of her situation, but she didn't want to harm her baby.

Ellen wrote about caring for her beautiful daughter, with whom she only spent a few weeks before having to leave her. She could barely write about the feelings of having her heart torn out as she handed her perfect Maisie Florence Simpson over for the last time.

The day Ellen's parents left her at The Queen Charlotte Hospital, her mother wept as her father supported her to their car. They drove away, and her mother turned and asked, 'did you remember to pay? I … I forgot … it was all, so … awful leaving her there.' She sobbed.

'Don't worry, I remembered to make the donation. It's going to be hard not seeing Ellen for weeks on end. Why does she have to stay there so long?'

'It's best for the baby if the mother can feed and look after it at first.'

'Seems so cruel, better to take the baby away soon as it's born, and forget it ever happened.'

'Maybe we could've …' Ellen's mother turned to her husband, but their decision had been made in the eyes of shame and God. 'I'll write to her every week to make sure she's alright.'

'It's going to be so hard for Ellen to leave the baby,' her father turned to look out of the driver side window, trying not to reveal his crumpled face to his weeping wife.

Her mother, rested a hand upon his arm, and gently patted it. He turned on the radio, and Brenda Lee's high pitched melodic voice rang out to, *Sweet Nothins*. They hardly spoke on the journey north.

CHAPTER 5
September 1980

Ellen Clarke woke one autumn morning in 1980, and went through the usual routine of organising her three daughters for school, with assistance, or one may suggest, interference from her husband, George.

Neve, the serious, studious thirteen-year-old eldest daughter, had her books at the ready and her games kit organised, calmly sipping orange juice at the kitchen table. Everything seemed to come so easily to Neve. She was, one could say, fairly ordinary; of average build, fair hair, with distinctive almond-shaped green-grey eyes, and perfect straight white teeth when she smiled, that stood out from her ordinariness.

What Neve possessed was a charming, yet forthright personality, and she appeared to take everything in her stride. Academically, Neve was near the top of the class in most subjects, and excelled in maths and science. She was so popular and gregarious not a day went by before a friend or two called in to see her, including many a prospective boyfriend, that she flippantly dismissed. Neve volunteered at a local stables; given her love of horses, and knowing the family would never be able to afford one, she mucked out the stables, fed the animals, and generally helped out, in return for a chance to ride her favourite pony, Candy, who she deeply adored.

Ellen and husband George had no concerns that Neve would get along just fine in life.

Eleven-year-old Jennifer had started high school this year. She arrived downstairs and preened in front of the full-length hall mirror, beside the seated telephone table in the hallway. Her brown hair had to be perfect; she checked every centimetre of her face, ensuring even the tiniest teenage pimple was covered with hide-the-blemish stick concealer. Her shirt and tie were neatly done up, exactly right; her patent black shoes gleamed, and she would use the adhesive lint roller to ensure each minuscule speck was removed from her blazer. She went through this ritual every day.

Ellen appreciated Jen was sensitive about her appearance and observed her endeavouring to make the effort to look the best she could. She often wished Jen would relax a little, and not worry about peer pressure. It was evident there was a little envy of the older, bright, popular sister, with the engaging personality; however, Ellen was convinced Jen would come into her own soon, even though she lacked Neve's natural, engaging personality.

Miniskirts, were still alive and kicking in 1980, and as Jen had inherited her mother's height, her legs went on forever. George was astonished at the mini-ness of Jen's skirt.

'You're surely not going to school looking like that!' Turning wide-eyed to Ellen, he spluttered, 'Ellen, goodness me, Ellen! ... she ... she can't go to school looking like that.' His head bobbing from side to side like he was watching a tennis match, between his wife's dismissive expression, and his daughter's disdainful look. His face turned a deeper pink. 'It's ... well ... that's ... well, it's ridiculous ... goodness me ... Ellen!'

Ellen popped her weary face out from behind the kitchen door, glanced down the hallway at Jen, and said, 'I've seen worse.'

She returned to the task of making sense of Alice's satchel. It contained crumpled bits of paper, an odd sock, a few bright fluffy gonk pencil toppers, four pebbles, and a squashed furry satsuma, with one of the gonks stuck to it, that must've been there for days judging from the smell. It made her feel nauseous, as she tipped the semi-liquid lump into the bin. She spread out some crumpled papers in case they were information letters for forthcoming events or school reports of some kind. They managed to make the last parent evening, they knew nothing about, by the skin of their teeth, as Alice had somehow lost the letter on the half a mile walk from school to home.

Nine-year-old Alice skipped into the kitchen, in a blaze of contrasting colours.

'Oh, what are you wearing today, Alice?' Ellen puzzled at the ensemble Alice had chosen to wear; neon lime rara skirt, orange print t-shirt, and brown lurex tights. Her hair was tied in uneven bunches with odd hair bobbles, one ladybird, one cat. She had accessorised the outfit with a plastic daisy chain belt around her middle, which she'd insisted on buying from a local discount store. This and her red patent sandals were her favourite items.

Ellen couldn't wait until Alice went to high school and had to wear a uniform. She noticed Jen's disdainful look and eye-roll at her younger sister's appearance, and was about to make some disparaging remark when she spotted Ellen's, *you dare say anything,* look. On occasions, Jen would compensate for her own low self-esteem by criticising others. Ellen knew there was a vulnerability there, however, nipped any bullying in the bud with all three girls.

Neve dashed to the radio, and Sting's dulcet tones strained out to, *Don't Stand so Close to Me.* Neve had turned the radio up full blast and was singing along. Posters of The Police, and Sting's face were plastered all over Neve's bedroom wall.

Alice recognised the song, and she grimaced, 'urrgh, it's Neve's boyfriend,' she said, swaying her head side to side and pursing her lips into a kissing shape. She began staccato chanting, 'Neve lo-oves Sti-ing, Neve lo-oves Sti-ing.' She spun around dancing, flailing her arms, and knocked her school satchel onto the floor spilling its newly organised contents.

'You little dafty.' Neve laughed with affection at her random little sister.

George piped up. 'What a flipping racket,' as he stooped to pick up the mess and place it all in a jumble on the kitchen table. 'Turn that down, Neve, I can't hear myself think!' Neve dutifully turned the radio down.

Ellen took Alice's hands, bent close to her, and told her to sit quietly and eat her cereal. Alice was affectionately named, *Dilly-Dally-Alli* by her father, who was constantly amused by Alice's detachment from reality. His youngest daughter was loving, funny, and energetic; she never knew what day it was, constantly lost her homework, gym shoes or pencil case, and was always bemused at where on earth she had put them. She dreamed her way through school, paying little attention to detail in Maths and English, however excelled at Art, Drama, and Sports.

Once the girls were bundled out of the door, and George had finally left for work, taking his outrage about Jen's mini skirt with him, Ellen sat quietly with a cup of coffee. The coffee was not satisfying at all. She checked the milk, but sniffing the top of the glass milk-bottle didn't produce the sour aroma she expected; something wasn't right. She poured the coffee away, and as she lifted the refuse bag out of the kitchen bin, she caught a whiff of pungent foisted orange, and the sight of the dead furry vole-like satsuma had her rushing to the bathroom to vomit.

Ellen recovered, and stood hands propping her up at the basin; she let the cold tap run before placing the plastic beaker beneath it. Gulping the ice-cold water, she looked in the mirrored wall-cabinet at her pasty face. She dipped the corner of a towel into the cool water, dabbing it on her forehead, cheeks, and the back of her neck. 'You look bloody dreadful,' she said to her reflection and was overcome with a deadening fatigue that drained every ounce of strength in her body. She lay on the bed, unable to raise even her little finger. Ellen recognised this overwhelming sensation; she had experienced it four times in her life. She bolstered herself, sat upright, and slowly padded down to the kitchen.

She took the wall calendar down, which was marked with full

days of activities and reminders, and tried to work out when her last period was. If her calculations were right, she could be ten weeks pregnant! Looking down at her chest, she realised why all of her blouses were popping open. The sensation of tender breasts against her underwear confirmed her thoughts, she wasn't simply putting on weight. Ellen didn't know whether to laugh or cry, and immediately rang her GP surgery to arrange a pregnancy test. She poured another glass of cold water at the kitchen sink, looked at her faint reflection in the window, and said, 'so ... another little one on the way.'

That night, as she lay in bed with George, Ellen spoke of when they would tell the girls there was another baby joining the family

'I think I may feel horribly guilty telling Maisie I'm pregnant,' said Ellen.

'Why on earth would you think that? George asked. 'She's just become a mum herself to our gorgeous granddaughter Kate.'

'I don't know, it almost feels as though I'm stealing her thunder in a way. I'd even wondered about not having this one, momentarily, to keep everything as it is now.'

'That's ridiculous,' said George, 'do you for one minute believe Maisie would think that?'

'No, of course I don't.' Ellen became emotional, 'it's just that ... she didn't have what our girls had, all the love and security, and it's all my fault.' She began crying.

'I'm sure Maisie will be thrilled to have another baby in the family. She's always been brilliant with her sisters, don't know what we'd have done without her help at times. She's so loving and calm with her own baby too. Maybe you can do things together. She's in her element in her own life now, married to Jimmy McLaine. He's a lovely feller, and he comes from a steady family. She's going to be alright, is our Maisie McLaine.'

'You're right. But the guilt never leaves you, when she sees me with another little one, it might, you know, bring up feelings of resentment. I wasn't a mother to her in her childhood, and I so wish I could change that.'

'I'm telling you; she'll be far too busy with her own demands to worry about yours, and have you seen any resentment from her yet? She's level-headed and understands you were forced into the situation. If you had kept her, how would you have looked after her? You needed money, a warm house, food, and everything. You were only sixteen, Ellen.'

'I am so grateful she found us, especially when I discovered the Blossoms hadn't told her I'd written to ask if I could visit, to tell her I missed and loved her … and I was so sorry I had to let her go.' The tears flowed. This happened on occasions when Ellen felt distraught she'd ever let Maisie down; her first beautiful, perfect daughter was abandoned.

George held his loving compassionate wife, rocking and shushing her gently, 'you had absolutely no choice.'

'Hm, yes, my parents would have had to take up the slack, and I don't think they were willing, apart from the obvious scandal of their jezebel of a daughter. I never forgave my parents, you know … ever, but I sort of understand now why they made me give her up. Who knows if I would've coped being so young. No wonder I became a rebellious teenager, cutting them off and moving in with my friend in Manchester as soon as I could get away from village gossip, nosy neighbours, curtains twitching, all of it.'

'You may have coped, but it happened, and everything has turned out ok. I can't praise you enough for being so gracious, encouraging Maisie to make peace with the Blossoms, even though Lizzie wasn't kind to you.'

'I understand Lizzie's misgivings, thinking one minute I'd given my daughter up for adoption, and the next I wanted her back; but it was Maisie who voted with her feet and left to come back to me, bless her heart. One person I will never forgive is her adoptive father. That Thomson bloke, returning her like damaged goods to the orphanage at four years old. He clearly mustn't have wanted her in the first place. I mean … it's tragic that he lost his wife so young, she would've survived sepsis these days, but still ... handing *my* child back like that.'

'True, but think about it, if she had stayed within that family, we would never have met her. Adoption was never spoken of, and parents were advised not even to tell their adopted children. I mean, it has massive implications for health reasons, genetics, and the like. People lived their whole lives never knowing their biological parents, so I, for one, am glad it's turned out this way.'

'You're a good dad to her, George, thank you for everything you do for her and all the girls.'

'I know, I'm blummin' amazing, aren't I? And another one on the way ... good job we moved to this bigger house from the two-up, two-down. It's bound to be another girl too, no son for me, I'm afraid.' He fake-scowled, knowing he'd be more than happy with another daughter.

A few days later, Ellen met with Maisie and held her three-month-old granddaughter, Kate, fussing and cooing over her. She noticed Maisie's soft, brown eyes full of love and tenderness, not being able to take her eyes of her perfect daughter. Inside, Ellen was conflicted; she had to tell Maisie she was pregnant, but didn't want to overshadow Maisie's unique happiness. That overwhelming joy you feel when you realise you've joined the exclusive motherhood club, the knowing nods and smiles with other new mothers you see everywhere.

'You okay, Mum? You look really tired and pale.'

'I have something to tell you.' Ellen was subdued. Her eyes met with Maisie's, and the recognition flipped a switch.

'I think I can guess ... are you pregnant?' Maisie asked.

Ellen nodded. 'I am, and I wanted you to be the first to know.'

'Oh, Mum, that's lovely news. Another little Clarke joining the family.'

Hormones, first-trimester fatigue, and reluctance brought tears to Ellen's eyes. 'I was worried how you might react; I don't want to take any joy from your gorgeous new baby, my beautiful granddaughter Kate.' Tears streamed down Ellen's face as she nuzzled into Kate's soft, peachy cheek.

'Mum, don't be so ridiculous, why wouldn't I feel happy for you and Dad. It'll be lovely, these babies will be brought up like siblings.' Maisie hugged Ellen.

'I sometimes can't bear the guilt, Maisie.'

'You need to stop all that, honestly, Mum. I am the happiest I've ever been in my life, look at how it's turning out. Both women smiled at the baby, who was now grizzling and squirming, stretching her delicate neck with an open mouth, searching for her next feed.

'Hungry again, Kate? I've no idea where she puts it all.' Maisie opened her blouse, and gathered her daughter up to offer her another feed. 'When are you going to tell the girls?'

'Tonight after school,' Ellen had relaxed, 'I've no idea what to expect from them. Will they be happy at the prospect of a new baby, or disgusted that their parents are still having sex?'

Six and a half months later, Ellen predictably gave birth to another daughter. The nine-pound healthy baby took a lot out of her, but she was perfect; she was named Grace. Ellen Clarke now had five beautiful daughters, Maisie, Neve, Jennifer, Alice, and Grace, and she couldn't be happier in her life.

Chapter 6

Ellen arrived home from hospital, and Maisie was waiting with her own cherished baby, Kate, now an animated ten-month-old. Maisie noticed Ellen seemed to be overcompensating, fussing and cooing over her granddaughter Kate, as if she was diminishing the birth of her own daughter Grace.

'She's absolutely lovely, suits her name, Grace,' said Maisie, we do produce beautiful baby girls in this family, don't we? Shall we swap so I can hug my new baby sister.'

Ellen passed her little bundle over to Maisie, carefully supporting her head, then gently lifted a smiling Kate out of her pram and held her securely.

'I remember you perfectly,' said Ellen. 'Your squished up little face, with that mop of thick black hair, and those big beautiful brown eyes. The nurse assisting the doctor who delivered you tied a pink ribbon in your hair, you had so much of it. I remember she seemed so kind, it's one of my nicest memories of becoming a mother.'

Ellen's overcompensating continued, and Maisie wanted to calm Ellen's fears that she was not feeling overshadowed. She was overjoyed Ellen had a healthy daughter; it had been a rough pregnancy this time.

'I looked like a baby chimp; I've seen the photo they gave to my adoptive parents,' said Maisie.

'You did not, you were the most beautiful baby that convent

place had ever seen.' Ellen appreciated Maisie's attempts to soften any awkwardness.

Since Maisie had Kate and experienced the overwhelming feeling of falling deeply in love with a little human being, she couldn't contemplate how awful it must have been for Ellen to give her up. Maisie often wanted to ask if she looked like her birth father, but it simply wasn't the right moment to be having that conversation. The trouble was, that conversation never happened. Ellen spoke of how Maisie came to be, not long after Maisie joined the family. All Ellen would say was, Maisie's father was Greek, called Manny, he was handsome, he was passing through her village, they had a love affair, and then he disappeared.

'I recall seeing you when you were seven at the Blossoms. It was awful, and lovely at the same time.'

'Did you understand why I was placed back at the orphanage after the adoption?'

'I never really knew until Bertie explained. I do know I lost all my legal rights. I had to sign papers when you were born, but honestly, I wasn't really sure what they meant. You did as your parents and the authorities told you to do. I received a letter from a catholic adoption agency years later confirming what happened with the adoption. I was so bloody furious, that Thomson bloke let you go, said he couldn't cope on his own.'

'Have you still got the letter? I'd like to read it someday … maybe.'

'I have somewhere, but think about whether you want it, only if you're sure. I wrote back to the agency asking if I could see you, and they refused initially. After I wrote again, they replied, saying you were placed with your new foster family, and they had agreed I could visit once, to prove your welfare was being looked after. Honestly, when I turned up in the village where they lived, I couldn't believe the size of the houses.'

Maisie said. 'Oh yea, the Blossoms weren't short of a bob or two.'

Ellen continued, 'there were strict rules. I couldn't let you know I was your mum or that I was even related. They said it had to be as if your foster family had bumped into someone they knew. I wasn't allowed to know where they lived.'

'That's terrible, Mum, how cruel.'

'I was under the strictest instructions not to rush to pick you up and had to wait and see if you would warm to me, but you didn't know who I was. I wanted to run away with you that day, but you would've been scared. It was bittersweet, they only allowed twenty minutes, and Lizzie Blossom was as frosty as ice. I'm sure she thought I was a stupid, cheap little vagabond who got herself pregnant. Cos you *can* impregnate yourself, did you know that, Maisie?' Ellen said with a scowl. They swapped babies, as Grace was grizzling for a feed.

'Anyway, I am grateful they allowed me to visit, and they took a polaroid for me to keep of you smiling at me. You were so beautiful; I couldn't believe it; running around and larking about with your foster brothers. You looked so happy. I knew I couldn't take you away, I had no right to and would've been done for child abduction if I'd tried to snatch you or something. I was penniless after I gave you up. I left home never having got on with my parents after they forced me to let you go. I was sharing a grubby flat with a girl I'd known from school; I knew I couldn't offer you anything like the Blossoms could.' Ellen looked dejected.

'I have a vague recollection of that day, but it was dismissed when I asked Lizzie about it. I was told you were someone who had worked for the family or something like that.' Maisie shrugged and continued playing with Kate, happily sitting upon her knee, Maisie squeezed her little bulbous thighs, and Kate, with her podgy dimpled fingers, was clapping and gurgling happily.

'I broke my heart walking away,' said Ellen, 'Bertie came after me, I think he wanted to be out of Lizzie's earshot. He reassured me they would take care of you and give you everything you needed. Also, if I wanted to write, they'd make sure you knew I had been in touch, which I did a few times. He's a lovely man.'

'I often wonder what Lizzie did with your letters,' said Maisie, 'obviously, I found the one that led me to you, but the photo you enclosed wasn't there, so she may have kept them from Bertie. It drove me mad thinking about having three little sisters and you asking after me.'

Maisie and Ellen looked into each other's eyes. There was a longing for both mother and daughter, a longing to have had the early relationship that was lost in time.

'Speaking of my little sisters, have they forgiven you and Dad for having sex now that they've got a beautiful baby sister,' asked Maisie.

'I hope so, of all three, it was Alice who was the most delighted. She couldn't wait to become a big sister. Neve was non-plussed, she's got her own life to live, and not really interested, but Jen was horrified, she walked out of the room when we announced it. By all accounts, Neve explained, Jen never mentioned anything to her friends at school and only replied with a nod if anyone asked her. But she's come around, and to be honest, is the most attentive and curious about Grace's needs, she's always ready to help.

'Alice, bless her, asked me the, *'where do babies come from,'* question. So I explained as best I could, and she seemed to accept it. She looked down between her own legs, looked between mine, and asked, 'where is the hole, Mum, can I see yours? Have I got one? Where is it? I'll need yours if I'm going to have a baby when I'm big.'

'That's a great idea, isn't it, a magic portal you can pass around the family, so it's no great effort to give birth.' They laughed.

'It may be confusing for others to work out that Grace is Kate's aunty, even though she's younger than her,' worried Ellen.

'Children accept things at face value. We can probably get away with saying they are cousins when they're young,' suggested Maisie. 'It hardly seems right for Kate to be calling Grace aunty, plus she'll be in the following academic year because of their birth dates.'

'True, the girls will work it out for themselves,' agreed Ellen.

Chapter 7

Kate and Grace were brought up as close cousins and never questioned why; when Kate became verbal, she had three Aunties; Neve, Jen, and Alice, but Grace, was simply … Grace. They lived through family holidays, supported each other through school, meeting boys and going out on the town, often amusing people with revelations of their true, and often disbelieved, genetic relationship. They shared similar life experiences, and met their future partners at roughly the same time in teenage years.

Maisie's daughter Kate was the first to become engaged at eighteen-years old, then scarily discovered she was pregnant when she and her fiancé Paul had an impromptu night of passion. Neither could believe it; the only time they had never used contraception. The couple decided it was meant to be. Kate was forging a career in the police service, and was a little dismayed at having to put her demanding job and studies aside to quickly arrange a wedding. She took maternity leave and couldn't wait to return to the job she loved, having reassurances there was an abundance of babysitters, so child-care wouldn't be a barrier to her career.

Kate gave birth to a healthy baby girl named, Francesca on 24 July 1999. At first, all seemed fine, when Maisie called one day to discover Kate sitting on the kitchen floor, looking pale, thin, and bedraggled, her hygiene fairly questionable too. The baby was nowhere to be seen.

'Where's Francesca?' Maisie asked, crouching to hold her distraught daughter. She cupped her face in her hands, 'Kate … Kate darling, where is Francesca, where's the baby?' A searing fear ripped through Maisie as she contemplated something terrible had happened.

Kate simply pointed toward the doorway.

Maisie entered the living room; Francesca was naked on her changing mat, showing initial signs of distress, with a crumpled expression, flailing her little limbs, and whimpering. There was a dirty rolled up nappy beside her and two open, clean ones next to it. Francesca had urinated, and the wee had pooled beneath her bottom, she'd also vomited up milk, which had trickled down the side of her face and became matted in her hair. Maisie went into mum mode; she cleaned up the baby and dressed her, constantly soothing her distress, humming and cradling her. Maisie didn't know how long Kate had left her baby in this vulnerable state. She took the baby into the kitchen and noticed the half-made bottle of formula milk. Francesca was beginning to express her hunger after the few smiles she had given Maisie.

'Francesca is fine, Kate, look.' Maisie sat beside Kate on the floor and presented the baby to her. She stroked Kate's hair as they sat together.

Between sobs, Kate said, 'Mum, I can't do this, I just can't. I'm no good at being a mum, my poor baby, having me as a mother.' Kate looked at her daughter and shrugged. 'Look at her, she's always crying. I can't help her, I can't make it stop, or make her happy. I can't even put a nappy on her.' Kate emitted a sob, then rambled, 'she keeps squirming away, and the sticky pads become unstuck with nappy cream from my fingers. I'm useless at this, Mum, useless.' Kate couldn't stop the tears flowing down her pale cheeks.

'Kate.' Maisie said firmly but gently, 'let's finish sorting out Francesca's bottle. Come on, we'll do it together.'

This seemed to distract Kate, and she looked at the feeding bottle with an amount of formula in the bottom.

Maisie was making a good job of not showing her own heartbreak at Kate's distress. 'Is that the right measure?' Maisie kept up the distraction tactics, the focus-on-something-practical dialogue.

Kate nodded. 'Yea, I put the scoops in and was waiting for the kettle to boil, and cool down. I went back in to check on Francesca, and forgot to press the switch, so when I returned to make her bottle, I hadn't even switched it on, she began crying, and I … I gave up. I'm so tired.' Kate looked down where she had been sitting on the floor.

Maisie tentatively tapped the kettle with a fingertip. 'You *had* switched it on, see it's warm. Make up the bottle now, Kate, it's okay. Let's get this little one fed.' Maisie took Francesca, who was very much letting her feelings known in an octave only babies can reach.

Kate mechanically made up the bottle; fortunately, the water was at the correct temperature, which she checked appropriately to Maisie's observation. This is a glitch, thought Maisie, her heart going out to her own daughter, recognising the immense responsibility of keeping another vulnerable tiny human alive. She encouraged Kate into the comfy chair in the living room, and handed Francesca over. The instant the baby's mouth sensed the bottle slide in, the gulping began, and she was quickly content.

Maisie looked at her daughter and granddaughter. She saw the rhythmic pull of the hungry baby feeding on the bottle, and Kate smiling down at her with her little finger stroking her downy-peach cheek.

'You can do this, Kate, you can.'

'I hope so, Mum,' she looked up with bleary, puffy eyes. 'I never imagined how tired I'd be. Everyone else seems to manage it so easily.' 'That's where you're completely wrong.' Maisie corrected her.

Kate looked up, surprised at her mother's admonishment.

'What you often looking at is a content baby who has been fed and cleaned, but what you didn't see was the bit before to get them into that state of contentment. It's really hard work. You are going through what every woman does after having their first baby.'

The room was silent, but for the gentle squeaking burbles emanating from Francesca as she fed.

'I don't know how to love her. I know I'm supposed to, and I do feel it most of the time. But I've had a couple of moments when … when I doubt myself, and I want things to be back the way they were before.' Kate said softly, 'I don't mean I don't want her here, nothing like that, but I'm struggling to see an end to the constant demands of feeding; cleaning, washing, bathing, shopping, and playing, with no sleep. It's never-ending, how do people do it?'

'Everyone feels a certain amount of baby blues for the first few weeks, even months. It's so overwhelming, and it won't last forever, I promise. Your life is very different now.'

'I feel sad all of the time, and guilty because I've got the most beautiful, healthy baby in the world, so I should be the happiest I've ever been. I was so looking forward to this baby, but motherhood is such a massive strain. I can't be bothered to meet up with the other mums; I can't think straight; I'm in a fog all the time. I went out for a walk and completely forgot to take her bottle, so when she became hungry and cried, I had to rush home to feed her. Everyone was looking at me, thinking, she's useless, can't even look after her own baby.'

The tears continued as Kate wiped her hand across her face. 'I have constant headaches, and want to sleep all the time. I don't want to get out of bed every morning to face the day. I can't think straight. If I'm asked a question, it takes me ages to work out how to answer. I mean, how could I have left her like that.' Kate was inconsolable as she looked at the changing mat, however continued to feed and hug her baby.

'Have you spoken to your health visitor, and does Paul know?' asked Maisie.

'Carol is lovely, but I haven't really told her how I feel. And Paul … well, Paul thinks I'm just tired from having the baby. I was fed up with being pregnant, not being able to do normal things, or even eat anything I wanted. How can I tell him, he'll think I'm a monster, he's so besotted with Francesca, but I'm lost in all this somewhere, like I'm being suffocated.

'Can you talk with him, do you think? Asked Maisie. 'You know, for men, it's different. Some men, anyway, as there's some brilliant dads being the main carer for children, but they haven't been through all of the physical and hormonal changes in their bodies. Most don't have to give up work, and it's cigars all around at their momentous achievement. I mean, what did they actually do in the process ... really?' She smiled at Kate, who reciprocated.

Maisie continued, 'I bet Paul comes home full of the joys of spring, and you don't even get a nod. I knew you'd be sad about having to take maternity leave after getting your perfect job too. It's all understandable.'

Kate nodded. 'I feel like I've been pegged right back to square one with work, behind everyone else. Even the wedding was a rush job. We should've waited until afterwards maybe, and had a proper honeymoon, or a family holiday with Francesca.' Kate pulled her daughter's content sleeping face towards her and gently kissed it all over. I do love her, I really do. If anyone tried to take her away or hurt her, I'd kill them.' Kate looked perturbed, 'they won't take her, Mum, will they, after this?' She clung to her baby.

Maisie shook her head. 'Over my dead body! It won't come to that Kate, ever.'

'But what if you hadn't arrived when you did?' Kate whispered.

'I'll tell you what would've happened, you would become aware of Francesca's cries, gone back in the room, held her, and done your best for your baby. You always do your best at whatever you do, this is no different. It's knocked you for six, it's like no other challenge you've ever experienced. You would have sorted her out and fed her, Kate, I know you. It may not feel like you're coping, but you must tell Paul. He has to know, maybe he can take some compassionate leave, or we can arrange babysitters, so you two can have a nice night out, or a quiet night in, and I'll have my granddaughter over to stay. Me and Grandad Jimmy would be delighted to have her, he's another one completely besotted with her.

Kate grinned this time at the thought of her dad Jimmy, who utterly doted upon Francesca. 'You're right, me and Paul should sort out some time together.'

Maisie stayed for the rest of the day and watched as Kate resumed her maternal role. It seemed a weight had been lifted as they got ready to take Francesca out in the pram for a walk.

'Thank you, Mum, I feel like maybe I can cope now. I mean, millions of women have babies every day, don't they. I know I'll wake up with the feeling of dread that I've had for weeks, but I can at least put some things in perspective, and start to enjoy her a bit more, instead of focusing on all the bloody tasks you have to do. It's so exhausting.'

'I know honey. Anytime you need me, night or day, I'm a phone call away.'

Kate was quiet, then asked, 'Mum, did you feel anything like this when you had me?'

'I was certainly overwhelmed at first and questioned my own ability, especially after the start I had in life. You know, questioning whether I was the right material to become a loving mother. Was I capable of looking after a baby when my early years were so mixed up, but I had Jimmy by my side and my mum; they understood. I was in good hands, mum had four babies by then. You're going to be fine; I know how much you love her; you'd never harm her in a million years. Please don't worry about that, try and focus on the joy.'

Maisie reflected upon her own mother, Ellen, forced to leave her baby behind in 1960. 'I can't imagine how it was for my mum in that nursing hospital, and returning home if she was hormonal, and her milk was still coming in … it must have been terrible.'

'Poor Granny Ellen.' Kate held Francesca upon her chest, patting her back gently. 'I've got to be honest with Paul about how I'm feeling haven't I? I'll try and make the effort to meet with the other mums too,' said Kate.

'Well, that's fine, but sometimes the competitive mummy scenario kicks in, and you can do without the stupid comments.' Kate looked bemused.

Maisie continued in the fake patronising tone of perfect parents;

'Our little Freddie is walking, and he's only eight months; definitely a professional footballer in the making. You may even hear idiocy like, Finty is so gifted, already showing signs of pure genius, we need to find a school that can manage her intellect, as she'll be heading for Oxbridge. Then we have the model child ... Benjamin, who has slept through since we brought him home; he's a dreamboat, no trouble whatsoever. He's perfection personified.'

Maisie paused. 'Load of old, pardon my language, utter bloody bollocks!'

For the first time in quite a while, Kate began to laugh.

Maisie said, 'in reality all babies do is cry, feed, vomit, fill their nappies and maybe sleep occasionally, and not for too long either.'

Kate looked into the pram as she pushed it along, gazing at Francesca's sleeping face and said, 'let's go visit Grandad Jimmy.'

The women linked arms, as they made their way along the sunny suburban street with a very content baby.

Chapter 8

June 2017

Jimmy McLaine adored his granddaughter Francesca, in fact, he idolised her. He treated her endlessly with gifts, and never missed an occasion; holidays, birthday parties, sports day, school productions, the nativity play. You'd find Jimmy with his handy camcorder recording every delightful moment. Christmas was particularly ridiculous, as she was spoilt rotten! The local neighbourhood saw an inseparable pair; the sweet little girl peering out of his van windscreen waving to passersby, as he took her on his delivery rounds at weekends.

In 2017, Fran was about to celebrate her eighteenth birthday, and Jimmy his sixtieth. They discussed a joint celebration; reaching adulthood, and reaching retirement. Jimmy had sold the business, and he and Maisie were looking forward to a holiday in the autumn to celebrate, though hadn't decided on their destination. Maisie and Jimmy had the where-shall-we-go-on-holiday conversation yet again over dinner. They watched television, before Maisie went upstairs to read for a little while until Jimmy came to bed. This was their routine, nothing much changed.

England was experiencing an early summer heatwave, the fifth hottest June since records began; being increasingly humid at night. The uncomfortable, sticky heat prompted Jimmy to get up a few nights in a row to get a cold drink of water; he had a raging thirst and, as a big man became quite overheated during the night. He would throw the duvet cover off himself in bed and had taken to lying on top of the covers. One particularly stifling evening, Maisie noticed beads of sweat forming on Jimmy's face and neck; the bedroom window was open, and the fan was whirring, which helped a little bit. They had ditched the duvet, and only had a cotton sheet for cover. Not much else they could do to cool down.

Jimmy leaned across to Maisie, kissed her and said goodnight. He said, 'let's not go anywhere too hot, Maisie-m'love.' Jimmy had called her Maisie-m'love every day since they began courting. 'This heat is really awful.' He lay on top of the bedding as he had been doing during this hot spell.

In the early hours, Maisie rolled over in bed, and felt the cold, clammy skin of Jimmy's arm. She roused and said, 'hey Jimmy, you're cold. Get under the covers.' She nudged him … he didn't move. As her panic was rising, she spoke his name over and over, louder and louder, then put the lamp on, leaned a little way over to see him, and knew immediately from his grey, vacant face, there was something terribly wrong.

Her neighbours heard the piercing screams; everyone had their bedroom windows wide open. Colin from next-door battered on the door, retrieved the spare key, entered the house, ran three steps at-a time upstairs to find Maisie kneeling on the bed shaking Jimmy's shoulder, screaming, 'I can't wake him up! He won't wake up, he's asleep, he's just asleep!'

Colin's wife, Heather, held Maisie and gently encouraged her downstairs until the paramedics arrived. Eventually Jimmy's body was removed. At the sight of the body bag carefully being transported to the ambulance, Colin leapt towards Maisie as her sobs faded into unconsciousness.

Maisie was anchorless, floating senselessly in a vast sea of grief. She should have been able to save him; she should have noticed the thirst and sweating wasn't right. She ran it over and over in her mind, his last words, he called her Maisie-m'love, but she wouldn't hear those words ever again. She couldn't live with the guilt; she should've paid more attention; it was all her fault.

The visits from family and friends lessened in the months following Jimmy's well-attended funeral; life had to return to some semblance of normality. No-one suspected Maisie had been secretly drinking heavily in the weeks after Jimmy's sudden death from the cardiac arrest. It was the only way she could deal with the encompassing shroud of feeling empty, lost, and alone. Going to bed in the early hours, half-comatose was her only solution. Maisie arranged to meet friends and family always after lunch, and never invited anyone over until the afternoon. This enabled her to have a few hours in the morning to sometimes vomit, then take heavy-dose painkillers for headaches, acid-reflux tablets, and her prescribed medication for depression and sleeping pills.

The days Maisie did have to meet people Started with the ritual of scrubbing herself in the shower, making the effort to dress, and look less disheveled than she felt inside; she had used clothing as armour in the past. Eventually she was able to eat a small slice of dry toast, and a powerful caffeinated coffee to enable her to cope with another day. There were many nights she didn't want to wake up. She was widowed at fifty-seven; this wasn't supposed to happen; Jimmy wasn't meant to leave her, she was alone. This life was too difficult to bear.

Maisie's mother Ellen and step-father George, popped in everyday initially, then every other day as time elapsed. Daughter Kate often called at the end of, or beginning of, her shifts twice weekly. Granddaughter Fran visited at weekends for a movie night. Maisie's four sisters kept in regular touch; it was a well-coordinated support network, however, all of them missed Maisie's deteriorating condition. She was not known as a drinker, far from it. Maisie had learnt the hard way to lock her emotions inside from being a small child. To be brave; not to show weakness; to never give anyone the key which would unlock the door to a chasm of limitless depths of loss, and grief. She was a mistress of deception.

Kate's job as a police officer working alongside the National Police Air Service covering the north west, did not prepare her for one particular evening as she walked, wearily, to her mother's door after a busy weekend shift over central Manchester. Her role, buzzing around with the helicopter pilot, tracking live criminal activity; vehicle pursuits, or searching for missing or injured persons and reporting to the ground crew, was exciting, but utterly draining. Kate was trained to manage emergencies of the most distressing kind.

A particular event that still weighed heavily upon her, was the case where a young mother; who had been texting whilst driving on a country road; lost control and her car slid down an embankment. She had frantically tried to turn the steering wheel to redirect it, but the rear of her vehicle clipped a relatively slow-moving passenger train, rotating the car aside, like a child's spinning top. The helicopter was first on the scene. A flickering floodlit crowd, surrounded a distraught mother trying to open the rear doors of her wrecked vehicle, scrunched-up like a piece of paper. It was an image Kate would never forget. Reading the investigation outcome later, she discovered the two-year-old died instantly, and the six-year-old had life-changing injuries. This was all part of Kate's professional world.

Kate let herself into Maisie's house, she hadn't intended visiting that day, but she wanted to talk with her mum after a particularly tiring shift. She missed her lovely dad Jimmy every single day, his loss was great. The shock of finding her mother in a drowsy state challenged even Kate's steadfastness to the limit. She could hear her voice echoing around her own brain, 'Mum. Mum, wake up!' as she tried to sit Maisie upright from her prone position on the sofa. The glimmering light from the tv screen lit up Maisie's face. Her breathing was shallow, her voice was weak, and her blue-tinged, cool, facial skin resulted in her needing immediate medical intervention. Kate was distraught, checking her pulse, while ringing 999; her innate emergency response kicked in, though she was shaking uncontrollably by the time the paramedics arrived.

Following intensive treatment from health services, including gastric lavage to reduce the effect of medication and alcohol, a brief stay in hospital was required before Maisie was discharged. She knew she could've been in serious trouble if it hadn't been for Kate's swift actions and the attention of the medics. Maisie was diagnosed with severe reactive depression, following Jimmy's sudden death and was referred to attend counselling appointments.

Maisie became insular for several months while the intensive mental health support services were engaged. She closed off her family and friends, telling them she had to deal with this on her own.

Maisie revisited the terrors of her past and the abandonment that forever plagued her life during counselling. Her grief was insurmountable. Dealing with loss was her biggest challenge, stemming from being that little girl wondering when her mummy or daddy would eventually come to liberate her from the children's home.

Maisie recovered, being discharged from counselling services after some months, but her family initially walked on eggshells around her. Her sisters were especially sensitive to her situation at family celebrations when alcohol was in the mix. Prior to Alice's birthday gathering, she visited Maisie.

After warm greetings Alice said, 'I want to be upfront with you, Maisie. How will you feel if there's alcohol at my gathering … and probably an awful lot of it, knowing my mates.'

'It's fine, Alice, please don't worry about me, I can manage myself in those situations. You don't have to change anything for me.' She repeated what was explained to her. 'Because I've never had an alcohol problem in the past, I don't feel at risk of recurrence. It was part of the reactive depression and shock of Jimmy's death.'

Maisie hugged her little sister Alice; she had a real soft-spot for her. 'There's nothing to suggest I have a long-term dependency, and I can have alcohol if I wish, with some protective factors, like never becoming maudlin, sitting at home drinking in the evenings.'

There were times Maisie could be resistant and sulky, even stroppy, but the family coped and forgave her. She chose not to drink alcohol for a long period of time as the family rallied around, and found their Maisie again ... almost. Maisie McLaine's heart had suffered another fracture that would never heal.

Chapter 9
April 2019

Sunlight bounced off the TrenItalia train carriage window. A young woman gazed out into the brightness, elbows resting on the table, her palms propping up her weary face. She closed her eyes, soaking up warmth from glinting rays, which enhanced her long golden-blonde hair. Sitting opposite, an older woman sat upright, face turned toward the window, her eyes shielded from the glare by huge sunglasses, her shoulder-length thick brunette hair, neatly tucked behind her ears. The young woman, Fran, turned away from the brightness, squinting. She tried to focus as the remnants of the sun's luminous afterimage faded from her retina.

Fran took out her ear-buds, and the tinny clicks of, Billie Eilish's latest album ceased abruptly when she tapped pause on her mobile phone. The display read, 12 April 2019, and the time 09.50 a.m. Fran leaned forward and spoke quietly to the older woman opposite, nodding towards a weary middle-aged business man sitting across the carriage from them.

'People are the same wherever you go. Nan, look, that Bank Manager over there has had another boring day at the office. Fidgety Girl beside him is on the way to meet her date, she keeps checking her reflection in the window.'

Tilting her head further, Fran added, 'poor Working Mum

is fussing with her heavy shopping, dreading going home to her demanding family, and Mister Perfect over there keeps glancing up to see who's admiring him.' Fran noticed Mister Perfect's self-satisfied smirk when their eyes met. 'Ordinary people going about their ordinary lives, just like any other city; it's like travelling in rush hour at home.'

The train jiggled and whooshed through a tunnel. Within seconds, the flickering figures beamed from black into brightness.

Fran's grandmother Maisie, a youthful fifty-nine-year-old, raised her hand and slid her sunglasses down her nose to reveal dark brown eyes. 'People-watching is a bit overrated, who cares about their lives? You know this may be a wasted trip, going off track like this.'

'It'll be fine, don't be so pessimistic. I'll find work to boost our funds if needed. We *are* doing this for you after all.'

'Go on, blame me, and if it goes horribly wrong, it'll be all my fault.'

Fran gritted her teeth. 'Lighten up, Nan, we'll be in Florence soon, you've always wanted to come here, to the city you were named after.'

Maisie straightened and looked away, 'I do wonder if embarking on this … this, ridiculous escapade, will come to anything.' She clenched the backpack, resting on her knee tightly into her body.

End of conversation, thought Fran as the train rumbled to a halt. They arrived at Florence Santa Maria Station. Fran understood there may be some reticence, and felt the equal weight of her enormous rucksack, and the responsibility of her grandmother, draining her physical and mental energy. If she got the directions wrong to their accommodation, she'd see the imperceptible signs of frustration as her grandmother would tuck her chin into her neck, and slightly pucker her lips. Not this time, Fran got it right. After several minutes, they arrived at the arched stone doorway of their pre-booked pensione.

Fran knocked on the vertically halved wooden door. The half

door opened, and out popped a balding man's cheerful plump face, welcoming them inside, even though they were almost an hour early for check-in. He opened both doors to reveal a pleasant, but dated hallway, with a huge bulbous vase of overflowing bright, floppy flowers on a side table. A bunch of room keys jangled in his hand. He continued his cheerful Italian dialogue as they followed his stout backside up the narrow staircase. They entered the tiny twin-bedded room, and their host left them to settle in.

Fran noticed Maisie's chin-to-neck lip-pucker from the corner of her eye. Maybe she was simply fatigued from the journey. Fran dumped the rucksack with relief, as it bounced on one of the sagging single beds, then entered the minuscule shower ensuite. She turned the ancient cross-shaped chrome tap, with a black, C, embedded in the ceramic circle. Fran recalled the confusion for English-speakers that, C, is caldo, meaning hot; whilst, F, is freddo, meaning cold. She trained her brain to think, F, for freezing. Thankfully, billowing steam swirled upwards as hot water gushed into the basin, which filled in seconds. She opened the ziplock bag she'd taken from her crammed rucksack, and pulled out some underwear, placing it in the sink with a squirt of travel wash, swooshing it around.

'Put your undies in there if they need washing,' she said to Maisie whilst looking at her own weary reflection in the mirror.

Maisie slid sideways into the ensuite. 'Lovely, washing my smalls in a tiny boarding-house basin.' She opened her backpack, pulled out some items, plopped them into the water, and vacated the bathroom.

They were four days into their trip, and Fran wasn't sure it would extend much longer. She dropped her shoulders, heaved a huge sigh, and gazed upwards. Painstakingly, Fran unravelled the clothesline she had placed on the bed. She tied one end to the window latch, looked around, and tied the other end to the rusted rosette, wardrobe door handle, ensuring the door was firmly locked with the ornate key beneath. Maisie, with her fleece jacket still zipped up to the hilt, sat rigidly on the toddler-sized bed, defensively gripping the backpack into her midriff. She seemed miles away, staring into the middle distance.

Fran sighed. 'Shall we go home tomorrow? I'm not sure this, *ridiculous escapade,* as you put it, is working out.' Fran hated disappointing her grandmother, feeling guilty as she noticed a veil of despair float across Maisie's face.

'We're here now, I suppose we'll just have to get on with it,' said Maisie.

'Be honest. Do you really want to find out about your birth father's family or not?' asked Fran.

Maisie said solemnly, 'I really don't know.' She dropped her backpack onto the floor, stood, unzipped her fleece jacket, and when it didn't slip off easily, she had to shake one arm to get rid of it, then flung it on the bed.

Fran almost laughed at this childlike behaviour.

'It's, it's ... this room ... these beds ... like the orphanage,' said Maisie.

Fran observed Maisie gazing at the small basic bed. How could she have anticipated that a room in a Florentine pensione would cause such vivid, upsetting memories. Life had been difficult enough lately for their whole family back in England. Fran hauled the rucksack on top of the wardrobe with a grunt, and went into the bathroom to wash the underwear. It was true that part of Fran couldn't wait to return home, with her parents, her speech therapy work, and her boyfriend Liam, soon to become fiancé. However, if her grandmother wished to stay on the journey, they would just have to get on with it.

'We're likely to be in for some revelations,' Fran warned, 'or maybe not,' she said quietly.

Maisie looked up, but she wasn't seeing Fran, lost somewhere in a time long ago. Recent conversations between the women were held without eye contact. Fran had seen this blank expression, mixed with anticipation a number of times.

'I mean, I hadn't expected having to wash my granny's knickers, and though I'm not thrilled, I'm doing it.' She noticed a flicker of a smile from Maisie as she passed the wrung-out items to hang over the clothesline.

'Good idea of mine to bring the washing line, wasn't it?'

'Absolutely, Granny.'

'Don't call me that, it's awful,' Maisie preened to her full slim height, 'makes me sound ancient.'

'Well … you are … I mean, sixty next year.' Fran said with a grin, 'you're almost a pensioner.'

'Youth is *so* wasted on the young.' Maisie gazed out of the open window. 'When you were a little girl, you thought my name was Nan, and you refused to believe I had a first name. I had to convince you it was Maisie, so you mixed the two together … and came up with, Nansie.'

Fran looked at the gently lined face and the few wisps of dark brown, slightly silvered hair wafting in the warm breeze, and realised she had not seen such tenderness for years.

'Ready for food, Nansie?'

Maisie enjoyed hearing the name, which Fran had shortened to Nan in recent years. Maisie nodded, leaving the line of knickers wafting like bunting in a breeze, they left their tiny room. As they reached the bottom of the stairs, Maisie said, 'that smell it's so … Italian … I'm ravenous! Shame it's only bed and breakfast here, they must be having dinner.'

The hosts popped out of their living quarters, releasing a powerful blast of oregano, pomodoro, and steam from pasta starched water. The mimed conversation with the stout proprietor and his diminutive crinkled wife, discussing directions to a nearby café, lifted Fran's spirits. Maisie couldn't help but smile as the crinkled lady, first with hands on her heart, her head to one side as she took both Maisie's hands, repeated Italian phrases to her.

As crinkled lady tread lightly back into the kitchen, their congenial host continually exulted, 'bella Firenze, bella Firenze!' Sweeping his arms wide, he ushered them along the hallway into the street, encouraging them to explore his precious city. He lit up a Marlboro Light at the door, the tobacco-filled air annulled the aroma of food.

The women stepped outside, their footsteps echoed along the crammed vehicle-lined, flagged pathway, leading to what Fran hoped was the direction of the recommended café.

Through the side of her mouth, she asked Maisie. 'Is he still there? I have no idea if we're going the right way.' She turned, and hoped the waving man had retreated back into the house as she had understood little from their conversation, wishing she'd paid more attention to her Italian phrase book.

Passing doorways, some with porticos, others with scripted bright canopies and ornate iron gates, Maisie asked, 'any idea where we're going?'

'Not a clue,' said Fran.

They came upon a café, whether it was the recommended one, was uncertain. They were seated immediately and enjoyed a swiftly served, sumptuous pasta meal and bread, the cheapest on the menu, which they devoured within minutes. The cacophony of the Italian staff, who appeared to be shouting in frustration with every word at each other, only enhanced the experience. Their waiter was constantly bustling about, responding to yells of, *'Andiamo!'* from the kitchen whilst efficiently managing several tables.

Fran swept a floury baguette slice around her plate to sponge up every morsel of the tasty pesto sauce. 'That was heavenly.' She relaxed, looked at Maisie, who had unlocked her shoulders.

With a devilish twinkle in her eyes, Maisie leant forward and said, 'shall we have another glass? Fran, this is lovely, so glad we are doing this.' Maisie took a large drink from the pale gold, cool effervescent Frizzante and raised her glass. 'To Italy and beyond.'

Fran raised her glass and, with a clink, she said, 'cin cin.' She'd read Italians preferred this toast, rather than the more formal, *salute*. Wandering aimlessly around bustling streets, Fran was relieved to notice a spring in Maisie's step, possibly an effect of the wine, as her eyes fluttered from visions of beautiful people, to glamorous shops and grand buildings.

A stunning young couple, arms around each other, were looking in a jewellers' window. Gold and silver rings displayed on a deep blue velvet stand had caught their eye. Fran wondered if they were getting engaged, as she would be when she returned home. She admired the athletic-looking couple, and doubted whether she could encourage Liam to visit Florence to buy her an engagement ring, she'd be lucky to get him to travel to Manchester. With abundant brunette hair falling around her shoulders, the young woman wore a cornflower blue, heavy-knit slouchy sweater falling to one side to reveal a beautifully tanned shoulder. Her slim black ankle-grazer jeans perfectly complemented the tan leather pumps. Her beloved, wore blue jeans, a white t-shirt, and a black lightweight overshirt, with a splash of colour courtesy of a thin, brightly striped scarf loosely wrapped around his neck. Such effortless style, Fran thought, only Italians could pull that off.

'Oh look,' said Maisie, pointing toward the Ponte Vecchio.

Fran was distracted from her admiring glances at the couple, and looked toward the old medieval arched bridge across Florence's Arno River.

'You up for exploring your city tomorrow, Maisie Florence?' she asked.

'Yes, it's all so wonderful,' breathed Maisie, eyes wide and hands in prayer pose, index fingertips resting on her chin.

The shops built all along the bridge were crowded, and they agreed to return in the morning when it would be quieter, they hoped. Neither woman had been particularly adventurous lately, but together they made a good team ... sometimes. They enjoyed a ramble around the streets and had to find their bearings as a deep fatigue set in from the journey. Fran had practiced using the interactive map on her phone before setting off. It was never needed at home, as she rarely ventured much farther than her workplace, and the city for an occasional night out with Liam.

Lying in bed that night, Fran breathed to the rhythm of the ancient aircon unit rattling above her bed. She looked across at Maisie's serene sleeping face. I could smother you with a pillow, she thought. Fran imagined her as a young child and wondered how awful it must have been for Maisie, returned to the orphanage after her adoption breakdown. Simply, the sight of these tiny beds had evoked traumatic memories from so long ago. Fran knew a little about Maisie's time with her foster family, who had rescued her from care. Fran heard Maisie's voice inside her mind often referring to the fact she did not need to be rescued.

Another look at the sleeping face and Fran knew her stoic, grandmother must, at times, feel quite lost and frightened. Fran expelled a luxurious yawn, and whispered, 'sorry, Nansie, I'll try and be more patient.' She then fell into a glorious deep slumber.

Chapter 10

January 2019

The four Clarke sisters, Neve, Jennifer, Alice, and Grace, were in the loft at their former family home at 74 North Park Lane, Swinton. It was either excruciatingly hot in summer up there, or feet and fingertip freezing, as it was today in early 2019. They huddled together, still wearing their bulky winter coats and boots, sitting on boxes, and the camping chairs they'd discovered in the darkest recesses. Their searing collective grief deepened at the death of their beloved mother, Ellen, as they embarked upon the task of clearing out seventy-four years of her life and memories.

It was painful and poignant, that Ellen had survived uterine cancer in her late fifties, only for cancer to sneak its way back into her lymphatic system, and re-emerge with vengeance in her seventies. The saving grace for her daughters was that she did not suffer long, and only failed in the final weeks of her life. Within four months of diagnosis, Ellen left her family peacefully whilst sleeping; she had seen every one of her five daughters that day.

'Brings back so many memories,' said Neve, looking around at the detritus they were faced with clearing out. The sisters nodded in agreement, in silence. Melancholy surrounded them, and grief filled the spaces in between.

'We were so lucky to have a wonderful upbringing because

of mum … and dad, when he was well. Remember his pride and joy, the garden and his shed. He'd build things that never really worked. I think Fran still has the old doll's house he attempted to make.' Neve smiled, 'it was a bit rustic to say the least. I loved the smell in that shed, would it be bitumen? Same smell as when they tarred the roads, you never see steam rollers these days.' Neve sighed her reverie away, tucking her tousled, bobbed hair behind her ears. She stretched her pullover down over the stomach, that diminishing gym sessions and middle-age was gradually expanding. 'You realise how young seventy-four is when you're in your fifties.'

Neve directed her comments at Jen, who, although approaching fifty, was as slender as she had been in her thirties. Neve was amazed at how well-presented Jen always was; not a twirled blonde hair out of place, hairdressers every six weeks without fail, fabulous dress sense, and high-end cosmetics.

Jen, looking down at her exquisite fur lined Italian-leather boots, said, 'don't remind me, nearly bloody fifty, how did that happen?' With a frown, 'I'm still furious about the settlement from Dad's health tribunal. I mean, how much do you put on all that suffering and maybe ten years of disability for him and all those other men. At least he seems well cared for now. Poor mum, so distressed when he was diagnosed with dementia on top of lung disease.'

'She worried about him until her dying day,' said Alice. 'I'm keeping an eye on dad's care; they know I used to work there, so I'll be on their case if he's not being well looked after. It's really painful that he doesn't remember anything. I go through the photo albums every time I visit, and he does recognise certain faces, but no clue who I am. Could be worse, some old fellers think you're their girlfriend or wife and start groping you. Thankfully he hasn't done that to me or anyone. Can you imagine?'

The sisters fell silent, remembering the rotational support for their dad George, whilst he was still at home, turning up regularly to help with his care, and to support their mum Ellen, with a husband suffering from a degenerative industrial lung disease, then dementia to compound matters. The sisters combined into one unbreakable force when it was needed.

Neve peeped into a box beside her and sighed. 'Mum must have kept everything. Our old school reports and baby clothes are packed in here.' She gazed longingly into the large dusty cardboard box she had opened. She inhaled musty dust particles that twinkled in the meagre light from the single bulb hanging in the centre of the loft. She looked up, and, ever practical, suggested, 'could one of you pop down into Dad's cupboard and see if there's any stronger bulbs.'

Youngest sister Grace, and consummate people-pleaser, leapt up immediately off a large plastic storage box. 'No probs, I'll do it.'

'She's the absolute double of you, Neve, isn't she?' said Alice

'Poor thing,' said Neve, holding her arms out, 'this is what she's got to look forward to in ten years' time.'

'Don't be ridiculous,' said Alice, who had maintained her petite athletic frame well. Still constantly colouring her hair to achieve weird and wonderful styles, this month's look was a sleek, magenta geometric jaw-length bob with a straight fringe.

Alice continued, 'Neve I honestly don't know how you do it. Top accountancy job, got your two still at home, supporting the women's forum, and still helping out running gymkhanas and stuff.'

'Hm, something's got to give soon; I do get tired these days. What about you? Three boys at home, running them around to all their sports clubs and classes. I bet the new house extension is helping with space, but still, working shifts at the care centre, it can't be easy having to lift and manage your clients either.'

'Well, my eldest will be off to Uni soon, so that'll make some space, and don't forget my doggies; they're my real babies,' said Alice. 'Yes two dogs to walk morning and night too, you must be mad.' Neve said, 'and now we have all this.' She looked around at the insurmountable task facing them.

'We could get a company to shift everything? It's going to take forever to go through all this stuff,' said Jen.

Neve glanced at Alice, noticing her frustrated look, and said immediately, 'well … I think it's important to try and go through everything. We've got time on our hands until the sale is complete, just as well, as I'm sure there'll be many keepsakes we want to sort out.'

Impatiently, Alice added, 'look, you don't have to stay Jen, we'll do this. Just go … get back to your precious little shop.'

Jen looked down, 'I didn't mean that … I—'

'We'll probably need to tackle this in shifts to be honest, so if you need to go Jen that's fine, we'll do the first stint,' interjected Neve with a neutral expression, not wishing to place her favour on one sister or the other. This was a constant pattern, keeping the peace between her socially and politically distanced middle sisters.

'Well … if you're sure, I'm around later in the week, it's only because I have a huge delivery from Spain arriving today, and the January sale stuff needs re-pricing, so I'd like to be there, rather than leaving it to the girls.' Without looking back, Jen cautiously stepped backwards down the loft ladders, first sweeping her hands down her classic tweed skirt to ensure not a speck of dust remained. The front door clicked.

'She's always been so ambitious for money and success. The only time she's happy is when she's talking about, *Jennys*, I mean how narcissistic can you get?' said Alice.

'She means well, she works hard, but sometimes comes across as … over enthusiastic about the shop, if that's the right phrase?' said Neve.

'Works hard my arse, she's never done a proper day's graft in her life.'

'She *is* a good business woman, her boutique has been successful for many years. People travel for miles to shop there; she's got excellent taste and knows what women want. A life of glamour was never for you was it, Alice?'

'Ah no, I love my job now, and who knew I was dyslexic, discovering that during my qualifications was helpful, all these years, I always thought I was just thick.' Alice sighed. 'It's tough for my unique and different children. I want to make their lives that bit better and advocate where I can; and support the families too, none of it is easy.' Alice shook her head slightly and the glow of light glinted on her hair, giving it a golden ruby hue.'

'I do believe Jen is jealous of you,' suggested Neve.

Alice looked puzzled. 'No way, why would she be? She's got everything.'

'When we'd go out on the town together years ago, you always got loads of attention. You'd be bantering away with the chaps, always bright and bubbly, always looked quirky and amazing, you'd get away with wearing the most outrageous, and if I'm not mistaken, scantily clad outfits on that petite figure. And even though she towered above you with those long legs, you were always better than her at sports.'

'You really think she was jealous?'

'I do. Jen is a classic beauty, but she may have really wanted to join in more, but …'

'But, she didn't have the craic.' Alice beamed.

Grace's head popped up through the loft hatch. 'Was that Jen leaving?

She probably wants to keep busy as a distraction,' offered Grace.

Alice softened. 'Yea, she's had some rough times with that wayward ex-husband of hers. What a prize prick he was.'

'What really happened?' asked Grace, 'I was too young to understand but I remember it being an awful time, lots of crying.'

'Jen's hubby was a professional footballer, kind of second tier. He was on telly a lot at the peak of his career, and earned quite a decent living. Great looking guy, fantastic physique. He had that typical footballer look everyone was going for at the time.'

'Bit of a Beckham maybe?' suggested Grace.

'Yea, exactly that, mid-nineties when they became rock stars, he really thought he was one with the adulation, and he did a bit of modelling, which Jen did too.'

'A proper WAG?' suggested Grace.

'They were the golden couple around here for years. Then it went horribly wrong when she'd just had their baby boy, and he was found having an affair. Stupid idiot, out on the town while she was at home with a toddler and a newborn. Anyway, as soon as she found out, it was awful because it was all over the local gossip columns, she must've felt so humiliated.'

'She came away with a great settlement though,' added Alice, 'and good for her, quite rightly. She built up her business, so I have to take my hat off to her for that. Her daughter has inherited their good looks, down in that there London working as a model.'

'She'll need to make as much money as she can while she's popular,' said Grace wistfully, 'fame is fleeting.'

'Yes, yes, yes, we all know about your fifteen minutes of fame on The Great British Bake Off, Grace, we don't need to hear about it again.' Alice grinned. 'I suppose Jen never could settle with anyone for ages, couldn't trust them I guess. No wonder she can be a bit defensive. But her hubby now is great … and he's loaded, so yea, good for her. Funny how Jen and Maisie inherited mum's height and figure, lucky them. They do look alike, even though they have different fathers.'

'We take after Dad's side of the family. So, come on you short-arses let's get cracking on this lot,' said Neve. 'Alice, shine your torch as I'll have to switch off the light to change this bulb.' 'What torch?' Alice asked looking around.

'The one on your mobile phone.'

Alice puzzled, staring at her mobile. 'There's a torch … on my phone?'

Neve laughed, the online world mystified her. Neve held up her mobile and clicked the torch on her phone, revealing the light fixture so Grace could replace the bulb. Once done, Grace switched the light on, illuminating both sisters' upturned faces.

Alice said, 'I wish I'd known I had that torch function when I visited old Mr Schofield on the home help years ago! He suffered from HAVS and—'

'From what?' Asked Grace, frowning.

'Hand-Arm Vibration Syndrome, it's a condition resulting from years of working with electric hand tools, which affects the nerves and joints in later years, causing hand tremors. The miserable old sod was forever launching his pills in the air out of the dispenser and losing them. I spent ages crawling under his filthy sofa looking for the bloody things amongst the manky food he'd dropped in the dust balls.' Alice grimaced.

'I visited one day and he was sitting in his mobility chair, swishing his hands at his threadbare swirly carpet. Alice mimicked an old man's voice, ''ere can you get these bloody cats out of my house! I thought he'd gone doolally, turns out he had a urine infection causing hallucinations.' Alice's glorious toothy grin, which no-one could identify where that genetic feature came from, spread across her face as her sisters laughed. Alice glowed in her sisters' joy.

'Honestly, look at these.' Grace had begun foraging in a nearby large suitcase and held up three pairs of denim culottes. 'Mum hung on to absolutely everything; I mean, look at these proper vintage eighties throwbacks; they're more or less the same! Why would she buy three pairs?'

Within minutes, the three were wearing a pair of culottes each. They donned some of Ellen's favourite items of clothing, draping scarves around their necks and teetering on spiked heels and platforms from days gone by. Neve found an original 1970s tie-dye top. She spoke fondly about memories of Ellen showing her how to wrap string around t-shirts, and dip dying them with purple Dylon in a huge pot on the stove to create unique patterns. 'I'm sure we boiled onion skins for an effect too?'

The women periodically held up items of clothing, ornaments, pictures, and toys, anything with poignant reminiscences about their young lives at home with their parents. A few hours passed, and the women were exhausted and grubby from sliding yet another huge dust engrained box full of stuff into the centre of the loft, and gently lifting up precious and, at times, hilarious items.

'Honestly, she kept every single Christmas decoration we ever had,' said Alice, stepping over three long boxes with Christmas trees inside, holding another box of treasures. 'Look at these sparkly numbers!' She held up two wall decorations that flooded the memories back into their brains. A snowman, complete with a bright orange carrot nose, striped scarf, and sticks for arms. The other, was a robin redbreast perched on a fence outside a snowy cottage scene, glinting in their glittery snowy backgrounds.

'I'm having those, love a bit of retro décor,' said Grace.

'You'll be wanting these I assume.' Alice held up several red, gold and green foil concertina ceiling garlands. She pulled a gold one apart and draped it around a nearby ceiling beam.

Grace said, 'there's retro, and there's pure bad taste.' With a sigh, she said. 'I think we deserve a tea break ladies?'

Grace popped downstairs, and soon, mugs of freshly-made tea emerged through the hatch. The sisters gratefully relieved her of the cargo. Neve sank a huge gulp of tea, as the three sat in silence surrounded by assorted items, relishing the refreshing elixir, sipping from 1980's era mugs.

'How was Maisie when you spoke with her?' asked Alice.

Neve replied, 'she was okay. The funeral was bloody hard for her, as it was for all of us. Losing her husband only eighteen months before is a huge double-whammy. I hope she hasn't gone off the rails again.'

Alice added, 'not surprising, losing the two most important people in your life within two years. Kate and Fran are keeping an eye on her, and Fran temporarily moved in as she wasn't eating well. We've got to be mindful of Maisie's vulnerabilities.'

'I've always included her in everything,' continued Neve, 'but she could be … you know … resistant at times. Can't have been easy for her living in that orphanage, after being adopted, then fostered. I wonder if she felt like an outsider, sometimes?'

'Possibly, but she is our lovely Maisie McLaine,' determined Alice.

Grace was rueful, referring to the twenty-year age gap between her and Maisie. 'I didn't know when I was little she was our half-sister, I just assumed she was … our sister.'

'I do remember when mum explained how Maisie joined us,' said Alice. 'I guess Dad knew from the onset about mum being made to give her up. Maisie could've been brought up with us if things were different.'

Neve said, 'forced adoptions in the 1950s and 60s were rife, and mum wasn't given any choice about keeping her baby. If she had, I doubt whether she'd have ended up meeting and marrying dad, so none of us Clarkes would be here. Strange how life turns out. I wonder if mum ever told her who her father was; I'm not sure they had that conversation.'

'Must be strange having that sort of genetic mystery in your background.' Grace threaded both her arms carefully inside another box after finishing her tea, and pulled out a large pile of yellowing flimsy papers, files, and notebooks. She opened a small floral diary, and emotion hit her like a bullet-train as she saw her mother, Ellen's neat, immature writing inside the first page.

'Oh look at this,' she turned the notebook towards her sisters, gulping away the compulsion to cry. 'Mum had such beautiful handwriting. Can I take these home and read them? They look like diaries from when she was young.'

'Of course you can, honey,' said Alice, putting her arm around her younger sister.

Neve nodded in agreement. The three sisters sat in silence and acceptance that their lives would change forever, once this family home was sold, leaving only fading memories.

Chapter 11

Grace read her mother Ellen's diaries and notebooks, and couldn't quite reconcile the image of her recently deceased mother, frail and failing, as the young vibrant woman she once was. One entry referred to a handsome, exotic newcomer she named, Manny Petaky who burst on the scene in their town.

15th July 1959 – Saw Manny today. Miriam told me about him. He is GORGEOUS! He actually looked at me, right into my eyes, I nearly fainted. Imagine him coming to live here, in my street!

Reading the diaries had become routine for Grace before returning to work following bereavement leave. As soon as her husband took the children off to school on his way to work, she had the luxury of sitting on the sofa in silence, with a coffee. She'd rummage through the box from the loft containing Ellen's early journals and mementos.

Grace continued reading, and with compassion, gleaned that Ellen had indeed been on a date with Manny. They'd walked around the local park, and Ellen described their first kiss as, *amazing!* Ellen wrote that he was, *handsome like a movie star. I melt when he looks at me with his chocolate eyes.*

Grace worked out that in 1959, Ellen would've been fifteen, and she read Manny was three years older. 'Sounds like a catch, no wonder she fell for him, hook, line and sinker,' said Grace into the ether. She was surprised at an entry which read, *tonight, it happened!*

Followed by a row of hearts Ellen had drawn, interspersed with crosses for kisses.

Grace was both pleased her mother experienced the flush of young love, but was quite surprised she had teenage sex as she knew her parents were staunch catholic. Grace thought, nothing changes, every generation has the same feelings and urges, but there were many more risks for girls in those days. She read further into the diary entries, and after a few more, *it happened again*, references, with loving words, hearts, kisses, and romantic ideas of, *when we get married*. The tone changed dramatically two months later. *That Miriam! Selfish sod. Can't believe I saw them together I could kill her.*

Grace, though not surprised, was saddened to read Manny had been playing away with Miriam, and likely several others. Her heart went out to her mum; whose dreams of white weddings, confetti, and a happy romantic life ever after, with a perfect baby, and the man she was completely infatuated with, must've come crashing down around her.

Grace's phone interrupted the heart-break. Alice called to ascertain how her sister was feeling about returning to the office following extended leave. Grace who wasn't forty yet, felt far too young to have lost her darling mother, and needed time from the demands of work.

'Been reading more of mum's diaries. It's adorable that she fell in love with a guy called Manny when she was fifteen.' 'Ah, young love, how sweet,' replied Alice.

'Well … it was until she saw him with, selfish sod Miriam,' said Grace. 'Seems Maisie's birth father was the, love 'em and leave 'em, type. The toe-rag. Wonder if Maisie knows any of this.'

'Maybe not. Are we all still meeting up tomorrow?' asked Alice.
'Yes, around sixish.'
'You'll have to give us an update, see you later,' said Alice.

Grace continued to read Ellen's diaries in as near to chronological order as she could, surprised there was none following the, *selfish sod Miriam*, entry. She'd rummaged through every box when she spotted a large decorative envelope full of notelets. She opened it, and read Ellen's immature handwriting.

This place is in London, I think it's called the Queen Charlotte Nursing Hospital. Mum and Dad have gone, but they'll be back in a few weeks.

Grace read the opening line again twice. 'They've left her in hospital?' She said aloud, then a dawning hit her repeating, 'a nursing hospital.' Tears sprung into her eyes as she read further about how frightened Ellen was in this alien place. She imagined the quiet, well behaved, polite girl being guided by the nuns and the doctor who did his rounds.

Tears dripped as she said to her mother's spirit, if there was such a thing, 'Oh no, they left you all alone, Mum, you poor thing.' Grace recalled Ellen telling them she had to go to a hospital to have Maisie, but assumed she was only there to give birth and her parents stayed with her to take her home afterwards, not that she had been left on her own there for weeks.

Grace imagined a young Ellen sitting, writing her thoughts about her circumstances. There was a brief entry describing Manny, and a little about his family background. Also, the domestic tasks she and her fellow *fallen women* had to endure, polishing silver cutlery, scrubbing floors, cleaning bathrooms, working in the laundry, and, praying for repentance twice a day. Ellen also wrote the women had to hand over all of their statutory maternity allowance. Grace was glad everyone was out of the house as she sobbed, reading the profoundly sad words of a heartbroken young girl, who had the double whammy of losing her first love, and her first baby, also being financially exploited by the organisation supposedly caring for her.

Ellen described lying on a bed alone with labour pains that took her breath away, and looking around, seeing medicine bottles on shelves with a desire to get up and drink the medicines, so it would take the pain away, or even kill her so she could end the terrifying ordeal. There was an entry a few days after she had given birth.

The contractions were painful I couldn't bear it, but I didn't dare cry. I heard the doctor say he could see the baby's head. A nurse kept telling me to push, push, push, but I couldn't do it, I was scared the baby was stuck. My body took over with a huge pain, it pushed the baby out. I felt a warm foot on the top of my leg, they placed the little thing on my chest. Told me it's a girl. Baby gurgled, and I said hello to my daughter. The nurse wrapped her in a blanket and placed her face close to my breast. She started feeding, it was a funny pulling sensation. I stroked her face, her body was really warm. I didn't cry. It was calm and quiet for a few minutes. I couldn't stop looking at her. It's amazing I've made a little person. She's so beautiful.

There were hearts, flowers and kisses drawn on the page. The symbols of a girl, too immature to become a mother, and quite badly let down by everyone. Grace continued her one-sided conversation, 'ah, Mum,' said Grace aloud again, her tears finally subsiding, 'it was barbaric in those days. I'm so sorry all of that happened to you.'

Grace held the book to her heart, walked to the kitchen, poured another coffee from the cafetiere, and as she stood in quiet contemplation, she wondered how much detail Ellen had told Maisie about the circumstances of her birth. She questioned whether Maisie would want to know.

The following day, the sisters met up for a final time at their, now sold, family home. It was completely cleared, and they sat on folding picnic stools, as they completed their final goodbyes to the childhood home, that had brought comfort and fun over the years. Jen arrived, and soon the pop of the sending-off bottle of champagne, was heard.

The sisters spoke again of loving memories of baking cakes with mum, and fighting over who got to lick the mixing spoon and bowl. How they loved the spaghetti bolognese Saturday nights, which their mum thought was a really exotic meal; playing cards or board games, and snuggling down together in their parents bed on weekend mornings. Crazy Christmases with masses of gifts, lazy summer holidays at the beach; helping dad digging his vegetable patch and meticulously storing his tools in the old shed. The times they broke a pane in the greenhouse and were grounded, a little face miserably peering out of the bedroom window as the others played together, taunting the culprit. The culprit was usually Alice, by her own admission. Then came teenage angst and arguments of pinching each other's new clothes, and all of the boyfriend troubles.

Chatter came around to the present. Grace kept them up to date with Ellen's diaries, but omitted much of the distressing testimony about Manny and the nursing hospital for now. She decided Maisie should be the first to read it.

'How are things back at work, Grace?' Maisie asked. Maisie had arrived after her Tai Chi class, to join her sisters as the champagne flowed.

'Mixed feelings. Good to join the team again, but I'll really miss sitting with my coffee reading mum's diaries every morning, it's become my routine, but now I'll be sitting at traffic lights.'

There was an audible groan from each sister in agreement.

Grace continued, 'I am looking forward to catching up with, *scabby scrotum* though.'

There was an audible wince this time from each sister, as Grace referred to one of her road traffic accident claimants. A young man was injured when he was knocked of his motorbike, and skidded facedown along the road, shredding his leathers, and his genitals which required stitches.

They enjoyed the reminiscences of weddings, holidays, arguments, laughter, tears, and the subsequent arrival of the many offspring that enriched their family. Maisie, Neve, Jen, Alice, and Grace, held each other in emotional tearful embraces in their final fond farewell for the life they enjoyed at 74 North Park Lane.

That evening, Grace contemplated what to do with the information from Ellen's diaries. She texted Kate, tentatively suggesting information about Maisie's birth father had come to light. She trusted Kate's judgement, especially because this information may have an impact upon her too. He was, after all, her birth grandfather. Grace ended the text with a question, should she say anything to Maisie? Kate called, and following a conversation with Grace, both agreed Maisie should be given the information.

Chapter 12

The following morning Grace called her sister, 'hi, Maisie, how're you doing?'

'Okay, some days are better than others. I've received a little more bad news, Lizzie Blossom isn't too well. Had a call from one of her sons, I really should try to visit soon.

'Sorry to hear that, I guess we all get to an age when this will happen more often.'

'Lizzie wasn't a bad old sort really; not sure I was the sort of daughter that she wanted. I'm glad I got back in touch and made peace with the Blossoms, after all, I did live with them for ten years. Old Bertie is in the rest home where I used to tend the gardens as a youngster, must pop and see him again soon. He's in his nineties now, still calls me Flossie when I visit. It's good to catch up with my brothers every now and again too. They taught me how to look after myself.'

Maisie recollected the rough and tumble memories of growing up with the family. 'It was mum who encouraged me to make contact with my foster family years ago, she was right about a lot of things, she had compassion and wisdom, didn't she?'

'She most certainly did, mum always thought of others first. I really can't get my head around the fact I won't ever see her face again,' said Grace. There was a long silence.

'I will miss her every day,' said Maisie, 'things could have been so different if she hadn't accepted me back into the family, when

I turned up on her doorstep all those years ago. You know, Grace, sometimes, I wonder what I've done to deserve losing everyone I love in my life. First, my adoptive mother, though I can't really remember her, but her death was the reason I ended up at the orphanage, as my supposed forever-family adoptive dad couldn't cope. Then Jimmy died far too soon, and now mum. George is the best step-dad ever, but he's not doing so well either is he?'

'Maisie. You haven't done anything wrong! None of this is anyone's fault, and our dad is your dad, he loves you to bits. I know it's hard losing mum, she was so special. But if we hadn't loved her so much, we wouldn't feel the pain we are in. Hey, listen, I'm going to pop over, will you be in this evening? Kate's coming along too. It'll be good to talk about mum and ... everything.' Grace's throat constricted, and tears pricked her eyes as she heard Maisie's quiet response, that she'd love to see them.

On the journey over, Grace questioned whether it was the right time for Maisie to learn about her putative father, Manny, as she was clearly suffering from all of her losses in one big fell swoop.

'Mum may already know about him,' said Kate. She was sitting in the passenger seat with Ellen's diaries on her lap. Kate read through the pertinent information Grace had pointed out on the journey over.

'Fran is so excited about all this; she wants to do the whole genealogy and ancestry searches. I didn't suggest she came along today as she may bombard her with too many questions. You know what nineteen-year-olds are like when they get a bee in their bonnet.'

Grace said, 'I do question whether we are forcing Maisie to make a decision she would rather not have to, it's a no-going-back situation, once the genie is out of the bottle, it's hard to put it back in.'

Kate said, 'I couldn't hang on to all this information, it wouldn't be right to keep it from her. It's her life history, she has never said much at all about her father; simply his name, and he was Greek. That's it. I do wonder if she knows more about her origins, whether Granny Ellen told her much or not.'

The car swept onto the drive at Maisie's house, in the spot where Jimmy's van used to park. Grace recognised how lost Maisie and Kate must feel at times with these reminders every day. Maisie had the tea brewed and a ridiculous assortment of biscuits out on a plate, reminding them of Ellen. After the usual catchup, Grace broached the subject of Maisie's paternity.

Maisie said. 'I never knew any more than he was a handsome stranger who briefly came to live in the town, and he must have seduced mum.' Maisie had no resentment of the actions of two young people who had given her the gift of life. She never punished her mother for giving her up and understood a sixteen-year-old Ellen, would never have had a say in keeping her baby given the times, and religious beliefs of her parents.

'If Ellen had been supported in keeping me, I'd imagine there would be stigma directed to us both, the fallen woman and her bastard child, and her parents may never have accepted me. One thing I do appreciate is that she was never legally tied to a man who may have treated her badly if they'd been forced to marry. I'm glad Ellen had a happy life, five lovely daughters, and loads of grandchildren.' Maisie leaned towards Grace, who was in close proximity, and took her hand.

Grace responded by squeezing Maisie's hand. 'You always were and always will be the first sister, and I'm so glad you were brave enough to return to us.'

'Have you ever thought about tracing your birth father?' Kate asked nonchalantly.

'To be honest, I have. You live everyday with curiosity. Did he know Ellen was pregnant, if he did, did he leave her anyway? There is little detail, and there never seemed to be a good moment to ask mum about tracing him. I know she carried a lot of guilt for the first sixteen years of my life, as none of it worked out. Once, when we spoke, she cried and said she should have been braver and taken me away from the Blossoms, but it would've been impossible for her. I often wonder what Lizzie Blossom's motivation was for me to live with her family. But Bertie, I know he really cared about me. Honestly, Bertie Blossom, his name makes me smile. What were his parents thinking? Lizzie hated being called Betty too.' Maisie laughed. 'Bertie and Betty Blossom, what a pair.'

The women laughed and sipped their tea. Grace was on to her fourth biscuit, not having had time for any lunch being back at work.

'It was odd calling them mum and dad, they didn't feel like my permanent parents,' said Maisie, 'they could have got a legal guardianship for me, but never did. I'm so lucky mum didn't send me packing when I turned up out of the blue.' The sisters squeezed hands again.

Kate was nothing, if not persistent. 'If new information came up about your birth dad, would you be interested in hearing it?'

'What have you been up to, Kate?' asked Maisie quite abruptly.

'Em … Grace may have some information.' Kate offered an almost imperceptible nod to Grace.

Grace said, 'well, okay … I found some diaries in the loft when we had the clear-out, that mum wrote when she was really young. She has written a little bit about a boy who may … be your natural father.' She glanced at Kate for reassurance, and noticed another imperceptible nod. 'It seems there is a little more information, and we wondered if you want to read about him?'

Maisie fell silent. There was a moment of stillness when the three women's spirits floated up into limbo, stopping time. Once their bodies settled back into their weighted present, Grace saw consternation in Maisie's face, and wondered whether it would open up wounds of resentment; it could be either a fulfilling revelation or a crushing disappointment. She also noticed a nervous edge in Kate's demeanor in that resounding silence.

Maisie stood suddenly, walked toward the patio doors, and gazed out into the neat garden. Grace and Kate looked at each other with anxiety. The genie was well and truly out of the bottle, freely swooshing around the room creating emotional chaos.

They were relieved to hear Maisie, still looking out at the garden, say, 'I suppose it could be interesting. I won't hold out too much hope of it meaning anything … but … yes, why not. Reading about how I came to be, might be quite enlightening.'

Grace said, 'I have to say, some of what mum went through as a young girl, the way the system was, is quite upsetting to read.'

Maisie replied unemotionally, 'oh I know. I still remember the dark, depressing, empty place I was returned to for re-sale.'

Kate wanted to cry. How could this beautiful, elegant, proud woman have once been a small frightened, powerless child being passed around at the adults' will. Grace sat on the arm of the chair and put a comforting arm around Kate.

Maisie walked back to the sofa and, with compassion, said to Kate. 'None of this is anyone's fault, darling. It's just the way it was in those days.'

'I know, but it's so unfair, so brutal,' said Kate.

Maisie said brightly, 'come on, show me what you've discovered.'

Grace sat beside Maisie on the sofa and lifted the diaries out of her bag. Kate went to make another pot of tea, and they didn't see the tears streaming down her face. She composed herself, and emerged, smiling warmly as they read out little bits of dialogue from the diaries. The evening ran on, and it was time to get home after Grace finished reading out the, *selfish sod Miriam*, passage.

Maisie was pleased she now had a name confirmed, Manny. Knowing he was Greek, and movie-star handsome resulted in her preening, stroking her hair and saying, 'so that's where my sultry looks come from.'

The women were saddened reading and talking about how Ellen's life must have been. It brought history to life and, more importantly, brought their mother back to them, but as a young woman with all of the hopes, that love and frailties innocent teenage years bring.

Grace placed Ellen's notebook on the coffee table. 'I'll leave this one for you to read on your own.'

'Mm, yes, that's the one that may bring on the waterworks,' said Kate. 'Please call me if you want me to pop over later and talk about it ... promise?'

Maisie reassured her daughter that she would, as she appreciated Kate worried about her emotional health since Jimmy died. They had an extended hug before parting.

Maisie began to read Ellen's diaries and notebooks that evening. The fragility of the girl who became her stable parent, and competent loving mother to five daughters, tore her to emotional shreds. Maisie reconciled her feelings that, had she remained with Ellen, their relationship may not have been so positive, and her sisters may not have even been born.

Maisie recalled the day she found out she was pregnant with her own daughter, Kate, and it was inconceivable to her that any parent could allow their child to be taken away, but circumstances were rather different when Ellen was sixteen years old in 1960.

In the morning, Maisie was feeling a little stunned at the revelations from the previous day; reminiscing about her early beginnings was often a painful process. Her family history had revealed some mystery, too. Ellen wrote – rumours of something terrible – had happened concerning Manny's father. Apparently Manny would never speak of his dad, none of the family did it seemed. Was there horrible dark secrets in her past, Maisie wondered as she pulled the duvet cover over the bed and smoothed it out.

Thankfully her recall of the night Jimmy died was less distinct. She kissed the tip of her finger and placed it on the photo of him on the bedside cabinet. She changed into a pair of smart cargo trousers and a cotton knit top. You'd never catch Maisie in a pair of scruffy old joggers and sweatshirt, some of Lizzie Blossom's early influence remained. She called Kate to reassure she was fine, and she would spend the day at home reading over Ellen's diaries. She invited Kate over after her shift that day.

Later that afternoon, Maisie took her coffee cup and sat outside on the patio. Walking through the ever-so neat and tidy rooms of her semidetached home, with its subtle décor, she listened to the silence of the ever-so empty house. She pulled a thick shawl around her shoulders in the weakening February sunlight. She missed Jimmy, looking at the empty chair of their mosaic tiled patio set, she imagined his familiar cheery greetings; he always looked on the bright side. She thought about how they met. Jimmy owned a fruit and veg stall she frequented, then worked hard to create his own successful business, opening a cafe and a bakery on the high street, then a chain of outlets in the local area. He was a robust, handsome man. Everyone loved Jimmy, he was larger than life, his loss left a gaping space.

Maisie recalled with fondness how thrilled he was when she said yes to his marriage proposal, saying he'd punched above his weight, marrying the most beautiful girl in town. They were happy, Maisie realised she took to him because he was dependable, and he offered her the security she yearned for. He was her anchor, the thing that stopped the ship from rocking and rolling in turbulent seas, and prevented her having that familiar feeling of drowning. She was safe with Jimmy, and now he was gone, and her mother was gone too; there was an emptiness inside which she accepted would last until her final breath.

A starling murmuration caught her eye in the hazy russet evening glow. The perfectly coordinated display, as thousands of birds synchronised as one, reminded her, she must visit Bertie Blossom soon, before it was too late.

Chapter 13

It was another chilly February afternoon out in the garden as Maisie sipped a hot chocolate; Fran would be arriving in an hour to talk about past revelations. Fran was enamoured with romantic stories of Ellen and Manny, and she wanted to trace her maternal family heritage. Maisie was looking forward to her visit, and had arranged to watch a movie that evening. Fran stayed over on a weekend night occasionally to keep her grandma company. Maisie wondered if Fran would choose a favourite childhood Pixar movie, or something more grown-up. Secretly, she hoped it was, *Toy Story*.

Fran arrived in a bluster of chatter, in skinny jeans, Doc Martens, and slouchy knit top. Her golden fair hair was bundled on top of her head, which tumbled past her shoulders in natural curls when she removed the hair band. She had inherited, what Maisie now knew, were Mediterranean features of dark brown eyes, and skin that turned a deep golden tan in the sun. She was a lovely northern and southern European genetic mix. Fran dropped her huge gaping bag onto the floor and gently kicked her boots off.

'How about something spicy tonight? There's a great takeaway opened nearby, and they do Thai.'

'Sounds interesting, why not?'

'I love trying new things. It's not too spicy, I think you'll really enjoy it.'

'Does Liam like Thai food?'

'Hah, you're joking! If it isn't fish and chips, bangers and mash, or steak pie and peas, or something with Yorkshire pudding on it, he turns his nose up. You'd never get a noodle past his lips.'

'What do you have when you have takeaway together.'

'Italian, usually share a couple of pizzas; plain Margherita or something with chicken on it, and a garlic bread.'

'What if you wanted something a little different, could you persuade him to go for that?'

'Probably not. But I get the chance to try things out when I meet up with the girls, or go out with Lucy and Greg as we share the dishes. But Lucy can't eat spices right now anyway, she's huge, have you seen her recently.'

'I saw her out shopping; ankles swollen up like balloons, bless her.'

'Yea, cankles.'

Maisie looked at her granddaughter, awaiting explanation.

'You know … when your calves join your ankles with no definition … cankles.'

'Aw, Fran, that's not nice.' They both chuckled, 'what if you end up like that if you and Liam have children.'

'That's not happening for aaages!' exclaimed Fran. 'No way do I want to be pregnant before I'm' … she pondered a little … 'twenty-five.' Then said resolutely, 'engaged on my twenty first, married eighteen months later, and kids a year, or five after that.

'Have you discussed this with Liam?'

'Yea, but he says he wants a baby straight away. Not if I can help it. No big belly and cankles for me until I'm ready.' Fran stuffed a cushion up her top, and imitated Lucy's waddling gait. 'We've visited some venues for our engagement party, and bigger ones for the wedding, but they are ssoo expensive!'

'There's no rush is there? Have some holidays, have fun before you settle down.'

'You and mum both married young and had children really

quickly. I was a shotgun, wasn't I?' Fran smirked, and her big brown eyes looked into Maisie's. They matched perfectly.

'Your parents were already engaged, so we had to … bring the wedding a little further forward,' Maisie grinned. 'It was very different in mine and your Granny Ellen's day though. You needed a man to look after you.'

'Worked out for you though, didn't it, and mum?' asked Fran

'It did, but I was doing an apprenticeship at a dressmaker's when I met and married Jimmy, and I always meant to finish my qualifications, but it didn't happen. I was a good dressmaker and thought about going into fashion, maybe becoming a designer, but I never really had the confidence to get the qualifications.'

The regret lay trapped like a bubble in a spirit level, never able to be released, only moving within the confines of its barriers. A quick shrug and the thoughts were gone. 'I've always had a leaning towards good clothes and fashion, probably after living with the Blossoms. I also shared the interest with your Granny Ellen, her first job was as a milliner's assistant for a local shop.

'Fashionistas!' Fran announced with a flourish, 'I'm much more of a casual gal myself.'

'And totally gorgeous with it.' Maisie opened her arms, and Fran fell into them, side by side on the sofa. Maisie could smell the faint scent of coconut hair products, and stroked her granddaughter's beautiful golden locks.

'Toy Story?' Maisie suggested.

Fran rolled her eyes, 'I suppose so.' Then scrolled her mobile to find the number for the new takeaway.

Maisie thought about Fran that night lying in bed, and her relationship with boyfriend Liam. Her observations led Maisie to conclude, Liam was the more content partner. Whenever she asked Fran what she had been up to, the responses inevitably seemed to be led by Liam's hobby and social commitments of playing football with his mates. Fran appeared to relish her role as a dutiful girlfriend, and didn't go out as often with her female friends.

There were parallels between her and Jimmy, in that Liam was hardworking and reliable. Maisie lived in domestic bliss, recognising she needed security, but could admit to feeling restricted at times. Jimmy's expectations were that she would be a homemaker, to feed and clothe him; their physicality and sex-life was mainly geared towards his needs, rather regular and straightforward, but, still satisfying for her too. Maisie never saw a spark in Fran's eyes when they spoke about Liam.

Fran didn't stay the night as she was meeting a friend in town to go shopping the following day, which pleased Maisie. As she rinsed out the coffee cups, she thought about asking Fran about the decision to get engaged on her twenty first birthday. She wanted to know if Fran was truly content; she wasn't yet twenty, and it seemed too young to be making the commitment. But, this grandmother concluded, she should not interfere.

A sudden rush of enthusiasm hit Maisie, following the previous evening's discussions with Fran.

She sent a message to Kate: *I think I'm ready to find out x*

Kate replied: *Ok coffee at ours 10.30 tomorrow x*

Fran was really excited about the prospect of finding out she had an exotic heritage, and said to Kate previously, 'I've told the girls at work, they're quite intrigued about the fact I'm Greek and we're going to trace my great grandad's family.'

Kate didn't want to diminish her daughter's enthusiasm, so tempered the situation. 'You can only go so far with genealogy searches, Fran, it could be a dead-end, but worth a try, especially if we're related to the Onassis family, or some other zillionaires. Doubt it though, can't imagine they'd be knocking around the outer suburbs of Greater Manchester in the 1960s if they were loaded.'

'True,' said Fran, 'I think it will help Nan; I know she has times when she's not so good … about her past and everything.' Their conversation was interrupted.

'Fran, Fran!' Liam was yelling from upstairs.

Fran sighed, and went to the foot of the stairs. 'Did you wash my kit?'

'Yes, it's in the middle drawer.' Fran referred to the middle drawer, which was assigned to Liam, in her bedroom when he stayed over. Fran had been with Liam since their last year in school. Once they became an established couple, her parents thought it futile for them to be forced into sneaky sex until they married, which could be years away. Kate had the contraception talk when Fran was a young teenager. The young couple were saving like mad to get a mortgage, so they could move to independence in their own home.

'What's he whining about now?' asked Kate, as she passed Fran on her way into the kitchen.

It was a continuing theme; the family playfully treated Liam as the butt of all jokes, always losing things, being forgetful, and unable to look after himself.

'Honestly, it's like having a baby,' she rolled her eyes at Fran, and with a smirk said. 'Just wait until you have children, he'll have to fend for himself then.'

Liam was adept at many homemaking skills his father had taught him, and had come in handy whenever they needed household repairs. To his credit, Liam worked hard as a mechanic for a national car repair company, and his skills were handy when family cars went on the blink. He pattered down the stairs with his sports bag in his hand, ready for football training.

'Dodgy eyesight or what?' asked Fran. 'Why didn't you look in the middle drawer straight away? You know your stuff is in there.'

'I thought you may have put them out somewhere.'

'Out somewhere ... where? Like right in front of your stupid nose.'

He gave her a playful hug. 'Don't know what I'd do without you.' Then a peck on the cheek.

'Me neither. Have you thought any more about going to the

cinema tonight? We could eat at the new Lebanese place for a change, they do chicken dishes. I get tired of us being stuck in here all the time,' moaned Fran.

'Not sure,' he replied, 'I'll have to wait and see if the lads have got anything planned after the match. May go for a few pints.'

'Can't you find out before the match, so we can make plans, we haven't been anywhere for ages.'

'Depends whether Howsy and Bilbo can be let off the leash,' he smirked.

'Let off the leash? Quite the derogatory way of putting it.'

'You know what Bilbo's missus is like. Honestly, her face is like a bulldog chewing a wasp, if he even mentions going out.'

'Don't talk about her like that. Honestly, sometimes your turn of phrase … she's probably got every reason to keep an eye on him, he's an idiot when he's had a drink.'

Liam's mate, William Bowen, aka Bilbo, had caused ructions when the lads took a summer holiday in Spain. There were rumours about girls being in their rooms, which were vociferously refuted by the lads cabal upon their return, sworn to secrecy. Fran was convinced Liam wasn't like that and hadn't cheated on her, or at least Liam had convinced her; however, when they were out, she caught his fleeting gazes at glamorous young women, but that was normal wasn't it? Strange how most of the holiday pictures seemed to be deleted from their mobiles.

'Yeah, but he is really funny. Always good craic on a mad night out with Bilbo.'

There were times when Fran despaired at Liam's willingness to be swept along by the madness of his immature mates on nights out. Like Bilbo's missus, she was not keen on Liam going abroad on holiday again with the lads after the antics they may, or may not have, got up to, led by Bilbo. Many Saturday nights would entail Fran sitting with her parents, sharing dinner, and watching tv. Or she'd pop along to spend time with her childhood friend Lottie, who also still lived at home on the same street; sometimes, they'd venture out for a drink.

On this occasion, an evening out dining, then cinema with Liam would be put on the back burner … yet again. Fran concluded not spending money on a night out would go into the savings for the deposit on the home she and Liam were saving for; and, of course, for the perfect wedding.

Fran's dad Paul would repeat, 'Liam is as easy as an old shoe. He's reliable, earns a good living, and there won't be any surprises.'

Fran accepted, and appreciated Liam's general ability to tootle along in life with his easy-going manner, but everything was routine; they rarely did anything spontaneously. She once tentatively mentioned starting a Ceroc dance class together, a work colleague went with her husband, and thoroughly enjoyed it; Liam had burst out laughing. Fran felt ridiculed, never again suggesting they consider something so out of the ordinary. Fran loved the cinema; Liam, more often than not, fell asleep half way through, so they're would be no dialogue afterwards discussing the plot, or characters. He would always yawn all the way home, slip into bed, and drop off to sleep, after having obligatory and enthusiastic sex, of course. Fran did find him attractive, he was great looking, and in good physical shape. They had always been a good fit when it came to their lovemaking. He was a kind and considerate man, and she could do a lot worse, as her dad constantly reminded her.

Chapter 14

At half past ten the following day, Maisie arrived at Kate's house, and before she had taken her coat off, or got the 'hellos' out of the way, Fran emerged from the living room door.

'How is it young girls went through such awful experiences like Granny Ellen? The men would have got away scot-free, all they had to do was have sex, then walk away, it's shameful!'

'The way of the world in those days, Fran,' said Maisie as she settled on the sofa. She could hear the hisses and gurgles as Kate made drinks with their new state of the art coffee-maker.

'Well, I think it's unutterably cruel and harsh,' replied Fran. Maisie and Kate offered each other a smile at Fran's indignant comment. A gorgeous, caramel aroma filled the room as Kate brought in the creamy lattes.

Maisie picked up her iPad, swiping, 'I did a little research about where mum gave birth to me. I discovered the Queen Charlotte Nursing Hospital was originally established near Marylebone in the mid-18th century. It was founded by, and get this, the Roman Catholic Order of the Sisters Servants of the Sacred Hearts of Jesus and Mary.' Maisie offered up a generous eye roll to the ceiling and continued reading. 'Queen Charlotte Hospital provided accommodation for unmarried mothers and their first-born babies.

'Girls were admitted free of charge, if they were destitute, on condition that they contributed to the earning power of the hospital by working in the laundry, and providing other domestic services. So … slaves, to be precise.' Maisie's voice was unemotional.

She continued, 'there were antenatal and postnatal beds in six bedded wards on the ground floor, with a labour ward on the first floor, and twelve cots ready for babies.' Maisie paused, then read with disdain, 'the patients, as they named them, not mothers, stayed for an average of ten weeks. The fees are in pounds, shillings and pence.'

Maisie noticed a confused expression on Fran's face, and continued.

'That's old money, Fran. A rough equivalent was one pound a week for expectant mothers, and one pound seventy-five pence for a mother and her baby. It would've been about a week's wage in those days. I guess Ellen's parents paid the fees.' She fell silent momentarily with Fran and Kate looking on.

'I don't know where to begin, to be honest,' said Maisie, breaking the silence, 'glad I've got you two to help fathom out where we go next to research who my father is. I use the term loosely, he was not my father at all, just the sperm donor.'

'Nan!' Fran looked up, giggling; Kate almost spat her coffee out.

'I'm only telling it like it is girls. Who knows how many half siblings I may have all over the place, but I am interested in the Greek part of the story if it's true.' Maisie made a flamboyant hand gesture. 'The land of heroes, hot sun, the beautiful Aegean Sea, and, of course, the goddesses and gods.'

'It would be good to get a DNA analysis,' suggested Kate, 'that may determine if Greek heritage is present. I'll send for a test.'

Fran summarized, 'okay, what we know so far is where you were born, and your birth father was named Manny Petaky, he was eighteen in 1959, therefore born in 1940 or 41, and he lived in Granny Ellen's Street. Without further details, finding a record of him may be impossible. We also believe there was a scandal, as Granny Ellen wrote of, something terrible, happening that he wouldn't speak of.

'Apart from the diaries and your original birth certificate which doesn't name a father,' Fran lifted the document, 'there is little factual information. However, I searched for Greek male names beginning with, m – a – n, and I thought there'd be loads, but the name Manolis is consistent. Is there anyone alive who would've known Ellen at the time, maybe they would remember something?'

'Gran used to visit an old neighbour, Aunt Rene,' said Kate, 'she'd take me and Grace to visit when we were young. She may know something. Think she's still knocking about somewhere; she'll be in her late seventies by now.'

'I remember Rene,' said Maisie, 'I believe she's now in residential care. I have mum's old address book upstairs.' Maisie retrieved the book, revealing an entry in Ellen's handwriting; Irene (Rene) Wilson, and the address of the residential care home was written beneath another crossed out address.

'I'll visit Rene to tell her about Ellen, as she probably won't know.' Maisie rang the care home and arranged to visit. The staff member was delighted as Rene's family rarely visited, and she was becoming more frail, as was her memory.

The three generations discussed the romantic prospect of having Greek heritage. They worked out a plan of how they would further the searches and agreed to meet if any significant detail was discovered.

The following week Maisie visited Rene, then recounted over a FaceTime call with Fran and Kate, what she revealed.

'Rene did recollect Manny's family,' Maisie noticed Fran's excitement, 'the surname sounded like Petaky. She knew the family were from a Greek island. Ellen told her something mysterious happened, as the family turned up out of nowhere, and a father or husband was never mentioned. She couldn't recall the mother's name exactly, and thought it began with Z. She said the mother was stunning. All the men in town knew of her and frequented the pub on the nights she was working. Apparently Manny worked in the local garage helping to fix cars.'

'Ooh, just like Liam!' Fran added, thrilled at the connection.

'Rene did remember the Petakys moved on quickly when rumours of Manny being the father of Ellen's child turned out to be true,' said Maisie.

'I'm sure Rene was upset to learn Ellen had died,' said Kate.

'She was at first, but when I left, she asked me to give my regards to Ellen, so I think the short-term memory is befuddled, but thankfully, the long-term memories were reasonably intact.'

'What Rene described was really sad, because Ellen was shut away when the pregnancy rumours began. Rene's mum must have been sympathetic, as she took her along to visit Ellen. Rene described going upstairs to see Ellen, who was lying on her bed, looking pale with, *a full tummy*, as she said. Ellen wouldn't talk about Manny or having the baby. I'm glad that visit happened, as those two young girls obviously remained good friends for many years afterwards.' Maisie fell silent, she couldn't begin to imagine how isolated and vilified Ellen must have been.

Fran piped up. 'Would you like to hear more of my research?' Without waiting for a reply, she continued, 'Granny Ellen's diary said Manny's birth place may have been Corfu or Crete. I've discovered the surname Petrakis is the fourth most common in Crete, and is pronounced without the 's' therefore Petaky could be Petrakis ... maybe. Online genealogy websites for Greece revealed the top three male names in Cretan records are; Georgios, Ioannis, and Emmanouil, which is more commonly known as Manolis. Okay ... it's tenuous, but Manny could be a shortened version of Manolis. I'll do more research with the National Archive Office in Athens for any trace of; a Manolis Petrakis, with a birth date between 1940 and 1942, born in Crete.

'You've been busy, Fran!' Kate was taken aback at her daughter's diligence.

'I love doing this sort of thing. As long as you make sure you're looking in the most likely of places; there are tons of databases. You're like a detective trying to identify someone from clues.' She beamed.

'I'll look into UK Census records for the family surname Petrakis,' said Maisie, 'but his mother may have remarried or reverted to her maiden name if there was some sort of scandal.'

Kate agreed to look through newspaper archives and The Historical Criminal Register for any activity related to the name Petrakis in the post-war period from 1946, but thought it unlikely that accurate records of domestic crimes were recorded.

It was looking like a lost cause until a week later when Kate rang Maisie, full of excitement, to say she'd discovered a news archive. She read out details from the written record. In May 1947: N. Petrakis was questioned in connection with a serious incident involving a travelling salesman. There was scant detail, apart from, N. Petrakis worked at a London warehouse. He was married, and had two young children.

'I'll keep digging in archive reports for a trial date, if indeed there was a trial. Maybe Mr Petrakis was a baddie, and his wife and kids had to leave him.'

'That's really worrying if it's true.' Maisie was dismayed, the last thing she wanted was to discover some heinous act in her background.

'Got to keep an open mind on all this, haven't we. Have you had the DNA results yet?'

'Oh yes, I have, just this morning. Tell you what, shall we meet, and I'll reveal all.'

'Sounds good, are you Greek?

'Yes.'

'Brilliant, can't wait to tell Fran.'

Fran and Kate arrived at Maisie's, with a bottle of Prosecco. Maisie revealed the results of her DNA test, and sure enough it confirmed she was 51% English, predominantly the Lancashire region with some Yorkshire thrown in, no surprises there. She was matched as being 38% Greek, 7% Balkan, and a surprising 4% Scandinavian.

'That must be where your love of Abba comes from,' Kate laughed, 'that tiny bit of Scandi DNA.'

The cool, bubbly drinks went down a treat as they thrilled at this information.

'So I'm nearly 20% Greek, and Fran 10%, though I'm not sure it works out like that,' puzzled Kate.

'Thank you for the great skin-tone, Nan,' said Fran, patting her cheeks. 'I know what! We should go to that new Greek restaurant, shouldn't we? To drink ouzo and eat souvlaki to celebrate our family heritage.'

'Great idea,' agreed Maisie.

Chapter 15

A further three weeks elapsed when Fran received an online acknowledgement from the National Archives in Athens. They confirmed a list of male children with similar names to, Manolis Petrakis within the data parameters. One, in particular, caught her eye; he was born on 28 March 1941 in Archanes, which she discovered was a small village north of the city of Heraklion in Crete. There was no further specific detail. The three women gathered together again, at Kate's house.

'Thankfully, they translated the records into English. I was half expecting those hieroglyphics,' said Fran.

Kate was now intrigued to discover who her long lost grandfather might be. She had never asked about her mother's paternity.

'I wonder if it's really him. Even if we locate him, he could have died, or will deny all knowledge.'

'Probably,' said Maisie, 'the rat buggered off sharp enough.' Then with a wry smile said, 'I've been as busy as Fran, putting all of my admin skills into this research.' Maisie had a meticulous eye for detail, having overseen the accounts, ordering goods, invoicing and keeping the records for the McLaine's company, before she and Jimmy sold the business.

'Look at this.' She handed a piece of paper over to her daughter. It was a copy of a passenger list from the, SS Homeric, a passenger ship that sailed from Athens to England in 1946. It showed entries of name, age, sex, occupation, nationality, and destination for passengers on the voyage. There was an entry revealing; Nikolaos Petrakis, and Xanthe Petrakis as passengers, including Manolis Petrakis, aged five, and Cora Petrakis, aged two. The copied record stated their nationality was Greek.

'That is amazing, Mum.' Kate was wide-eyed.

'Seriously?' said Fran, snatching the paper from Kate. 'This is brilliant! It must be him … them, I mean, it's too much of a coincidence. How on earth did you find this, thought I was good at research.'

'Good old fashioned local library assistant called Catherine, who is like a dog with a bone, she wouldn't give up no matter that we kept coming up with nothing. Bless her heart, she spent hours at the ancient microfiche machine that I couldn't bear reading, but Catherine didn't mind. She directed me to the most likely archived data bases, and came up with the idea of families who migrated after the war to England. We've made good friends actually, and sometimes meet for a coffee. A clever, interesting, and pedantic woman is Catherine. She looks exactly like a traditional librarian should; no frills, thick glasses, pleated skirts, cardigans and sensible shoes, with a wicked sense of humour when you get to know her.'

'Fantastic, Manolis must be your birth dad. Far too coincidental not to be, surely,' said Kate.

There was a slight downcast look on Maisie's face. 'Would've been lovely to share this with your dad.'

'Ah, Mum, I know.' Mother and daughter hugged. 'He'd be thrilled for you … well, maybe?'

'He could be over protective, I know.' Maisie acknowledged.

Fran became animated, 'shall we go to Crete, Nan, to Archanes? It would be an adventure.'

'It could be a waste of time as we don't really know if this Manolis is my birth father, though some of the information does strike a chord from what Rene said, mum's diaries, and the secrecy about the family, it's too coincidental.'

Kate added 'you could stop off in Florence too, we always said we'd take Granny Ellen there, but never got around to it.'

'You're right,' said Maisie, 'it's why mum gave it as my middle name, she always wanted to go. But when George became poorly, she lost her enthusiasm and wanted to stay close to him. I wonder what she'd make of all this?'

'Doubt we would've started the whole shebang if she was still here. Maybe would've upset her, and we'd never want to do that'

'We can go in her honour,' Fran implored, 'come on, Nan! What do you say?'

'Oh … I don't know if I'm up for travelling into the unknown, who knows what we may find.' Maisie was pensive, it didn't take much to disturb her equilibrium.

'You should go, Mum,' said Kate softly, 'if Fran is up for tagging along. I'd love to go, but would never get the time off. Plus, I'm hoping for that long awaited extended leave to travel to the Caribbean for my fortieth. Twenty years I've given to the Police so far. I deserve a great big holiday, lying on a beach with unlimited cocktails and swimming in that azure sea.' Kate closed her eyes and sank back into the sofa. 'Does dad know of these plans, Mum?' asked Fran

'He'll find out soon enough.' Kate's eyes remained closed.

Fran said again, 'how about it, Nan, a trip to Florence, then Greece and anywhere else you'd like to visit before you're too old and decrepit,' she laughed.

'Cheeky thing, and are you made of money, honey?'

'I have some savings and wanted to go on holiday with Liam, but he's planning a lads final tour as a few of them are getting married and having twenty-firsts soon, so it's one big last lads hurrah.'

Maisie observed Fran; was there disappointment in her neutral expression? Kate was still Caribbean dreaming on the sofa.

'Okay, let's do it.' said Maisie impulsively.

'Great! Mum, me and Nan are off to Greece.' Fran was already scrolling for airline tickets and accommodation.

Kate roused with a jolt, 'oh, I was onto my second rum punch sitting on a sunny beach.'

'You look tired sweetheart, you do work so hard,' said Maisie.

'I know, it's not been easy over the years, but not long now before my big holiday break,' she smiled at her mother, then turned to her daughter. 'Fran, how long can you take off work? I'm assuming you can only have a few weeks in one stint.'

Both mother and grandmother were surprised at Fran's response.

'I'm thinking of taking a sabbatical, extended leave, or a career break or something. As long as they can cover my post. Josie did it last year to travel around India for three months, and they got a temp in.' 'That's quite adventurous for you?' said Kate.

There was disparity between mother and daughter. Kate had always been adventurous, seeking the adrenalin rush in her chosen profession. Fran however, enjoyed her employment as a speech therapy assistant with the health service; no dashing around or shift work for her. Further disparity was in the genetic mix too; Kate had inherited her father's robust stature, his blue eyes, fair hair and skin, whilst Fran's genes incorporated only the fair hair, with Maisie's olive skin and brown eyes.

'Well, let's be honest, it's the only chance I'll have before I'm married and settled with kids; then I'll be your age, before I get another chance.' Fran stood abruptly, from her prone position on the floor, walked out of the room, and closed the door. Her footsteps resounded as she ran upstairs.

'Is she ok?' Maisie asked Kate, looking at the closed door.

'Think so. She gets frustrated with Liam. You know what he's like, a bit boring and routine, but he is a lovely lad, steady and reliable.'

This comment inspired Maisie to be even more determined that the trip should happen. 'He is, that's for sure. Wonder if there's some preengagement nerves, bound to be, I suppose. Maybe it will do both me and Fran good to have this trip away.'

'Not sure what Liam will say about her buggering off for a month or two,' after a pause, Kate asked, 'how are you doing, Mum?' It was a regular request, with meaning.

'I'm fine, sweetheart, please don't worry about me. I've had the odd tipple now and again, but never once been tempted to wallow in it. It's a good balance, and I have the counsellor's details if I want to book further sessions or to call him. Don't need any sleeping pills now either, still have some in case, but honestly, never think about them.'

Kate peered across at her with a gentle nod, she seemed reassured.

Over the next few days, Fran busied herself arranging a travel route that would incorporate a stop off in Paris, Florence and Athens. She applied for extended unpaid leave for two months which was approved. Fran's parents were a little hesitant about her taking extra time off work, however, they saw the benefit of enriching her life experience before she settled down.

Later that day Fran rang Maisie, 'you should've seen Liam's face when I told him of our plans, he went ballistic.'

Maisie asked, 'why is he so cross? I thought he was planning a few last hurrahs with his mates?'

'He said it's a ridiculous idea, questioning why I'd go away for so long, and why don't I book a holiday with the girls instead? But I was adamant. He doesn't get that this will be it for me, because it wouldn't surprise me if he still goes on football trips, and stuff with his mates even when were married.'

'Once you're settled down, especially when children come along, it's not so easy to please yourself and have the freedom to travel.' Changing tack, as Maisie was irritated by Liam's response. 'How are you getting along with the plans to reach the destination where it all began? Or should I say, where I began.'

'That's it, Nan. Destination Maisie McLaine, here we come!'

'I'd like to pop in and see old Bertie Blossom en route if you can add that into the schedule?' said Maisie, 'maybe the last chance I'll get.'

'Of course, we can do a quick detour.'

'I know the area well, and Bertie now lives in the residential home where I volunteered as a kid.'

'I've always wanted to go on the Eurostar,' said Fran, 'hey, we could travel by rail, instead of flying, to really *see* places. I can get an under twenty-five rail card, and you'll be able to get a granny one, so it may work out quite reasonably.'

'I'm not that old!'

On 2 April 2019, a gathering was arranged at Maisie's house to celebrate her fifty-ninth birthday; a week later she and Fran would be setting off on their adventure across Europe to Crete. Liam had called in on his way back from football practice and offered a resigned, 'good luck, enjoy the trip.'

Fran's dad, Paul was insistent on running through their itinerary, and kept checking Fran knew how to store her euros safely. All Fran wanted to do was drink fizz and enjoy the excitement with the whole family; aunts, uncles and cousins were all present for the grand farewell.

On Tuesday 9 April, the date of departure, Kate arrived for Maisie, with Fran looking a little tense in the rear seat. Maisie thought the parting with Liam may have been difficult. She turned to Fran from the front passenger seat, 'you ok? We really don't have to stay away so long; we could have a shorter holiday instead.' Maisie was relieved at Fran's response.

'No, Nan. Think Liam is feeling a bit strange about it all, I honestly wouldn't miss this for the world.' Fran forced a smile.

'How about a big fat hot chocolate in the station to set us on our way?'

Kate joined them at, Manchester's Piccadilly Station, and after huge hugs, and many tears she waved them off. A few hours later, and a change of trains, Fran was occupied reading a Lonely Planet publication about Crete.

On the train journey, Maisie recalled the day she left, The

Blossoms to find Ellen in 1977, and the kind people she met on her journey. She was astounded sometimes at her own naive bravery; she thought about the kindly guards, who may no longer be alive. Also, when she punched that idiot who was harassing her, with hindsight, she realised how stupid that was. She often wondered what sex the baby was of the memorable, monochrome pregnant lady she met in the powder room in the department store. The baby would now be forty-two! If she had a time machine, Maisie would go back to that day and thank them for being a positive part of her life journey.

The two women arrived at the small, exclusive, Windmill Hills care home where Bertie resided. The same home where she'd volunteered to tend the gardens when she was a young girl. Fran had cheered up and was full of enthusiasm; she loved hearing the amusing stories about the tricks Maisie's foster brothers played on her. As their footsteps crunched up the graveled path to the grand entrance, Maisie pointed to a twenty-five-foot silver birch tree. It's huge canopy was producing the earliest of spring leaves, which fluttered in the breeze. 'I planted that tree, she said.' Fran offered a doubtful look.

'I did, honestly, you can ask Bertie.' Maisie took a moment to really look at the forty-five-year-old tree. It represented some happy, but also troubling times in her early teenage years. She was overjoyed to see her beloved Bertie Blossom, though dismayed at his pale frailty. He recognised her immediately and, in a withered voice with emaciated arms outstretched from his wheelchair, said, 'ah my little, Flossie.'

They hugged, and Maisie was immediately concerned at how bony his back and shoulders were. She and Bertie reminisced about their time together, the trouble she got into with Lizzie, and the pranks with the boys.

Fran enjoyed the tales Bertie revealed about her wayward grandmother when she was a young girl.

'Nan tells me there is something in the garden named after her?'

'That's right, the Maisie Blossom Birch,' replied Bertie, 'she worked hard planting trees, and that one survived. He took Fran's hand. 'Of course it did, takes after your Gran, a survivor.' He winked at her, then smiled at Maisie, but his face was drawn and gaunt.

Bertie spoke of Lizzie and her beauty until her recent death; his sadness was palpable. 'I don't mind when I go now, Flossie darling. My faith has often been challenged, but I do believe I will be with Lizzie once again. I'm ready.'

'I always hoped she forgave me for running away, but ...'

'She did forgive you, Flossie.' Bertie nodded resolutely. 'At first, she was rather disappointed, then realised it wasn't about her, but about you and your happiness, and where you belonged. I'm so sorry to hear about Jimmy, and your mum Ellen. Poor Maisie, you don't deserve this much sorrow, but I'm pleased Ellen got back in touch with us so we could see you again. Lovely woman.'

Bertie looked deeply into Maisie's eyes. She looked into his sunken brown eyes, with the tell-tale signs of old age; the blue-grey opaque edges around the iris.

'You will always be my first dad; you know that don't you? I love you, Bertie, you were so kind to me.'

'I love you too, my little Flossie.'

They held each other. Maisie was determined not to cry as she reached out to hold his weak, tendon-thin hands, covered in age spots. The absence of this once powerful, strong man's secure grasp gave Maisie the feeling she'd never hold his hand again. Maisie promised she'd return on her way back from the trip to tell Bertie all about her adventures, if indeed, there was anything to tell, knowing deep down it was highly unlikely.

As she and Fran left, walking past her tree, Maisie was bereft and sobbed for Bertie; for his kindness, for the fun they had together, the stability and tender care the family had offered to a lonely child they claimed from an orphanage.

Fran and Maisie travelled to a basic motel for an overnight stay, ready to take the Eurostar to Paris the next morning. When they arrived, the receptionist said the booking hadn't been confirmed, despite Fran showing the receptionist the online booking receipt. It was an unusually warm spring weekend, and both women were emotional, overheated, and tired.

'Okay, so the situation is, you've booked someone else into our room? Well, I want my money back,' said Fran with authority, looking at her watch. 'I'm here with my grandmother, it's after seven, and you're telling me there's no room; what do you suggest we do now?'

It wasn't a good start to the trip, however the receptionist did make a call and booked them a room at a nearby sister hotel. The combination of Fran being upset that morning; the sadness seeing Bertie so poorly, the anxiety of travelling, and the fatigue, rendered a sleepless night for Maisie, and it was only the first night of their trip.

In the morning they were directed to Eurostar, and although they missed the original planned connection, thankfully got the next train.

They were on their way to Crete.

CHAPTER 16

Maisie and Fran arrived at the Gare du Nord in Paris on 10 April, having added an extra overnight stay to their itinerary, as an opportunity for a brief tour of Paris. They had to hang around in a cafe with their baggage until they could check into the budget city hotel, which took an age to find, despite using a street map and asking for directions. Fran carried a large rucksack with the majority of their clothing and shared toiletries. Maisie had a smaller backpack, which she wore hooked in front of her, as it contained their passports, tickets and money. Fran was glad she had offered to take this responsibility.

The women checked in to the cheap tourist hotel, then enjoyed a boat ride along the Seine, and a trip up the Eiffel Tower which lifted their spirits. A stunning evening meal, which only the French know how to do, proved incredibly expensive and way above their daily budget, however, it was difficult to find anywhere reasonably priced in the beautiful city.

The next morning, Maisie was extracting the wallet from the backpack, to buy some patisserie at a stall. A hooded, skinny youth grabbed at the bag, but she fiercely held on to it as he tried to tug it away. Fran grappled with him, and kicked at him until he let go and ran off.

Maisie was shaken but reassured Fran she would be fine. 'I used to wrestle my brothers, that little squirt wasn't going to take anything from me.'

They filled in time after checking-out, peering into classy clothing boutiques, taking in tourist sights, and enjoying Paris' vibrant café culture. Both were tired and relieved when the seven o'clock evening service arrived in the station. It was time to get their overnight train to Milan from the Gare de Lyon. They settled into their cabins and agreed they loved taking in the sights and sounds of the most reputed romantic city in Europe.

Maisie vowed to return to Paris someday.

The overnight train was a little cramped, and washing facilities were limited. They arrived in Milan early on the morning of the 12 April, and as they left their sleeper cabin, Fran realised she had forgotten to brush her teeth, and felt unclean. They were fatigued, and disheveled, alighting the sleeper train. Fran was bewildered with the effort of communicating in a language other than her own, she had brushed up on tourist French and Italian, however could only manage the most basic of conversations. Fran and Maisie agreed they admired, and were grateful for, the ease at which many European citizens were able to switch between a few languages, especially English.

It had not been a restful night; though the clickety-clack of the train was soothing, it did not induce sleep for Fran. Maisie said she had slept, but Fran doubted her words. Changing trains at Milan to get to Florence was confusing. Milano Centrale Station was stunning, vast and extremely busy. The incredible stone architecture, and marble flooring was amazing, as were the many beautiful retail outlets. Their prebooked tickets, allowed fifty minutes to make the connection, which seemed ample time. However, it was not clear which service to use, as the departure times on the electronic board did not match that shown on their tickets. There were long queues at the information desks and no guards available to ask if they were heading for the right platform.

Fran knew Maisie was trying to be patient, and she wondered if she had misjudged the situation taking a fifty-nine-year-old on a journey more suited to a student gap year. They arrived on a platform which, as clearly as they could ascertain, had trains heading for Florence. Fran resolved that if it was the wrong train, she would simply plead ignorance, show the electronic tickets on her phone, and hope to get away with it. Fran was resigned to the fact they'd simply have to pay a further fare; she'd also printed out their itinerary, including QR codes, in case there were any issues with her phone signal. She hoped she'd covered all angles. They got on the train, trying to glimpse what they could of Milan as it rolled out of the station.

Maisie vowed to return to Milan someday.

The seat numbers on their tickets did not correspond to those in the carriages, so they tramped through the compartments to find empty seats. Ahead of her, Fran spied two vacant seats opposite each other at a table; the window seats were occupied by two people shrouded in dark clothing. As she neared the seats, she realised the two figures were nuns. Fran hauled her rucksack to a conveniently empty space above the opposite seats, and the nuns graciously shuffled about, making space for them with welcoming gestures.

Fran wasn't thrilled to have to engage in any conversation. It wasn't the right time to pop open the two small bottles of fizz she had bought for her and Maisie, to celebrate them finally travelling to Florence. Fran recognised the last thing Maisie ever wanted was a conversation with nuns. They were, however, pleasant company. Their spoken English was limited, and they insisted a weary Fran took a small leaflet entitled Sorelle della Misericordia. It had a picture of Jesus in the centre, complete with surrounding golden halo, a red outline crucifix in the bottom corner, and a glowing candle in the other. The word Charitas was printed in between. The word meant, as explained by the nuns, charity or benevolence, and Fran, in broken Italian, gleaned the nuns were Sisters of Mercy from their basic interpretations.

Maisie kept her sunglasses on and feigned sleep the whole time. Fran could see her eyes were open at one point, and she was staring at the crucifix worn by the nun beside Fran. The nuns alighted the train at a stop half an hour into the two-and-a-half-hour journey, and Fran visibly noticed Maisie relax. Fran jumped up and grabbed the two small bottles of fizz from her rucksack with two plastic flute glasses, and they slid along to the now vacated window seats.

Maisie lifted her sunglasses onto her head, looked into Fran's eyes, and said, 'thank fuck, Sister Act has buggered off.' She meant it.

Fran, wide-eyed, laughed aloud; her Nan said fuck!

Maisie joined in with a devilish giggle. 'Last thing we need is their divine intervention, cheers.' They tapped their fizz-filled plastic flutes, and settled in for the journey, chatting happily.

'Only another hour or so, and we should be able to enjoy our stay in Florence. It's been eventful so far, hasn't it?'

'You're not kidding. Can't wait to sleep in a proper bed.'

Fran immediately had misgivings that the basic pensione she had booked in Florence wasn't going to be as luxurious as Maisie may have anticipated. It was just after nine a.m. on the 12 April 2019. Fran began listening to Billie Eilish's latest album on her ear buds. She gazed out into the brightness, elbows resting on the table, her palms propping up her weary face. She closed her eyes, soaking up warmth from the golden rays. In an hour they'd arrive in Florence.

Chapter 17

Two nights in Florence did the trick, Maisie seemed genuinely relaxed, and was found on the second afternoon chatting away with the stout proprietor of their Pensione, sharing a tot of Grappa in the communal sitting room. A Finnish couple, an American family, and a Ukrainian photographer were all enjoying the hospitality, and each other's company.

Fran emerged, a little shaken, having suffered a debilitating bout of period pain, which rendered her in a fetal curl for two hours that afternoon. She'd taken the strongest painkillers known to humankind; wishing she'd continued her contraceptive pill, or had prescribed medication to delay her period, at least until she was settled in Crete. She felt washed-out, and if it wasn't for the golden tan naturally emerging on her face, she would have looked deathly pale. Fran believed the overland train journey from Florence via Zagreb, Belgrade, Thessaloniki, and Larissa to Athens was just a bit much, and was so grateful she had arranged flights instead.

Early the next day, they packed up and bid a fond farewell to their friendly stout and diminutive hosts, who had kindly provided a takeaway breakfast for their guests. As the women headed for the rail station, Maisie said with true sentiment, 'Mum would have absolutely loved it here.'

They took the direct T2 tramline to Amerigo Vespucci Airport. They punched their tickets in the yellow automated box system, and watched the huge Duomo di Firenze which dominates the skyline, diminish into the background. They were on the way to their next destination ... Athens.

Maisie vowed to return to Florence someday.

They landed in Athens at ten-thirty a.m. only two hours since take off, and took a half-hour taxi ride into the city. The transport system was incredibly organised; they had time for a ninety-minute bus tour taking in historic sights of the Acropolis, Parthenon, and several magnificent statues adorning the grandiose city. Sustenance was provided at a street food outlet where Fran and Maisie demolished large gyros packed with delicious lamb, onions, tomatoes, feta and tzatziki. Fran commented it was the best thing she'd ever tasted in her entire life. They then took the fifteen-minute metro ride to Piraeus passenger port.

Maisie vowed to return to Athens someday.

Fran was relieved to find they were on time, and on track, and she could now relax as the three o'clock ferry departed, heading for the northern coast of Crete to their destination ... Heraklion. Fran had prepared Maisie for a lengthy eight-hour journey and had the foresight to book internal air type seats, which to Maisie's delight, found they reclined, like on a flight. It may have been a little extravagant from their budget, but Fran was so pleased she had done so, having read the sun's rays could be deceiving on the deck seats, even in mid-April, and she'd fortunately secured window seats,

Once the ferry set sail, Fran accessed the onboard café, returning with two iced frappés and sugary Greek bougasta pastries; she thought they may need the caffeine and sugars to boost their constitution during the journey. They chuckled as they tried to contain the abundant sugar sprinklings, and wisping flakes of filo pastry floating onto their chests and knees. Fran decided to explore, leaving Maisie to read her magazine and rest, with the large rucksack tucked securely under the seat, and the smaller one squeezed in beside her, in case she nodded off.

Fran checked her phone as she stood on the outer deck and

sensed the relieving breeze from the Aegean. There was no message from Liam. She had sent a number of, so she thought, entertaining and informative texts to Liam with the occasional call, but he seemed not over enamoured with her tales of travel in Europe. She could tell he was probably distracted, playing on his games console, or watching the footy. It crossed Fran's mind that Liam would never have tolerated this trip. It was all she could do, to get him to book a week in the Balearics. He was specific about which hotels they stayed in, usually geared for British tourists with 24/7 streamed football. Her mind wandered to her last week at home before she left for Europe; she had a headache, and a strange, unsettled sensation in her stomach. As the ferry listed gently, her eyes had glazed over with fatigue, and she became entranced by the blurry sparkles reflecting off the sea.

A splash of sea-spray was blown into her face by the breeze, and a sharp downward momentum of the ferry, broke her thoughts as she returned into her present. As the ferry continued to charter its course, and her eyes focused, she became aware her forearms, resting on the metal rail, were hot to touch. She experienced how deceiving the sun's heat could be, masked by the brisk breeze. Time to move indoors.

Fran tried to quell the disappointment at Liam's dismissiveness about her trip of a lifetime. Feeling quite pissed off, but hungry, she headed for the café again. Returning to her seat, she observed Maisie in deep conversation with a dark-haired older man, probably Greek, sitting beside her. She didn't want to disturb the conversation; her grandmother looked distinctly pleased with the attention from the swarthy gentleman. Fran waited a few minutes before heading towards them.

Whilst Fran had been mulling over the last week she was at home with Liam, Maisie was napping in the recliner seat.

'Hello, madam.' A gentle, accented voice roused her from the drifting snooze. She sat upright.

The voice continued. 'Sorry, I noticed a document has fallen from your bag.'

Maisie looked down at the unzipped pocket of her backpack; she mustn't have closed it after she took her magazine out. Their document folder with passports, and tickets inside had slid onto the floor. It could easily have been picked up by a random passer-by without her being disturbed. How could she be so remiss!

'Oh, how stupid of me. Thank you so much for pointing that out.' 'It's a pleasure, madam.'

Maisie, a little taken aback, was pleasantly surprised at the gentleman's polite demeanour and smiled broadly at him. Maisie was an attractive brunette; constant exposure to the sun recently, brought out natural copper highlights mixed with a light speckling of silver-grey. You could take ten years off Maisie's age, and most guesses assumed she was still in her early fifties at most. Her Greek skin had absorbed the sun, releasing a golden tan; although she was meticulous about using sunscreen, the sun's rays had given her a natural healthy glow.

'I guess you knew I was English from the passport, most people assume I'm not.'

'Ah yes, I am the Greek Poirot.' His tanned face was pleasing as he held up an index finger, then stroked his goatee beard with the discerning, thoughtful style of many a tv detective. His pale blue linen shirt and cargo shorts revealed tanned, healthy limbs. Maisie guessed he was in his late forties.

'You must be … Italian, Spanish, or maybe Greek, in your background?'

Maisie recognised his hopefulness of her heritage, and recounted the story that led to her sitting on a reclining chair, on a ferry in the middle of the Aegean Sea heading for Crete, and it was as natural as any conversation she'd ever had.

'It may be impossible to discover where my origins lie, but as everything points to Archanes in Crete, we thought we'd head there.'

'We?' he gave a questioning look. He really did have a lovely smile, and he smelled of an attractive, light cologne.

'I'm with my granddaughter, Fran. Lost my husband James two years ago.' Maisie was talking openly to a man she'd met only moments ago, and wasn't perturbed in the slightest.

'I am so sorry to hear that. You are too young to lose your husband and must miss him terribly.'

Maisie nodded, and changed the subject as the desire for a large vodka overwhelmed her, to drink away the hurt and grief; it hit her heavily at times. 'We're travelling to Heraklion, then taking it from there. Do you know Archanes?'

'I don't know it well, but what I can tell you … is you will have a wonderful time. I am Cretan, and we love to welcome visitors and make sure their stay is happy. There is a lot to see, and I hope you do find your roots; you should be proud of your Greek heritage.'

'I am, it will be interesting to see if I feel … somehow, at home.'

'I understand this.' He paused. 'You will always be at home wherever you go. Your husband is with you in spirit. He is by your side, I do believe this.'

'Sometimes I feel him near to me, and that he is guiding me.'

'He is, and he is looking after you.'

An elegant woman dressed in casual floaty summer clothing, hair piled on her head, looking as cool as a cucumber, walked up to the pair, and the gentleman introduced his wife. He gave up his chair for her and perched on the window sill with Aegean blueness shining behind him. His wife was kind, and interested in Maisie's journey too; they spoke of the delights she could partake of in Crete.

At this point, Fran walked towards them, brandishing two small tubs of honeyed frozen Greek yoghurt. The couple suggested they meet up in the bar after dinner, where they would introduce Maisie and Fran to various delights of Greek alcoholic beverages, and, with a polite goodbye, they wandered off.

'That's something to look forward to later,' said Maisie, and added, 'continental women always look so relaxed, they don't seem to suffer from sweaty armpits, red faces, or hair plastered to their foreheads, do they?'

'You're not so bad yourself, Nansie, I thought you'd scored there. Getting hit on by a middle-aged Greek lothario.'

'Not bad for fifty-nine eh?' Maisie spooned a serving of her yoghurt.

'I wondered if you would be sneaking off to his cabin, until his wife arrived.'

Maisie winked, 'you never know.' She had to admit she was flattered, as she did sense the chap was attracted to her, and in fact, she was not dissimilar to his wife in looks and stature. Maybe he has a type, she mused. For all of the insecurities that filled Maisie's being, she was aware of the male attention that had often amused her, yet also plagued her life.

Maisie and Fran enjoyed two hours in the company of the couple that evening, and gleaned lots of detail about travelling in Crete. They insisted on paying for dinner as a welcome treat, despite Maisie and Fran's objections. The elegant couple advised the best taxi services to use in Heraklion, and which to avoid. They gave advice on different meals to try, looking out for scam tourist trips, and the must-see tourist attractions, including ancient Knossos, which Fran added to their travel itinerary. They parted from the couple, and gathered their baggage in readiness to depart.

Maisie was weary from the journey and the intake of alcohol, definitely finding a taste for Ouzo. Fran, however, had taken one sniff and decided it wasn't for her. The aniseed aroma reminded her of being horribly ill at a friend's party when she was seventeen, drinking Pernod, and she never recovered from hating the smell. Not the information she wished to reveal when they were in company with the classy couple; however, Maisie knew and gave her a cheeky knowing glance.

The two travelers, which Fran and Maisie could legitimately now claim, took a twenty-minute taxi ride east of Heraklion, and arrived at the Anemios Apartments that were to be their home for the next month. Fran had negotiated a good deal with the Airbnb owner, and although it was basic, it suited their needs. The block was on two levels consisting of twenty-two studio apartments, surrounding a small pool with dozens of sun loungers on each side. Their room was on the ground floor with a private patio space, a small table, and two chairs. The patio led into the main living area, comprising a compact kitchen, a sofa and chair, a small tv, and a coffee table.

Two doors off the main room, led to a large bedroom with a small ensuite; the other door led down a hallway to a bathroom and another bedroom. They were pleased with the freshly laundered bedding and cleanliness of the apartment. Fran offered Maisie the larger bedroom, and it didn't take long for them to settle in. They arrived in the early hours, so didn't unpack before they both said a weary goodnight, and gratefully climbed into their respective beds.

Maisie slept late, and wandered through to the crisp, bright living area to find Fran pouring cold frappe, from cartons she bought on the ferry, into glasses. They finished-off the Greek pastries they had saved, then unpacked. Within an hour they had donned trainers, in case they would do a lot of walking, t-shirts; shorts for Fran, and capri pants for Maisie, ready to discover the small town.

Following the divine smell of freshly baked bread and cakes, they located a bakery, which it seemed was popular with tourists and locals alike. They found a small café, which had an ice cream stall attached, with the most delicious range of flavours. They called in for strong fresh coffee and a traditional breakfast of Greek yoghurt with berries, nuts, and honey.

They shopped in a half-covered local fruit and vegetable market, and scouted local supermarkets, trying to avoid the main tourist outlets, which may be more expensive. They were mindful to calculate how much the produce came to, and what was cheap for future shopping trips. They consumed the sights, smells, and sounds of this foreign island, absorbing it's intoxicating warmth. They filled the apartment cupboards and fridge with an array of breads; meat, olives, feta cheese, snacks, crackers, milk, and lots of earthy-scented fruit and vegetables.

'I love how the fruit still has their leaves attached,' said Maisie as she held up a bunch of lemons to her face, breathing in the sharp scent.

Fran was slicing open a huge watermelon. 'Everything looks and smells so fresh compared to the supermarket at home.' After a pause, she asked, 'are you ok, I mean, are you happy you came, Nansie, you seem really chilled-out. Does Crete feel like home yet?'

'I feel as though I'm on a lovely holiday right now, and I'm really pleased I practiced basic Greek phrases from that app you put on my iPad. I'm going to keep it up, but it's not easy.'

'I was impressed with your attempts in the shop,' Fran added, 'apart from the woman thought you were Greek and started babbling away.'

Maisie laughed. 'I'm determined to master it so I can at least have a pleasant conversation.'

'You're a natural.'

Maisie stopped arranging the produce, became quite still and said, 'I do feel different … inside, can't really explain it, probably the sun, sea, and the ouzo of course.

Fran nodded in agreement. 'Now, to the beach!'

The temperature in April in Crete, they had read, averaged over 20°C, just right for British skin. They applied sunscreen, rolled up their towels, took a book each, iced water bottles from the freezer and placed it all in a huge striped beach-bag. They wore swimwear under their shorts, t-shirts, and a light hoody in case it was breezy, and headed towards the beach. It would cost a small fortune to pay for sun loungers every day, so they used the lightweight folding beach-chairs provided by the apartment, as their money had to last. It was half an hour until midday; the sun had warmed the air they breathed and the sand they walked upon.

They found a calm space on the beach, where the rows of tourist sun-beds ended, and set up for the day, nothing else to do. The low beach chairs were remarkably comfortable, and the sun parasols that fitted onto the chair gave relieving shade, perfect for reading.

After some time, Maisie stood, gazing towards the horizon. It was mid-afternoon and even in the shade, the sun had warmed her skin; the slight relief of the sea breeze was deliciously welcome. Breathing in the saline air, she began walking toward the sea, and couldn't prevent luxurious tears rolling down her cheeks. It had suddenly hit her. Greece was part of her, it was embedded in every cell in her body, it was part of her DNA. Fran looked on from her chair, then followed, and took her grandmother's hand as they walked in silence, with damp faces, feet sinking in soft white sand, toward the gently rippling, azure sea.

Chapter 18

Maisie and Fran were gathering information from locals about Archanes and what would be the best and cheapest way to get there. Using the unreliable bus service in the heat was eliminated, and a taxi would be too expensive. Renting a car would be economical, but they had to gain the confidence to drive along mountain tracks. They briefly considered mopeds but ruled it out after watching the treacherous method of tourists, and locals zipping about, slicing through traffic, with no helmets. They decided they couldn't bare the dreadful whiney noise or the smell of polluting, raw fuel.

'Can you imagine a whole line of traffic following us pootling along the road, beeping and yelling at us to get out of the way,' suggested Maisie, 'how embarrassing would that be?'

'I know, everyone looks so cool and confident, breezing along in their shorts and flip-flops. You and I would have to wear protective clothing, helmets, and adopt the sit-up-and-beg pose, using only peripheral vision in case we slightly swerved and fell off.'

The women laughed, doing impressions of how they'd look. They enjoyed this first week of nothingness. Sitting on the beach, eating natural produce, exploring the area, and learning how to fathom the oven and water temperature system in the apartment. They rarely used the pool, preferring the beach, but enjoyed the atmosphere of happy tourists taking breakfast and supper on the patio with the faint wisp of chlorinated water. It was idyllic, until a particularly lively day at the pool, when a young girl got into difficulty in the water and had to be rescued from the bottom.

They witnessed the tiny body lying motionless on the side of the pool, soaking wet with her turquoise, *Little Mermaid* costume, stuck to her plump little frame. The colourful grinning Ariel, and Flounder characters seemed incongruent with the drama. The child's thin plaited hair stuck out almost comically at each side of her head. This vision, accompanied by the sound of her wailing parents, was treacherous to behold. Fran and Maisie stood watching in disbelief as their insides turned jelly-like. The little girl was breathing by the time the medics arrived, who zoomed the family away in the ambulance, lights flashing, sirens howling. The family did not return to the apartment, but details from the owners suggested the little one would make a full recovery.

'That's put me right off having kids,' said Fran after the scary incident.

'Don't worry, you'll grow a pair of eyes in the back of your head,' remarked Maisie, who was convinced the incident wasn't the only thing putting Fran off having children right now.

Maisie and Fran had been in Crete for only a week and felt at home with their new routine. Their daily budget was working well, so they agreed to dine out one night a week. There was a restaurant they passed every day on the way to, and from, the beach; they had surveyed the menu, which seemed reasonable. The drifting smells of charcoal roasted meat with onions, and a mixture of, garlic, dill, basil and thyme were utterly mouth-watering. They were staying at the quieter end of the resort, and The Pallas Taverna wasn't the most upmarket place; no neon lights or flashy discount cocktail menus to attract younger clientele, and in truth looked a little downbeat with old traditional seating.

The vine-strewn trellis roof was adorned with fairy lights in the evenings, and it had a welcoming appeal, attracting more local custom too. The owner, they assumed he was the owner, was a tall, lithe man probably in his fifties, with walnut skin, thick greying hair, and a luxurious moustache; he gave them a wave and a hearty, 'yassou!' as they passed by.

As they approached The Pallas Taverna this first evening out, the owner welcomed them graciously, seated them in a cosy alcove; lit the candle in the centre of the table, and offered them a welcome drink on the house. A Mythos lager for Fran, and he was clearly impressed with Maisie's choice of Ouzo on the rocks. He introduced himself as Socrates Vasilakis, known to all as, Sox. He asked what foods they liked and offered suggestions according to their taste. Once they had ordered, and received their freebie drinks, Maisie and Fran raised their drinks with a, 'yamas' as they clinked glasses.

They shared tzatziki and taramasalata with pitta bread, and a Greek salad with creamy feta to start. Maisie enjoyed a sumptuous serving of lamb kleftiko and vegetables, whilst Fran opted for pork souvlaki with rice. They were satiated and mellow as they sipped the recommended wine to accompany their meal, and refused dessert as they couldn't have eaten another thing. It was a most enchanting evening. The constant level of conversation with the staff and other diners, and calming traditional lyre music in the background was sublime. The women walked out arm-in-arm, Maisie with a tipsy gait, vowing to Sox they would return to the Pallas Taverna.

Maisie was becoming entrenched in the open, easy style of beginning a conversation with complete strangers, which Fran enjoyed observing, however, recognised seemed out of character. The morning after their meal out, they headed for the beach, and heard a familiar, 'kalimera ladies!' from Sox. Maisie suggested they stepped inside for a coffee and a chat. They settled at what would become their usual table, and Sox brought delicious omelets and joined the women, at their invitation, to breakfast with them.

They discovered Sox had been quite the athlete as a young man, rowing for his country, and the team narrowly missed out on qualification for the 1984 Olympics. He had lived in Canada, having family links there with his wife, and worked at a college coaching a basketball team. His eldest son, Adam, now plays and coaches basketball there, whilst Stefanos, his other son, is a chef and works in the family restaurant.

Sox told them the sea was his life, and he had a small fishing boat where he and Stefanos would catch produce for the restaurant. He invited the women to sail with him one day. His wife passed away many years ago, and whilst he had many romances, he assured them with a wink, he hadn't met anyone who could take her place. Sox looked emotional as Maisie asked if the photos of the beautiful woman hung behind the bar were of his wife.

He showed an enormous amount of interest in Maisie's quest to trace her Greek heritage in Archanes, and promised to offer help in any way he could.

'Do you know your name, Maisie, translated into Greek, is, Margaritári? It means pearl, which suits you.' Sox could charm the birds out of the trees.

Both Maisie and Fran enjoyed his company; he was informative, polite, humorous, and helpful. He took to calling Maisie, Margarita, because she, *shone like a pearl*. She liked it; it felt pleasant, even though it could be a load of old rubbish; she knew he said similar to all of the middle-aged women looking for a bit of sun, sea, and maybe sex with the charming chap. They got to know his son too, who Fran found rather attractive and confessed this to Maisie after one too many glasses of retsina.

Sox took the women on a trip to Archanes the following week, which was fourteen kilometres inland from Heraklion. He helped Maisie alight from the open top four-wheel drive, and she slowly took in a panoramic view of the area. Archanes lay between two mountains in an elevated position, commanding a stunning view of the surrounding countryside. Sox advised the village was one of the most historic in Crete, dating back thousands of years.

Maisie had researched the history of the village and offered knowledge of the Turkish and Byzantine influences. They enjoyed a wander around a group of ruins thought to once be a Minoan palace. There had been ongoing restoration work to preserve the area's history, which had won awards, Sox imparted, for the harmonious, authentic atmosphere, mixing the old and the new perfectly.

The trio walked by a mural painted on an ochre-coloured wall. It was around three metres high, with a young woman's face with blonde hair and blue eyes, not typically Greek, maybe a goddess tribute. The image showed her hair flowing out sideways, intertwined with green leaves and red roses. They stopped for a moment and admired the enchanting image, then found a charming cafe further along the street. The cafe was adorned with fuchsia draping from the roof, and huge urns were placed intermittently along the street, bursting with abundant bright, colourful plants. They sampled the local delights of; olives, lemon minted tzatziki, stuffed vine leaves, soft village bread, and local grapes fermented into a refreshing crisp white wine.

They passed by the small Town Hall, externally painted in a sunny yellow; they delighted at the vision of hillside houses with red-tiled roofs, and pastel-coloured walls in cream, lemon, and pale blue. Maisie and Fran were captivated, wandering down the cool, flagged, narrow alleyways that led toward the main square, then emerging into bright white heat that took their breath away. No sea breeze here.

Maisie stopped at one point on a residential street and said, 'I wonder if this is like the area where Manolis and his sister lived and played before being taken away to England?' She imagined a dark-haired, brown-eyed toddler in shorts and t-shirt playing with other children. She could almost hear a child's laughter ringing out.

'I feel quite sorry for him. Imagine the life he would have lived here, but he was dragged away to a big anonymous scary city. If our research is accurate, and we have the right person, he would have been seventy-eight a few weeks ago on the 28 March, if he's still alive.'

'There must have been reasons for the family to move away,' Sox suggested. 'If crops failed, and after the war, you know there may have been no jobs, and poverty in the villages; his father maybe wanted a better life for his family.'

Quite suddenly, Maisie confessed, 'there seems to be a horrible family secret his father was involved in, but we really don't know if it was Manny's father ... or, even if Manolis Petrakis from Archanes is my actual father.' Maisie turned away and walked at pace back to the village centre where the car was parked.

Fran and Sox looked dolefully at each other. Fran said, 'I never wanted Nansie to become upset by all of this. I often wonder whether we should have started this whole thing.'

Sox patted Fran's shoulder gently. 'It is simply time that is needed. Time to get used to discoveries about the past. Not easy for Margarita.' Sox had begun using this endearing nick-name. Fran sensed there was something brewing between the pair, but knew her grandmother could be quite defensive if someone tried to become emotionally close to her. Fran had a protective affection for Sox, he had enriched their time in Crete.

Fran scanned the scene, 'I'll be really sorry to leave here in a few weeks. England sometimes feels like frosty February all year round.'

'I hope you both can stay longer to finish your search. If you need to boost your finances, I could always do with paid help at my Pallas.' Sox enjoyed the phonetic similarity with the English word palace.

'My brother, he has a cocktail bar in Heraklion, he always needs extra staff for the busy months. This may be more exciting for you.' He winked.

'But, I don't have a work visa or anything.' Fran shrugged.

Sox gave a hearty laugh. 'I will speak with him. It doesn't matter about such things as visas; we talk, we shake hands, we make agreements; it is the Greek way.' His broad smile lit up again, 'should I ask about a job for you?'

'Yes, why not, it would be fun. If it means we can stay a little longer, then great.' Fran ran ahead to tell Maisie the news. She realised Sox's motivation may be to get her out of the way, so he could charm Maisie on her own. Fran desperately hoped her grandmother would be willing to extend the trip, rather than disappear back to the mundane safety of their old lives.

Chapter 19

In early May, Fran commenced her job at Suzanna's Cocktail and Gin Bar in Heraklion, a ten-minute walk from the sea front. She was initially overwhelmed by the array of bottles stacked behind the bar; the different mixers, the fruits, and other decorative paraphernalia to adorn drinks. She was nervous when serving the first few nights, however Sox's brother and the bar team were incredibly helpful during her initial training days, serving mostly brunch with beers.

Crowds of holidaymakers arrived, ordering snacks and drinks, ravenous from the previous evening's shenanigans, looking rather shabby and bedraggled indeed. Fran was conscientious and took the cocktail menu home to learn the measurements of different liquors, and shots which made up the most popular drinks on the extensive list.

A few days after her first shifts at Suzanna's, Fran arrived at The Pallas whilst Maisie breakfasted with Sox. This had become routine.

'Thank god I can sleep on the beach all day; I'm knackered.'

'My brother is very pleased; he tells me you are a hard worker, with always a good attitude.'

Fran tipped her head, and looked discerningly at Sox, with squinted eyes.

'I know.' Sox nodded, 'you have to keep smiling even at the

malakas. Margarita has been busy too, earning her free breakfast helping me behind the bar.'

Fran was quizzical. 'I didn't expect that we'd end up with the same jobs. Fancy my Nansie working behind a bar.' She smiled, reached out and squeezed Maisie's hand. 'Good for you, and don't take any crap off the punters … I mean, the malakas.'

'I would never allow that to happen,' added Sox resolutely.

Fran noted the admiration in his eyes, fixed on Maisie's now serene face. I wonder if they're *at it*, she thought briefly, and wasn't sure if she was delighted or disgusted at her grandma having sex at her age. They could be getting up to all sorts whilst she was at work. In a split-second, she chose to be delighted that Maisie may have found some affection, even love, after the devastating loss of her beloved Jimmy McLaine.

'It's a slow pace here; I've mastered the perfect frappe; want one?' Maisie asked Fran.

'Love one,' Fran closed her eyes, 'make it a triple shot.' She was desperate for a sunny, snoozy beach day, but the caffeine would be enough to propel her weary limbs to the beach.

After her lazy day, and an afternoon nap, Fran took the bus into Heraklion to Suzanna's for her shift; she felt more like a local taking the bus and not relying on Sox or Stefanos for a lift into work now.

Fran made loads of temporary holidaymaker friends from all nations and had a riot with some of the groups. The majority of people only wanted a good time, but there were some malakas, of course. She was invited to beach parties on several occasions, once with the *Scottish Heathers*, Scotland's netball team; there were the hilarious Irish junior doctors, and a bunch of Aussies on sabbatical from work. Fran was intrigued to learn it was not unusual for employers to allow an extended break, for up to a year, to enable employees to travel, returning to their jobs all the richer for their experiences.

Ashley, Jake and Sam from Brisbane were part of a larger group of working tourists, and the four friends gelled immediately. Ash was the ringleader, brash and bolshy, but full of fun; she wouldn't hurt a fly. Her huge brown eyes, shone beneath black brows that always appeared raised in surprise. Her abundant curly hair framed her innocent-looking heart-shaped face, but the broad, dimpled grin showed she was jam-packed with mischief; always ready for the next prank. She tanned easily, showing off the small yellow Tweetie-Pie tattoo at the top of her hip. She played county cricket and had a physical strength that belied her size. Ash was of aboriginal heritage, and very proud of this, often recounting ancient tales to Fran, that her mother had told her, passed down through generations. Fran was fascinated, besotted and loved Ash's impulsivity. They say opposites attract, and these two did.

Occasionally, Donna from Slough, a lone traveller, would join in with their group at after-work parties. One morning, Ash and Fran met at a beachside cafe before their respective bar shifts commenced when Ash said, 'I'm convinced she's on the game, as she often leaves the bar with middle-aged, um … gentlemen.' She peered over her sunnies, revealing sparkling eyes, and winked with a knowing smirk on her face.'

'Could be, but she needs to be careful who she's getting off with, there's always some wierdos around,' responded Fran.

'What about, Posh Pommy Pete, wandering around on his own in those dodgy red shorts every day; they must be really stinky by now.' Ash grimaced. 'He spills bullshit all the time; always shit-faced, said he'd been a Red Devils pilot, only because Sam said he flew bush fire planes, which thank Christ he doesn't, by the way. We set Pommy Pete up with lies, and he always has to go one better.'

Ash laughed. her tinkling, pleasant, infectious laugh. Fran relished the lilting lift at the end of conversational Australian, and couldn't help but mimic the style in their company. They were enjoying their early caffeine-loaded coffee to spur them onto another busy day of work, when Ash said, 'Jakey-boy has been keeping me entertained on this trip, if you know what I mean. He's one beautiful bloke. Do you miss your fella, Liam, what's he like?'

'Similar type, good-looking, fit as anything, plays footy.'

'Great in the sack?' Ash grinned, then curiously said 'but ...'

'But ... what?'

'Dunno, you don't mention him much.'

Fran clicked her tongue. 'Not much to say, he's fine, the steady kind. Be good to see him when I get home.'

'He didn't fancy this adventure then?'

'I came out with my grandma, so he'd have been like a spare part.'

'Surely now he'd love a holiday out here ...' Ash spread her arms wide ... 'in this paradise island for a week of booze, sun, sea and sex with his gorgeous girl?'

'Says he may come out for a few days before I go home.'

After a few moments finishing their coffees, Ash said, 'you do know I'm bi, right?

'Of course ... but Donna, come on Ash, thought you had better taste.' Fran grimaced.

Ash hung her head in her hands, 'I know, a moment of weakness; at least she didn't try to charge me fifty euros. And by the way, you're my mate; I do not fancy you one little bit,' said Ash.

'Pf-ft, I'm way out of your league anyway!' replied Fran, leaning toward Ash. 'You can't punch this high, mate.' Holding her hand high above her head.

'You cheeky Pommy ...'

Fran had run off, across the sand, and a game of catch-chase ensued into the sea, shorts and vests soaked, limbs flailing. Ash caught up with her, rugby tackled her, and they both fell about, laughing and spluttering salty water as they made huge splashes, and tried to duck each other under. Ash was mighty strong, but Fran was the faster swimmer, and she wriggled out of her grasp.

As they walked from the shore, Fran said, 'I really better get going; I hope my clothes dry out quickly,' pulling at the vest clinging to her body.

Ash turned and suggested, 'we're off grape-picking later in the summer, Fran, if you want to come along. You can earn amazing money, it's hard work but worth it. Late August to September, what'ya think?'

Fran agreed if she was still around, she would certainly consider it.

Ash continued, 'I can't wait to leave my accommodation to be honest with you, I made the mistake of sleeping with Dimitri, and now he's madly in love with me, pleading with me to stay.'

Ash had told Fran about the villa where she was staying. The owner, Mika, and his business partner Dimitri; they owned the bar where Ash worked, and lived in the villa too. It had five bedrooms surrounding a pebbled courtyard with a kitchen, and they mainly rented rooms out to seasonal workers.

'The pair of them are always off their tits on something, playing Bob Marley really loud and wandering around stark bollock-naked. They are lovers for sure, but both bring loads of girls back too, so why is he begging me to stay?'

'It's your wit, charm and beauty, Ash, anyone could fall in love with you.' Fran truly meant it, she loved her too, she was often surprised by how much she revealed to Ash; she trusted her implicitly. The two friends hugged before they went their separate ways to work. Ash would be moving on in a few days when her time in Heraklion was done, and Fran knew she'd be bereft.

The day Ashley and the Aussie's left, she and Ash hugged and cried. Ash begged Fran to come along with them, and they made promises to meet at the end of August for a jaunt into the mountains to go grape picking.

One quiet early shift a few weeks after her Aussie friends had left, Fran was cleaning the bar and straightening the bottles when a voice behind her asked, 'could I get a Campari and soda, please.'

Strange drink, Fran thought as she turned to look into a pair of sparkling deep jade green eyes, with the longest dark eyelashes she'd ever seen on a man. She fumbled with the bottles, most unlike her, as he chatted freely and introduced himself as Jonah. He had arrived from Köln, Germany, with some university friends, and heard the beaches were ideal for snorkelling and water sports. Fran served his drink, and after a brief chat, he wandered outside to three others sitting together playing cards.

Fran observed his profile. He had rather delicate features, and defined cheekbones; his tousled light brown hair was bleached by solar light around the hairline, and the ends flicked up around his neck. He wore a small shell pendant, a white vest top, dark pink shorts and leather thong sandals. Fran thought he epitomised the casual beach dude look perfectly. Jonah was not her usual buff, muscled, sporty type, if indeed, that was her type.

Fran was disappointed not to see Jonah the next couple of nights and wondered if he had found another bar that his group favoured. He did arrive one night with his friends, obviously having had a number of beers. A few effortlessly casual, and naturally beautiful girls were hanging around with them. Their cosmetic free skin, tanned athletic limbs, and long veil-like sun-kissed hair were to be envied. Fran felt foolishly disappointed. Jonah approached the bar and ordered a huge round of drinks, which she expertly served to their table from a large tray. Fran took her break, and walked to the chairs outside of the bar by the bins, where the staff could grab a few minutes of peace and quiet.

Jonah appeared beside her and said, 'sorry, I did not catch your name.'

Over the thrum of the music, she said, 'It's Fran.'

'Just … Fran?'

'Francesca, think my parents were trying to give me something exotic for an ordinary lass from the North.'

'There's nothing ordinary about you, Francesca. You seem to like fun, and are very competent too. But …' Jonah hesitated, 'I think there is something deeper …' He flushed, and lowered his gaze.

Fran noticed Jonah appeared to be embarrassed by his forthright comments. To ease the slight tension, Fran announced, 'I do have a professional job back at home. I work in speech therapy with young children, but decided to take a few months out …' she was going to say, before she settles down and gets engaged, but changed midsentence '… to help my grandma find her Greek roots.'

Fran offered a brief explanation of the scenario. Jonah conversed with ease; he told her he was studying marine biology and hoped to qualify later in the year and travel all around the world. Fran couldn't help but compare to her world being so tiny and insignificant compared to the interesting, vibrant people around her from all over the world.

Jonah then really surprised her. 'Could I take you out to dinner one evening?' he asked.

It was the most polite request for a date, Fran had ever heard. She thought he was going to bow, then she'd need to curtsey in response like Liesl Von Trapp in the *Sound of Music*, before they waltzed around the bins. Amused, a brief smile crossed her mouth.

'It's okay if you're not interested.' Jonah's deep green eyes looked downcast.

'Oh no, I'd love to!' Fran responded, before he changed his mind. 'But aren't you with someone?' She nodded toward the bar.

'Sort of, but I'm not too interested.' He gave a sheepish grin.

'When is your night off?'

'I don't really get one, but give me your number, I'll let you know.' Fran was relieved at his response and, for the first time, noticed his lovely white teeth as he smiled directly at her; she didn't take her eyes off him as he returned to his group, watching his relaxed gait.

They had exchanged numbers, and several glances that night; as Fran took her taxi back to the apartment, she couldn't get Jonah out of her head. What did he mean, *there is something deeper*? Could he see inside her brain, were her thoughts vulnerable and exposed? Had he been metaphorically rummaging around in there, and found her discontent lurking? Fran arranged a night off and wondered if they should meet at The Pallas, but what would Maisie say if she thought Fran was on a date?

She'd make a convoluted suggestion that Jonah may like to speak with Sox about sea-related things, that may suffice as subterfuge. Another panicky thought was … Jonah was drunk and would realise his error when he awoke the next morning with one of those long-legged lovelies wrapped around his hips in bed. Fran questioned why she was envious, and also resigned herself to the fact Jonah would now avoid Suzanna's, to dodge her, and return to his prospective spectacular future, and she'd never see him again.

Chapter 20

Fran and Maisie became ships that passed in the night. Fran returned from work in the early hours, whilst Maisie would rise at dawn and take a beach walk before calling in at The Pallas for breakfast with Sox. Fran would appear a few hours later, either at the taverna or on the beach and doze. Maisie headed for The Pallas around five p.m. most days to help out, leaving Fran to a couple of hours peace and quiet until she left for work around eight p.m. returning usually after two a.m. It became a pattern and one that worked well. Like cat burglars they'd creep around the apartment while the other was sleeping.

Sox had taken the lead with Maisie's quest to trace her birth father, or any relatives that may reside in Archanes, as Fran simply didn't have the time. He was best placed to do so, given he could make enquiries easily. He offered to ask questions of the locals to discover if anyone knew of, or had links with the Petrakis family. Maisie was initially reticent, but wasn't really sure why. One morning, before dawn, when Sox had taken a day off, he and Maisie arrived at Heraklion harbour, and parked up.

Maisie said, 'How can you find your boat,' grinning at the vast number of vessels moored, with masts bobbing up and down like the poles on a carousel, all around the harbour. The sea glimmered pink, as the initial rays of sun hit the water, flickering to yellow, then settling as bright gold in minutes. They walked towards three similar wooden fishing boats; all were white with a blue and red border. Huge piles of tangled yellow netting rested on the harbour in front of each vessel. Sox leapt onto one engraved with Greek writing, which he said was, Katrina, named after his beloved wife.

Facing the pointed bow end of the boat, there was a small jaunty white wooden wheelhouse cabin with, what delighted Maisie was an old-fashioned style ships wheel, and other instruments on the dashboard. Towards the stern, there were large brown and grey tubs and blue plastic trays ready to house the day's catch. It looked like a mess of ropes, cables and metal hooks to Maisie, yet Sox swiftly and expertly prepared the boat for sailing. He turned the engine, and with a gentle, *put-put-put*, merged with a faint smell of gasoline, they were on their way heading to the open seas. As the boat sliced through the water, rhythmically bobbing and swaying, Sox noticed Maisie looked pensive, gazing out over the side of the boat.

'Margarita, do you like sailing at sunrise?' It was six a.m. on the second day of June 2019. Warm golden rays streamed onto the boat, reflecting off the water lighting up their faces. 'What is going on in your head today?' Sox now had the confidence to ask Maisie directly what was troubling her, after her initial resistance to divulge any of her thoughts and feelings.

'I'm really not sure about trying to trace Manny's family or any relatives. Why not accept I'm having a lovely extended holiday and be happy with that.' She turned and smiled, but it wasn't heartfelt; it was one of her learnt behaviours; don't let anyone in, or let them see what you are truly feeling. Don't let them in, they'll only hurt you, disappoint you, or leave you.

'I can't prove anything. What if all we have is a false lead? I don't want to upset anyone. Me turning up out of the blue claiming I somehow belong to complete strangers,' she shrugged. 'I could be rejected or called a liar, a fake.'

'Okay, that is a possibility, but if you leave this island not having asked the questions, it may be more painful in the long run.'

Maisie knew Sox was right, travelling all this way and leaving before she'd even contemplated further searches. What then, was the point in this wasted trip?

Sox said, 'I wouldn't let anyone or anything hurt you. The coincidences are too much for Manolis not to be your father, especially if we trace a Petrakis family who left the island for England. Nothing will happen to you, I promise.'

'You can't promise that!'

'Okay, that's true, but if we don't try anything in life ... well ... after my Katerina died, my life was hell. I wanted it to end, but couldn't because of my boys who needed me. Life can be cruel, Margarita, but we are here, and we have to keep going if not for ourselves, but for others ... like your lovely Fran.'

With calm contentment, Sox guided the boat further out, into the vast deep blue, sparkling ocean. Maisie felt reassured somewhat; however, the feeling of unease and being an imposter never quite left her. Could she bare to be rejected again, it always hurt like hell, but she was beginning to trust Sox in the time she'd known him.

The searing June heat was whipped away by the warm winds, and she relaxed, encouraging herself to enjoy this experience. What was it her counsellor said; try to live in the moment, stop everything, just breathe, use your senses. She wandered to the front of the cabin, where Sox was perched on a chair in front of the dashboard.

'Come on, time for you to navigate,' he encouraged.

'Really, you sure?'

Sox nodded, so she stepped in front of him and sat on the seat. He stood beside her with a hand resting gently upon hers as they guided the boat through the water together. Maisie was comforted by Sox's proximity; there was a naturalness in the way they walked, talked, sat and ate together. As he leaned closer to flick a switch, causing the engine to die down, they floated with the amazing deep blue below and the startling white ball of fire overhead. There was nothing else, nothing at all.

The undulating motion of the gently rocking sensation,

reminded Maisie of her summers with Bertie Blossom. She drifted back in time, in a trance, mesmerised at the glinting water, she couldn't look away. Without warning, she was a young girl; it all came flooding back as if it was yesterday. She and Bertie were in the rowing boat on the lake, with scary deep-water creatures approaching; the evil water dragons would terrorise them. She recalled them yelling for the brave tree warriors, the friendly cloud-ghosts and lake-nymphs with their flashing magic powers to aid their fight. They would always overcome the monsters together.

Ripples of glinting sunshine reflected on her face. Maisie was lost. Lost in a time long ago when she was secure. She wanted to stay here forever, on this boat, and never go back to dry land. She was free, and at home again, as she had been with Bertie. Maisie had received the news of Bertie's death a few days ago, yet as she gazed at the water, she sensed him with her, not the old face she'd last seen, but the handsome man in his forties who made her feel so safe. She looked upwards and internally said thank you, Bertie … for everything. She felt peaceful.

Maisie turned and impulsively gave Sox a peck on the cheek.

'Thank you, Sox.'

Sox became quite coy and dared to put his hands upon her shoulders. Maisie turned the swivel chair to face him, looking into his hazel brown eyes; she cupped his scratchy chin in her hands, leaned upwards to his face and gave him a gentle kiss on his mouth. She enjoyed the bristle of his abundant moustache. It was a risk; she could have totally misconstrued the affection Sox had shown her; however, he reciprocated and held her in a warm embrace. What had developed between them was more than friendship.

Maisie remained in the driving seat with Sox behind her, arms placed gently around her shoulders. They would nuzzle into each other, and his brief kiss on the side of her neck awoke something physically visceral inside her she hadn't felt for many years. Maisie was glad he couldn't see the flush on her face, as she was burning up, and bristling with the thrill. Sox switched the engine off again;

they remained in an embrace for who knows how long. Two lost people finding comfort and warmth, marooned in the soothing, peaceful Aegean surrounded in beautiful sunlight.

Sox was a physically strong, virile man, a few years younger than Maisie, with a healthy appetite for sex, which she was about to discover. Making love out in the open sea on a tarpaulin was never the way Maisie envisaged she would begin a new relationship. She imagined a courtship of at least several months, and financial scrutiny of any potential suitors; she'd definitely find closet skeletons if they had any. But this, giving in to the natural emotion and basic human need for the instantaneous gratification of physical comfort, was never on her cards.

They had lain in peaceful contentment afterwards, dozing, until a ship's horn startled them. Popping their heads above the parapet, an oncoming small tourist boat was heading directly toward them. Maisie was horrified; how would she cover her exposed body without anyone seeing her. Sox laughed as he stood, his generous-sized genitals visible to all, as he quickly grabbed for his shorts, whilst Maisie scurried naked into the wheelhouse and cowered, thoroughly mortified. As the ferry passed, Sox, his nakedness now covered, gave the gaping tourists a flamboyant wave. Maisie had frantically wrapped her sarong around her and faced the opposite way as the boat passed. Sox thanked Maisie on the return trip, saying he had a good birthday this year. Maisie was astonished, he had not said 2 June was his birthday. He roared with laughter until they reach the harbour.

Later that day, when Fran and Maisie were chatting on the beach, before Fran went to work, Fran introduced the concept of inviting a lovely friend she had met for dinner to The Pallas. She explained Jonah was studying marine biology, and thought he may like to talk with Sox about the coastline and maybe arrange to go out on his boat, so he could scuba dive, if it wasn't too much trouble. Maisie thought it a good idea and was sure Sox would be agreeable. Maisie got the impression this may be a date, but knew better than to say anything.

Chapter 21

On her way to the beach after a busy shift with a few work friends, Fran had observed the various British holiday makers coming into the bar. She mused that her former routine consisted of; rushing to get to work, chatting with friends, watching the telly, wondering what to wear for a night out, or how to style her hair, longing for that really pricey cosmetic range, and saving up to buy an expensive skin serum. It all seemed so long ago, so far away, so trivial.

After a particularly raucous shift, a group of bar workers settled on the beach, far away from the blaring noise, and glaring lights of the town. Fran lay back, resting on her elbows, quite exhausted, looking toward the rippling ocean, when existential thoughts swirled around her mind. She was a tiny dot of an organism laying on a beach, on an island, on a huge planet slowly turning in infinite space. She was not immortal, and the realisation this was it, this was her only time to live her own life, was overwhelming. Fran had never really wondered about her insignificance, or relevance within the history of the universe, and the futility of her ordinary life. Why would she?

In the early morning hours, Fran became aware of the group conversing, laughing and discussing trivial matters in general. Fran embraced a mixture of exhilaration and dread simultaneously; the vast possibilities of life, but not wasting the time you have been given. The Marlboro tobacco smell from the smokers in the group hit her nostrils, which brought her back to reality. There was something about that smell; something distinctly Mediterranean.

Fran stared up at the deepest black sky with the brightest array of twinkling white stars, some with a blue or red haze around the circumference; she wondered if they were red dwarfs, and why some shone blue. She had read, or had heard from tv programs, stars that had exploded eons ago, emitted light, which was only just visible to earthlings after millions of years. Fran contemplated the depth of the cosmos, lying here, on the beach at night, which she'd never dreamt of doing at home in England; she would never think to lay on the ground staring into space; there was too much light pollution for one thing, and, it was too cold!

Fran was at a crossroads and didn't know which path to take. She gazed hypnotically into the night sky with wonder at the layers of those trillions of stars, and emotion welled up from a deep place within. She questioned what she was doing with her life; would she return home, could she ever go back to work and continue as normal, when there was a whole world to explore? She closed her eyes, and a trickle of warm, tiny tears squeezed out. Simultaneously she sifted the cooling sand through her fingers. Listening to the gentle rolling swoosh of the waves, she wished she never had to return home. Home, to her ordinary, tactile-less, boring life, and … to Liam. This island was changing her.

It was unusually quiet in Suzanna's the next day. It always was on one of the main change-over days for flights, when the current fortnightly bunch would be replaced by another fortnightly bunch of new, *Lemonikis*. A Greek colleague referred to the pale skin of northern European tourists having, *'skin the colour of a lemon.'* The Lemonikis wouldn't arrive until much later that night, looking resplendent in their new holiday gear, preening with perfect hair, until they realised they could relax and, for the men, ditch the hair wax, and the women ditch the teetering strappy sandals.

Jonah walked up to the bar, Fran was cleaning a table, out of his peripheral vision, and she noticed he was surreptitiously looking around, hopefully for her. One of the bar staff served him an espresso with a tall glass of iced water, and he sat in a quiet shaded corner.

'Guten morgen Jonah,' Fran sidled up to his table, 'bit of a heavy night?' She smirked.

Jonah grinned back at her, peeping over his sunglasses, but beneath the cap shielding his face from brightness. He nodded, looking rather queasy. Fran wondered if he had recalled their conversation? Was he here to apologise, and retract his proposition of their date, explaining it was a drunken mistake? He may have had a great night banging away with Emilia, Sabine or whoever wrapped around him, and although he didn't want to be with Fran, he was a gentleman, and had turned up to explain.

Fran sat at the table, and they chatted; he asked if she was free to go snorkelling that evening. He wanted to show her the wonders of swimming at night when bioluminescence was at its height. Fran agreed she would, as this was her early shift. She had a nervous afternoon; she'd have to reveal her body in a bikini. She didn't possess the long, lean legs of those other girls; she tipped towards what she deemed was typically English, short and pear-shaped. She was fit however, swimming every day had defined her muscle tone and streamlined her body; eating fresh, healthy produce, made her skin glow and her eyes clear. But … she'd have to go without her contact lenses! She had visions of snorkelling in the dark and head-butting rocks, or picking up interesting items from the sea bed, only to discover it was some discarded tourist detritus, and not the interesting shell or creature she thought it was. The embarrassment.

Later that day, Fran ate a delicious meal prepared by Sox's brother after her shift, a huge bowl of Yuvetsi, his speciality lamb and orzo stew, saying she would need her strength for her activities later. He winked, and guffawed like Sox, with that hearty gruff bellow. She insisted, *it wasn't like that*, but couldn't help engage with the joyous frivolity, but ignored the suggestive innuendo. Fran always kept some spare clothes and swimwear at the bar, so she changed, and borrowed fins, snorkel and a mask from the diving hire shop nearby. The owner was friends with the Vasilakis brothers and shouted that she could keep the items with a wave of his hand.

As prearranged, Jonah arrived promptly at a quarter past eight. They left in his hire car, a small open-top jeep, and she enjoyed the journey to one of the remote parts of the coastline. A cool breeze swept her hair back, and she felt relaxed. Jonah was good company, easy to converse with, and she forgot her insecurities within minutes in his company. They arrived at the rocky bay; with feet sinking into soft pebbles, they waded into the water. There were a few other snorkelers there, but it was peaceful. The huge red ball of sunset disappeared with a final flash, as it sank beyond the horizon.

They had donned their masks and snorkels, Jonah ensured Fran's mask was secure and water-tight, with the snorkel at the right angle, so as not to drop below the waterline. He was attentive to her, adjusting her fins so they comfortably fitted her feet. Their bodies were close; she enjoyed him fussing; she wasn't used to this. His helpfulness was attractive. She watched the gentle waves breaking across his shoulders, which glinted in the darkness.

The rubbery claustrophobia of the mask and snorkel passed after the first few reassuring breaths; testing out the equipment face down in the water. Both gave a thumbs up, and flipped their fins, propelling them along the surface of the sea towards the rocks.

As darkness surrounded them, the bioluminescence was beginning to sparkle blue-green and white, as gliding bodies broke through the water. It was a perfect evening; Jonah had planned it on a new moon phase, when it was least bright, to maximise nature's glow. They looked at each other's hands and arms glinting as they swept the water aside; lifting their hands, and watching split-second luminous drops.

Fran couldn't stop smiling. Her fears about not being able to see clearly diminished as soon as she placed her face in the water.

Not only was her vision clear, her future was clear too; she wanted to stay here, forever.

Maisie, and her now lover, Sox were sitting in The Pallas after a hectic night, when all the patrons had left, singing and dancing their way back to their respective accommodation. Maisie relished their joy, and enjoyed the gossip; also the traumas as holiday-makers would reveal their deepest sins, and boastful triumphs to her on late evenings after too many rums, ouzos and wine. She had become quite the agony aunt. There was a keen wisdom present, Maisie had learnt a lot about life and especially relationships.

Maisie wondered about Fran's acquaintance with Jonah, as she seemed quite enamoured with him: she looked forward to meeting him. Maisie spoke to Sox about Fran's planned engagement to Liam, 'I'm not sure Fran's heart is really in it?' Maisie worried.

'It is difficult. You cannot choose your children's and grandchildren's friends or partners. Liam sounds like a steady man who will take care of her,' Sox reassured.

'I'm sure he will. But … does she really need taking care of? I've never seen her so happy, and I do wonder about this Jonah chap she's bringing along tomorrow.'

Sox said, 'Maisie, maybe don't interfere; I know you want the best, but our children, no matter how old,' Sox shrugged, 'we have to let them make their mistakes, and—'

'But she could be marrying the wrong person! I need to know if it's right. There is such a change in her. She seems, so free … so confident … outgoing … enjoying the nightlife, the food and the friendships. I met her friend Aussie Ash, a real Tasmanian Devil, she's wonderful.' Maisie smiled.

There was silence, apart from the glasses clinking and the low hum of the dishwasher from the kitchen. There was the constant sharp chirruping of the *tzitzikas*. A distant moped whine broke her reverie. Sox suggested they close up the bar and head for a walk on the beach, to which Maisie agreed; she knew Sox recognised she was at her most relaxed in, or near the sea.

After a lengthy walk, over some low rocks onto the next tiny deserted cove, Sox took Maisie's hands.

'Stay … stay here, Margarita. Stay with me. We can be happy, and make a life here.'

Maisie took a sharp intake of breath, and attempted to withdraw her hands with an automatic head-shake, and before any defensive words were emitted, Sox gently placed his hand on the side of her cheek.

'I only ask you to think about it. Think before you say no. What do you really want? Even if you go home for a while, think about coming back to me.' He spoke softly, 'if it doesn't work out, you can leave anytime.'

Maisie was at a loss. Sox could often pre-empt her next defence with a rational comment. In a way, it irritated her, how easily he stepped lightly over her emotional barrier into her protective inner layer. They stood facing each other; she slid her arms around his waist and rested her head against his warm shoulder, his beating heart soothed her. The thought of returning home had occurred to her many times, but she pushed it away; she didn't know whether to go or stay. Sox squeezed her close, and she could feel his passion rising. His penchant for making love outdoors freaked Maisie out initially. Her English voice told her it was disgraceful behaviour at her age, but her Greek voice told her, *endaksi*, it's fine.

On a previous walk along this quiet cove, Sox began his expert technique of kissing Maisie's neck and caressing her backside, gently pulling her groin towards his. She enjoyed his touch and the feelings that started to arouse within, even though she resisted at first, breaking away to suggest, 'this is a bit animalistic, isn't it?'

'Yes … but we are animals,' a broad grin spread across his face as he asked, 'what did humans do before they had houses, before bedrooms and switching the light off, like you English?' Enjoying his mocking perspective of British prudeness.

As Maisie dropped her dress and unzipped Sox's shorts she replied, 'we British are not all frigid and uptight, you know.'

'Good to know,' said Sox as his eyes grew wide, and his passion grew stronger.

They dropped onto the sand, Maisie astride him, and the rhythmic physical experience was echoed by the rush of waves. The cool sea breeze on the back of her body felt good; it enhanced the warm touch of her lover's hands as he stroked her thighs. Afterwards, they giggled and skipped into the water, skinny dipping being a favoured pastime on this nudist beach. Maisie had found this out inadvertently, and was a little disconcerted, when she had wandered along the shoreline previously, to which Sox roared with laughter as she described the naked visions she encountered.

The following evening Fran arranged a night off; she and Jonah met Sox and Maisie at The Pallas. As they approached the restaurant, Maisie noted Fran kept a distance from Jonah, though she suspected she would enjoy closer proximity.

'Nansie, you look amazing!' said Fran, turning to Sox, 'you've been treating her again, haven't you?'

Maisie looked resplendent in an ecru dress with a cowl neckline that draped across her bronzed shoulders, tied with a chain belt at her waist, then flowed to her ankles, revealing gold gladiator sandals. Maisie's hair was entwined with tiny beads, a string of which framed her forehead.

'I've gone for the Greek goddess look.'

'You have certainly … erm, pulled this off … is that the right expression?' asked Jonah as he held Maisie's welcoming hand and brushed a gentle greeting of a kiss on her offered cheek. 'I am not sure if that is also something rude in English. I apologise if it is.' It broke the ice, as they laughed.

'My cousin, she has a spa, and a ladies shop, where they …' Sox waved towards Maisie, sweeping his hands to show her off.

'It's a boutique,' corrected Maisie, 'next door to a beauty and hair salon, so Chrissy, Sox's cousin, treated me to the full works.' She held out her arms. Those early deportment classes had certainly made their mark on Maisie McLaine, the once defiant little orphan.

Fran winked. 'Totally smashed the look, Nansie, beautiful.'

Fran took photos and texted the images back home to her mum Kate, and Aunties Neve, Jen, Alice and Grace, who were intrigued at their adventure.

'Let me take one of you, Fran; you look absolutely gorgeous tonight, such a pretty girl. We can send it to your mum and Liam.' Maisie, noticed Fran's noncommittal response. 'I love you in fuchsia pink; you've always suited it with your skin tone since you were a tiny girl.' Maisie noticed Jonah's adoring eyes; he smiled in acknowledgement, though he kept any comments to himself. The pair looked relaxed in each other's company, maybe a little guarded.

The evening was amazing, full of lively conversation and excellent food. Maisie got the sense there was something between Fran and Jonah and later mentioned it to Sox, who agreed he noticed it too, despite their efforts to keep distant. Maisie wondered if Fran had suggested Jonah keep at arm's length for her benefit.

The two men got along brilliantly with their common love of the sea, its creatures, and it's wonder. They shared a mutual passion for ocean conservation and held deep discussions about the plight and effects of global warming. They arranged a trip out on Sox's boat. Fran and Maisie arranged a visit to the spa for a day of pampering Greek style. Fran had saved a lot of money with tips on top of her wages; she was a popular hard-working member of the team and fully earned the additional income.

Following that special evening, the four met up again, this time in Heraklion and enjoyed a meal out so Sox could relax, and have a well-earned night off. They arranged their respective activities of spa and sea.

Chapter 22

Maisie and Fran booked in at the spa, which was part of an exclusive leisure club attached to one of the notable hotels in Heraklion, and as they were 'family', Chrissy, the manager and Sox's cousin, arranged a free session. The women were draped in light toga-style robes as they lay on sumptuous thick wadded sun-beds in the shaded area by the leisure club pool. Drinks were included in the package, but Fran kept to the minimum as she was working that evening.

'I'll need a nap today. It's the weekend, so I'll probably not get finished until about four in the morning.'

'Well done you, Fran, you work hard. It's great having these little luxuries instead of scrimping and scraping. Sox wants to pay me at the restaurant, but honestly, I'd work there for free. He has offered to pay our next month's rent on the apartment to make up for it, if we want to stay longer?'

Fran rolled her head towards Maisie. 'Do you want to stay Nansie?

You seem to be really enjoying Greek island life.'

'I love it here … Sox has asked if I want to stay. But, I really don't know whether I should. I have you, your mum, and all my sisters and family back in England. I can't make up my mind.'

'You'll know when the time is right to make the decision; it suits you being here. Is there any news on Manolis and his family?'

'We're going to take another trip to Archanes, and stay for a couple of nights to make enquiries if anyone knows of the family. But I'm nervous about it, letting sleeping dogs lie may be a better option.'

Fran leaned up on her elbow and repeated, 'staying for a couple of nights, eh? ... separate rooms?' She laughed. 'I knew you two were ... em, bonking!'

'Bonking?' Maisie laughed.

'I had to choose a word you'd know, that wasn't too crude. I haven't got a potty-mouth like you.'

'Well, if you must know. Yes ... we are bonking. Bonking on the boat, bonking on the beach and bonking in bed. I'm bonking for Britain!' Maisie waved her hands skywards.

They broke into fits of giggles as a wealthy-looking couple of women walked by and sneered.

'They can sod off too.'

'Nansie! Shush, they'll hear you.'

'Don't care.' Maisie took another sip of the extraordinarily ornate cocktail she had chosen from the menu. 'It's good, sitting here, people-watching.'

'You've changed your tune from our train journey to Florence, and the Sisters of Mercy will be absolutely disgusted at your language.'

'Good!' said Maisie. 'You know I do feel different Fran. But I'm not sure if it's still the holiday spirit, the new romance, the sun, sea and everything ... I think Jimmy would be happy for me.'

'Grandad would be content knowing you are alright ... and loved. I'm happy for you; Sox is an absolute gem; you wouldn't meet anyone like him back home.'

The alcohol mix in the cocktail influenced Maisie's next statement; otherwise she wouldn't have commented. She slid her sunglasses down her nose, looked into Fran's eyes, and asked, 'what about Jonah? He is absolutely lovely.'

'Ah yeah, he is, I meet loads of lovely blokes, and girls, of course, in the bar.' Fran shrugged.

But Maisie was not going to be shrugged away, she saw through Fran's fake nonchalance.

'I do sense he really likes you, not just fancies you, but admires you … you know what I mean?'

Fran fell quiet for some time.

'I'm getting engaged to be married, and I haven't come here for a final few shags before I get wed, you know that.'

'I know that, of course, and I'm not suggesting anything—'

'I need the loo.' Fran stood abruptly, cutting off this line of conversation.

Maisie persisted upon Fran's return, even though she had been warned previously by Sox not to interfere. She said, 'I think I know what's going on. I think you really like Jonah … really like him. But you don't feel you can do anything about it because of loyalty to Liam.'

Fran's frustration was rising. 'Look, with respect, you have no idea how it is for me and Liam. We get along great, and I love him. I'm going to marry him, and we will be happy. The end.'

'As long as you don't have any regrets.'

'What's that supposed to mean?'

'All I'm saying is, don't rush into marriage; you're still young with your whole life ahead of you. Happy ever after doesn't always come true.'

'I know that, I'm not stupid, and it's up to me how I choose to live my life. So, was it a big disaster getting married young for you and mum? How old were you, eighteen, and mum hadn't even had her twenty-first birthday before she was married with a baby. Do you mean, don't rush into marriage with Liam specifically. You've never really warmed to him, have you?'

'It's not that at all, I love Liam, but you must admit you're having a great time here though, with the likes of Ashley and all the people you have met.'

'And Jonah, I suppose? Life won't be like this all the time; you can't pretend your life is one long holiday. I have responsibilities at home, my family, my job. I'm saving for a house, and yes, I'm going to be engaged to be married for fuck's sake.' Fran said in an angry whisper, as their raised voices were becoming noticed.

'Well, yes, I do mean Jonah.' Maisie became animated. 'He is exciting to be with, handsome, intelligent, seems he's going to have a great career travelling the world, who wouldn't want to be part of that, instead of stuck in England—'

'With Liam?' Fran tilted her head with a grimace. 'He's not exciting enough, eh? He isn't exotic like Sox; in fact, he's quite ordinary. Or is he just too thick and boring for your liking?'

'I really don't mean anything against Liam, he's a lovely lad; but take your time; there's a world out there full of interesting people and experiences.'

Fran swung her legs around, sitting on the side of her sunbed, face leaning in toward Maisie's as the argument became more heated.

'You can't talk. You didn't even want to come here, and you complained about everything at first with that sneer on your face when things didn't suit.'

'What sneer?' Maisie thought this unfair.

Fran stood abruptly, grabbing her towel, book and sunglasses, 'I need to go. I've got to get ready for work.'

'But … Sox is picking us up later.'

'I'd rather sort myself out.'

'Fran, all I'm saying is don't settle for ordinary because it's expected of you, not yet, take your time.'

'It's okay; I know exactly what you're getting at.' Fran said in her low, menacing whisper. 'Maybe there's nothing wrong with ordinary.' She walked away.

Fran returned to the apartment and got changed for work. She didn't want to face more scrutiny, questions or criticism of life choices about her, and Liam and their future. Fran stomped around knowing she would be in a foul mood with the Lemonikis tonight if they started any nonsense. Should she go into work feeling this way, she wondered? Fran wanted to be out of the apartment, away from the awful truths that had been chipping away into her mind and soul. She questioned whether she really did love Liam. If she did, how could she feel so passionately about Jonah. She longed to be physically close to him; swimming alongside him when they went snorkelling was thrilling; to feel the brush of his leg against hers, or when they held hands to dive to the sea-bed guiding each other to an interesting find.

The realisation that Fran had to go home hit her. She must know whether she should marry Liam. All this could simply be stupid holiday romance stuff, and she'd been far too busy to really miss Liam hadn't she? Sometimes, she did a little after one of their less frequent calls these days, and it was a comfort to hear his voice. Nothing seemed to happen at home, he had nothing much to say apart from how the match went, and recounting inane experiences from nights out with the lads. Fran had lots of infinitely different experiences, many of which she didn't impart, because Liam wasn't interested, and kept asking when she'd be back as he missed her. Fran couldn't stop the tears which flowed in abundance, as the familiar stomach-churning sensation was back.

Chapter 23

Fran took a taxi to work; she couldn't be bothered with the bus that night. She was distraught, and still shaking from the antagonism of the earlier argument with her grandma. They had never argued, and had always been able to resolve issues in the past. She decided to be civil; further conflict would get them nowhere. She was beginning to become tired of working in the busy bar; the summer season was at its height, and every night was hot and sweaty despite the aircon.

The Australian contingent had left, and Jonah was leaving soon. She thought about his bright, engaging face, his lean, strong body, the way he sliced through the water when they swam together and their bare flesh touching. The thought of him again sent a direct emotional arrow from her brain to deep inside her being; her senses exploded from his touch, the sound of his voice … everything. She must deny these feelings. Fran had been unable to confess to Maisie the effect Jonah had upon her, however, it was clear her grandma knew, although the spa disagreement was never brought up.

Fran met with Jonah on the two nights before he left; he abandoned his group, and their groupies, for her. She couldn't resist his kiss after a few drinks, on his last night as they sat on the beach, but she came to her senses and had withdrawn from the embrace. But why, she couldn't understand it as she wanted him so much, and now, as she sat in the apartment feeling hopeless, he was gone.

She recalled their last moments, and shook her head with embarrassment. Fran regretted her lame comment as their kiss was leading to the impulsive passion she must deny, 'Jonah … I … I'm so sorry … this shouldn't have happened—'

'No, Francesca, I'm sorry, I should not have done this. You have done nothing wrong. I deeply apologise.' was Jonah's immediate response.

She recalled the desperate look on Jonah's face, eyes closed as he leaned away from her, resting his head in his hands.

Fran sat on the edge of her bed, and cried desolate tears. She was confused and conflicted. She had desperately wanted to be intimate with Jonah; to be close to him always, to hear his voice, to talk about the sea, to laugh, to learn more German language, but the guilt thinking of Liam at home overwhelmed her. Was she as bad as Bilbo and the lads when they were on their holiday shagging around. Her feelings certainly weren't in the category of shagging; she had a deep connection with Jonah. No-one would ever have known if they'd had sex … although she would have, and would have to live with the guilt.

Liam was a good man; he could be kind and helpful. They had fun together, sex with him was good; they had plenty of practice over the years managing each other's expectations … but … she had never felt the unbridled passion and yearning she had for Jonah. Maybe she could talk with Maisie about this, but was aggrieved that it would only play into her gran's suggestions that Liam was not the right man for her, then what happens? She must find out for herself.

Fran lay, tired and sobbing on the bed; she had to get ready for work again, it was becoming tedious. She had enjoyed her role in the bar so far; everyone was happy, apart from the odd miserable malaka, who would never know the meaning of happiness, returning their drink out of spite, when there was nothing wrong with it. She needed to go home to the safety and security of her parents' house, her bedroom, her office and her work in the health service, and to Liam. He was safe and reliable, it matched her life, and, yes, she could be fulfilled with that.

Fran rationalised the rush of feelings she had for Jonah, as a typical holiday romance. As she lay on the bed, she found herself identifying with her great Granny Ellen, who must have experienced the same enthralling passion when she fell for Manny all those years ago. Fran inwardly sensed a connection. If their love affair had not happened, she wouldn't even be here. Thoughts turned to Maisie, the product of Ellen and Manny's union. Maybe she had been harsh on her, with her immature strop at the spa.

Her phone pinged, and she retrieved it from her bag. There were a number of texts she had neglected, and one message was from Jonah.

> *Dear Francesca, I leave for Köln now. I am sorry if I have upset you, I did not mean to do this. I have enjoyed our time together and will think of you often. Please keep in communication if you feel it is right, but I understand if you do not want to, which makes me feel sad. I wish you a happy future. Your swimming soul-mate. J x*

Fran sent a reply, reassuring him, he had not offended her in any way, and she too, wished him well. Jonah was gone, she may never see him again, and it hurt like hell. She was about to delete his contact details, and as her finger hovered over the red minus icon, she could not do it. She lay on her bed and wept, when she heard a gentle tap on the bedroom door. Who could it be, her gran was supposed to be in Archanes with Sox.

'Fran, sweetheart, are you okay?' it was Maisie's soft voice.

Fran realised they must not have stayed over because of her, and felt guilty. 'I'm okay, Nansie, but I've got the most dreadful period pain. Don't think I will make it in to work. Would you contact Suzanna's and apologise for me, please.'

'Of course, honey, don't worry about that. Can I get you anything?'

'No thanks. I have painkillers, and should rest for a while.'

'Alright, Fran … listen honey, I'm really sorry about the things I said. I—'

'It's fine, really. Think we're both a bit weary … maybe.' The tears spilled, Fran's throat rasped, 'I just need some sleep … that's all.' 'I'll check back on you later, okay?'

'Okay.' Fran managed to squeeze the word out, before the silent crying began, she stuffed her face into her pillow, and sobbed once she realised Maisie had walked away.

The following day, Fran emerged with a steely resolve to make a go of her life at home with Liam. A sense of calm flooded through her, arriving at The Pallas. Maisie was full of apologies, saying she had no right whatsoever to criticise Fran's life, and reassured that she recognised Liam was a good man, and Fran would have a great future with him. They had reconciled their differences to a degree, but there remained a rift.

'You never know, I may still be around to see great grandchildren, as I fully intend to be. How fantastic is that?'

Fran appreciated the comments, also Sox's deep Greek-Canadian accented, soothing tones, that everything would be, *endaksi.*

Maisie told Fran information had come to light from Sox's enquiries about the Petrakis family. It seems Manny's sister Cora may be living on the island, though not in Archanes.

'We would never have been able to search for the family if not for you, Sox. I'm really grateful for your help and support.' Fran gave him a huge hug; he was the most compassionate man she had ever met, apart from her Grandad Jimmy.

'We need to get ready for the next exciting episode,' Sox reached his arms out wide. 'The quest to search for Maisie's destination continues!' They laughed at his intrepid explorer pose. 'I have arranged for cover for the restaurant and hired a better car than my old beat-up buggy, so we can get going, and maybe find Cora, as soon as my girls are ready.' Fran fell silent.

Maisie recognised her reticence. 'Honey, you really don't have to come if you don't want to; I'll be okay with this old goat, I'm sure,' 'Hey!' Sox retorted.

Fran saw the admiration and trust in Maisie's face as she looked at her lover; at five years her junior, there didn't look much of an age gap, given his leathery, weathered skin and greying hair, compared to Maisie's youthful appearance. No-one would ever guess she was approaching sixty. Fran loved their playful, oppositional banter; he brought out the best in her. She looked … fresh and liberated.

'It's probably time for me to get back to my responsibilities. It's my birthday soon, and I should get back to spend time with my family; I'll sort out the travel arrangements today.' She looked into her grandmother's brown eyes, and there was a deep mutual understanding that it was the right thing for Fran to do; though both recognised, and would never admit, it was also very-much not right.

The following evening, Sox laid on a wonderful celebratory goodbye meal with friends, family, and holidaymakers. The Pallas, festooned with lights was bouncing with the jollity of family shenanigans, and holidaymakers being unleashed from their regular routine lives for two weeks in the sunshine on a Greek island. Fran's work colleagues called in, and her former boss, Sox's brother, made a huge fuss of her, suggesting she could have a job anytime.

As Fran packed her bags the next morning, she glanced through her phone messages, checking her electronic boarding pass for the flight, and responses from her family about her forthcoming return. She spotted another message from Jonah; it was simply the kiss emoji, that's all. Fran thought this rather odd for Jonah; he wasn't the emoji type. Had he sent that meaningless response because he'd cut off from her, or as a joke, or as a sarcastic kiss my arse? That's the thing about emojis, Fran considered, 'who the fuck knows what they mean.' Knowing Jonah's personality, she thought it was with affection.

When people go back to their real life, responsibilities, and their day jobs, she knew holiday romances were simply a brief fantasy. Fran found the selfie with Jonah on the wonderful bioluminescence night; she slid her phone into her pocket, and picked up her rucksack. She should forget all about him, as they would never meet again. Fran scanned the room for any rogue belongings before she left, and said, 'but … you never know.'

Chapter 24

London 1946

Nikolaos Petrakis was married with two children when he arrived on the south coast of England in 1946, after the Second World War. He was searching for a better life for his family, and was prepared to work hard to provide for them, but lacked any skills or qualifications. He obtained employment at a fruit and vegetable warehouse, working from the crack of dawn every day to get fresh produce off the wagons and into storage areas, for stallholders to collect. Niko, as he was known to his friends and associates, was a good, honest, well-mannered and loyal man. His wife, Xanthe, was stunningly beautiful, with sultry brown eyes, full mouth, and thick brunette hair. Her voluptuous figure encased in figure-hugging dresses, and shapely legs propped up by stilettos, raised eyebrows, heart-rates and other parts of male anatomy wherever she went.

Whilst Niko was working hard each day, and once Xanthe dropped the children at nursery, she would shop, then go to the Green Dragon Inn, where she had secured a few hours work serving in the bar at lunchtimes. She entertained the patrons with her fun personality, sexy figure, chatter and songs. The men were enraptured with her vivacity, and thrilled when she accepted an invitation to slow dance. Xanthe was great for business in the post-war, jitterbug euphoria of the recently ended conflict.

Xanthe caught the eye of one man in particular. With his smart, clean-cut suits and trilby, she found him the height of sophistication. His blue eyes shone, and his fair hair was swept back in a neat side parting, perfectly in place. He had a reluctant air about him, and she couldn't resist his reserved reaction to her the few times he frequented the bar. Eventually, he asked Xanthe to dance, then they chatted in a cosy corner over cigarettes and cheap brandy. He told her he was leaving the area soon, suggesting they meet up before he left. He whispered an address to her, adding, *'in half an hour.'*

Within the hour, Xanthe was naked, straddling the fair stranger; he could not resist her, nor could she resist him. They met daily over the next few days.

Niko noticed a reluctance lately from his wife to make love; always tired, avoiding bedtimes, waiting until he was fast asleep; also faking sleep herself when he rose early each morning. She kept repeating, she did not want another baby.

A stallholder, and trusted friend, had a quiet word with Niko one day. He could never have anticipated, nor wanted to believe his friend's words about Xanthe's infidelity. Niko watched her for a few days. His heart was shredded as he witnessed her emerge from the bar; hair coiffed, bright red lips, and high heels clipping the pavement, as she walked swiftly along the two streets to a rundown bedsit. After half an hour, she'd emerge to pick their children up from nursery.

Niko was patient; he waited and watched. He couldn't believe what he saw, and each lie she told him about her whereabouts seared into his heart and his brain, lie after lie, day after day. He was prepared to wait until the affair was over. Niko had often wondered if their marriage would be beautiful, but short, and he convinced himself he could overcome her indiscretions, he loved her that much.

One rainy, wild, winter afternoon, he could not take it any longer. He watched from the corner of the opposite street. Xanthe entered the building, Niko planned to catch them red-handed, chase that, *piece of shit,* away and beg her to end the affair, and become his loving wife once more.

He spotted the landlady of the building; he knew Mrs Marsh well from her visits to the market. As she approached her front door, Niko walked toward her and asked her to let him in. Mrs Marsh looked bemused to see him standing there, and as he pushed past her, she cried out. It was too late; she saw something glinting as he ran up two stairs at a time until he reached the room. Niko knew which one it was, as *he* always closed the curtains right before Xanthe arrived. The landlady heard the screams and shouts from upstairs and yelled from her doorstep for help, shouting for someone to get the police.

Niko only intended to use the knife to threaten the man to make him disappear forever; he never intended any harm. Nothing could have stopped the jealous rage inside Niko, not even Xanthe's frantic screams. Niko stabbed the fair-haired lover, time and again, in his back as he lay on top of Xanthe. By the time the police officers arrived, the scene was blood-soaked and heavy with a thick metallic aroma mixed with sweat, fear and tragedy. Xanthe remained curled up in a corner, hands bleeding as she'd tried to hold Niko at bay, and blood was matted in her hair.

The police took Niko away; he was never seen again by any of his colleagues, or his family. Xanthe told the children there had been a terrible fight at their father's workplace, which ended in a deadly accident, where a man died, and their father was blamed, so he would be going to prison. Xanthe never spoke of Nikolaos again.

Manolis cried and cried for his loving, kind joyful father. The man he had hero-worshipped in childhood. His sister Cora was too young to remember her father, but for a faint sense of being held tightly but tenderly by him, and being sung to sleep when she was upset. Xanthe moved out of the area as soon as she could find accommodation and work elsewhere. First, she travelled to

Liverpool, where she worked in bars and engaged the support of friends, and lovers until she moved on again.

In later years, Manolis, at seventeen, had an affair with a married woman, and it was clear from her expanding waistline she was pregnant, after seven years of trying to conceive with her husband. The family quickly moved on, Xanthe could not risk the truth, or any scandal being revealed. Manolis left the woman; he could leave anyone easily, with no loyalty. He was without his father to help guide him through his teenage years.

There were many more men, but Xanthe never stayed or bonded with any of them, and when it all got too much, or there was debt, or another scandal, she moved the family on yet again. More towns and villages, more pubs, more men until she reached a quiet town in Greater Manchester, where she felt safe enough to hide her sinful past of betrayal, that took her husband away, broke her spirit, and fractured her family.

The family settled well in this sleepy town. Manolis pottered around car garages, an untrained grease-monkey, but he helped out and learned from the older men he worked with. They ribbed him about his handsome looks. *'Hey, Tony!'* they would shout with an Italian inflection as he passed by, offering their reference to Hollywood heartthrob, Tony Curtis with his brooding dark looks. They'd repeat, *'how's Sophia?'* further reference about Italian actress Sophia Loren was directed at Xanthe. The family brought an exotic eroticism to a sleepy north west town.

Manolis and Cora made new friends easily; having many years practice at fitting in. They were courteous to neighbours, and Cora made a few schoolfriends. As always, Xanthe took work in the local hostelry, working long hours to make ends meet, and Cora, when she was old enough, helped out a few evenings each week working in the kitchen, preparing basic meals for the punters and cleaning up. Cora was never going to be the beauty her mother was, but Manolis had inherited his mother's glamourous attractiveness.

Manolis had his pick of the young girls, and women for

companionship and sex. He was particularly drawn to a pretty girl named Ellen. She was a challenge for him. Most of the other girls fell at his feet, he didn't have to try, but Ellen was different; she ignored him for the most part. Until one day, Ellen was shopping for some fruit at a local market when he made an approach, and finally she succumbed to his charms. He claimed his prize, then discarded it when another glinting conquest passed before his eyes.

Chapter 25

Archanes Village

The day after Fran's departure, Maisie and Sox made the forty-minute trip to Archanes in search of Cora Petrakis. Maisie often got the impression Sox had been life-long friends with everyone he met, because of what she perceived as over-familiarity. Eventually she stopped asking if he knew them. They were inevitably invited to sit and take food or drinks as he chatted with everyone they met, interpreting for Maisie. However she had picked up several phrases, and understood the flow of repeated conversations, always using Greek to thank people for their help.

Sox was diligent in his scrutiny of archived records and found an address where the Petrakis family may have lived in Archanes. He had been given a lead to an elderly couple, who had lived and worked in Archanes all their lives, and may have knowledge of the family. There was a reluctance initially by the couple to divulge any knowledge of the Petrakis family; the rumoured legacy of the family scandal in England ran deep. The woman repeated local gossip that Cora had returned to the island, however she had not visited Archanes as far as was known.

The husband of the couple was losing his memory and his faculties, though had moments of distinct lucidity. He immediately pointed to Maisie and called her a name, something similar to,

Santhy. The old woman commented there was a remarkable likeness between Maisie and Manolis' mother, Xanthe Petrakis. The old woman believed a cousin of Nikolaos lived near Rethymno. Maisie and Sox bid a fond farewell to the couple. The old man waved, repeating, 'Xanthe, Xanthe.'

Sox and Maisie researched Petrakis families currently living in Rethymno, Sox made enquiries by phone, and it was by chance one of his calls was productive. The guy he spoke with was a Petrakis, but not connected to Nikolaos, however, his friend married a woman with that maiden name, and he believed her family came from Archanes. He was happy to pass on a telephone number. Sox made contact with the prospective relative named, Theia, and she confirmed her father was indeed, Nikolaos Petrakis' cousin, and invited them to visit.

Sox and Maisie drove from Archanes back to Heraklion, then travelled west for one hour along the coast to Rethymno. Maisie discovered a lively Venetian harbour, filled with cafes and shops. Sox explained it was an ancient town, similar to Heraklion, with a rich medieval history. Maisie vowed to return to Rethymno soon.

They found Theia's home, and she immediately offered them drinks on the terrace of her worn-looking villa, which overlooked a stunning panorama. Sox apologised, for speaking in English to translate. Theia raised her hand and wafted away any objection, as she poured homemade, sharp lemonade packed with ice and wild mint leaves. She adorned the wooden table with small offerings of fresh homemade bread, olives, cheese, figs, and huge slices of cucumber and tomatoes all generously doused in olive oil.

Theia vaguely recalled Manolis was about her age, and after the scandalous but scant recall of the family history, she confirmed Cora had returned to Crete many years later. She indicated no-one really knew the truth about Nikolaos, but that he was imprisoned for some crime in London, and the circumstances were vague, and he was never mentioned once word of a serious crime reached Crete.

Theia knew Cora was divorced from her English husband, and had remarried a Greek man here on Crete, and they had a child. She estimated Cora would be in her mid-seventies by now. Theia had spoken with Cora when she initially returned many years, and advised Cora would not say what happened … ever. She simply repeated her parents were dead, that was all. The only detail about Manolis was, he remained in England, but moved around so much, Cora lost touch with him, but Theia did not believe this.

Theia scanned her memory banks and came up with the surname Angelakis; she believed this was the Greek family Cora married into, and he had something to do with the wine trade. Theia suggested searching for a winery near Spili, a small inland village, where she believed Cora Angelakis had settled. It seemed a reasonable place to start. Further internet searches revealed two locations. Sox suggested enquiring at the more commercial of the two businesses, as the remote winery only had road directions, no specific address. The name on the map reference Sox translated as, *unmade road*.

Sox suggested to Maisie, 'we could travel to the Kourlou winery and continue our search today, it isn't too far, maybe forty minutes.'

'No, I'm exhausted,' was Maisie's swift response. She thanked Theia profusely for the information and hospitality. The ancient concept of Greek hospitality, *Xenia*, was not lost on Maisie this day. The moral obligation to offer friendship, generosity, food and gifts to foreign travellers and guests, often played out in real life.

In the car, Maisie said, 'I'm scared Sox. Part of me really wants to know, wants to feel I belong here, to meet a woman who could be my aunt. But part of me fears hearing information I may not want to learn about my father, or this terrible incident … I don't know what to do, or think.'

Sox said, 'if we meet Cora, I will ask the questions, you will not understand the reply, but I will tell you the truth of what is said, and I will keep you safe. The truth *can* keep you safe, even though it is difficult to hear.'

'I imagine Cora speaks English anyway, she lived there long enough.' Maisie added.

'If we find her, it may be more ... comfortable for her to speak her native language. We'll see ...'

They journeyed in silence; watching the scenery rolling by, Maisie enjoyed the cool breeze from the open road.

'Okay, let's do it!' She said suddenly, 'let's go now; I can't leave this hanging over me for the rest of my life.'

Maisie and Sox arrived at the Kourlou Winery within forty minutes, and settled at a table, on a bright terrace in front of the small retail area, where a range of different products were displayed. A guide asked them if they would be joining the tour. Sox refused politely, however ordered a very expensive bottle of wine and asked about other products. Sox knew the hospitality business well, and was persuasive in gleaning details from the young man about the history of the winery, and the people who worked there. The guide, who was a member of the extended family that owned the winery, recognised the name Angelakis, suggesting he was maybe a marketing manager, but he retired many years ago.

Maisie sipped a glass of cold white wine, taking in the wonderful vista of rolling hills, covered in the vivid green strips of the extensive vineyard. She tapped her mobile, amazed she had a signal, and now adept at internet searches, thanks to Fran, who removed any mysticism about it. She tried the name Angelakis and the winery company name, and an image of an older Greek man, Hector Angelakis, appeared. His brief bio confirmed he had indeed worked for the winery as a marketing manager during the 1990s, retiring in 2005 when he was seventy. Another link revealed his obituary. He died three years ago, and it also confirmed his wife was named, Cora.

Without giving Maisie an opportunity to hesitate, Sox encouraged her into the car once the wine was consumed, and they headed for the village of Spili. After some fifteen minutes driving, he announced, 'Theia recalled the Angelakis' address in Spili, I didn't want to say earlier.'

There was silence, apart from the sound of tyres crunching along the rough gravelled track, which seemed amplified because of the open four-wheel drive. The huge golden globe of mid-afternoon sunshine warmed the back of their heads and shoulders as they travelled south from the winery to Spili village centre. Sox glanced a number of times at Maisie, who remained silent, steadfastly looking forward, expressionless, half of her face covered in huge sunglasses.

'I feel as though I've been ambushed.' Still not turning her head.

'If I explained, you would have found an excuse not to go.'

Both knew he was right. Another ten minutes into the journey went by without communication.

Meekly, almost child-like, Maisie asked, 'how do you plan to introduce me to some woman who doesn't even know of my existence, and who may consider I'm insane.'

'We can look only first. We don't have to talk with her.'

'Then what's the point?'

In five minutes, the car pulled up in Spili, set in the foothills of the Kedros Mountains, twenty-seven kilometres inland from Rethymno. They strolled along a street to the centre, and came upon the row of twenty-five lions head fountains, carved in stone from the sixteenth century. Fresh, filtered spring water flowed directly from the hills above the town through the lions mouths. They took a drink from a lion's mouth near the centre of the row, and saw a waiter filling jugs with fresh water to take to diners' tables. They wandered further into the streets bustling with shoppers, and bought some essential oils and Aloe Vera products from Spili's renowned Maravel Shop, specialising in local organic herbal and aromatherapy goods. The scent in the shop was enthralling, no-one left without a purchase.

'Let's sit a while,' said Maisie, which they did at a quiet cafe away from the main tourist area. Sox was good at finding these small, out-of-the-way local places.

'Exactly where is Cora's house? This feels like voyeurism, like I'm stalking her.'

Sox noticed Maisie's, rigid posture. She had a habit of pouting when she was anxious, almost like a sad child, though he hadn't observed this for many weeks. She had been a version of Maisie-light, softer and blurry around the edges, not the sharp-edged, restrained woman he first met. He loved her defiance, and her resilience and decided in this moment, he would do anything to support her; in fact, he'd do anything for her. If she wanted to turn back and return home, either to his villa, as she now lived with him, or return to England if it is what she truly wanted; he would support her decision, but one of those outcomes would break his heart in two.

Sox held Maisie's hand and asked if she was feeling okay. He apologised if he had cajoled her into pursuing the woman who could be her aunt by birth.

'It's fine, I know you try to do what's best. Sometimes, it takes a while for me to get used to situations. You know a little about my past, but not all of it.'

'I have always known there is a … history, let's say.' Sox took her in his arms and kissed her forehead, as she rested her head against his shoulder. They finished their drinks at the café, and wandered to a pleasant park full of flowers and sat on a bench.

Cora Angelakis awoke that morning. She rubbed the small of her back as a pang of arthritis radiated from her back to her hips. She watered the abundant, beloved plants in her garden, replaced the watering can, and stepped back into her modest bungalow, on a quiet street in Spili village. Cora had changed her bedding and was lugging the heavy basket of damp laundry out to the rear garden, and proceeded to hang the bedding out on the line. Her octogenarian neighbour popped his head over the fence and offered his usual wave and, *'kalimera.'* Cora took good care of him; recently widowed, she recognised that lost look he portrayed, and worried whether his memory was going, or it was simply a response to grief.

Cora thought about her husband, Hector Angelakis. He was a good man, and had been the best husband she could have hoped for as a divorcee from England. Their daughter had produced two wonderful grandchildren who would be visiting soon. After her contemplation and finishing her glass of iced coffee and a pastry for her breakfast, she headed into Spili centre for a few items of produce.

'Yassou, Cora!' She was greeted everywhere by the many shop owners she regularly visited; choosing oranges, lemons, olives, aubergine, and cheeses from their stalls. She was casually wandering around the fish market and spotted a couple ahead of her. Something about the woman stopped her in her tracks. There was a familiarity, even though she only vaguely heard the tone of voice. Cora stopped to absorb every nuance of that voice. The woman was tall, slim, and had dark brown hair and eyes, and as she turned to speak to the man, her profile was unmistakable.

Cora whispered under her breath, 'mama.' She was immobilized, the world swirled around her, as her memory was dragged back, kicking and screaming, to a dark, dreary house in northern England where she'd lived with her mother, Xanthe and her brother, Manolis. Cora was stunned and statue-like; only her shopping basket was shaking, revealing the tremors her body was responding to. The couple turned to walk by her, and as they passed, the woman smiled at the man. It was her mother's smile.

'Cora, Cora!' Her old neighbour was trying to draw her from her reverie, asking if she was alright and guided her to one of the market stalls, where she was seated and given a warm brandy with water until she steadied. The stall holder asked what was wrong? What had caused such a shock? Cora replied that she thought she had seen a ghost, her mother, alive and walking through the market. The elderly neighbour and stall holder looked tentatively at each other, wondering if Cora had experienced some form of episode.

Even in his own befuddled bereaved state, her neighbour recognised she was in emotional distress. 'You know the woman could not possibly have been your mother?' he suggested.

Cora nodded, 'of course, how could it be? But her voice, her face, her hair, she was the exact copy, how can that possibly be?'

'They say everyone has a double.'

Cora was pensive. 'This woman isn't Greek, she spoke in perfect English. I lived there as a young girl, I know.'

Cora roused, and her neighbour took her arm, suggesting they take a stroll around the local public gardens. During their casual wander, Cora chatted happily, then stopped again, with a disbelieving look of apparent horror on her face. She stared at the same couple sitting on a bench amidst some pretty flowers.

Maisie gazed into the middle distance and became aware of an elderly couple; the woman was staring intently at her. Maisie raised her head and glanced behind her, wondering what, or who on earth she was staring at. Sox became aware of the couple too. He straightened up and offered a polite, 'kalispera.' The man responded, but the woman could not take her eyes off Maisie. He realised in this chance meeting who she must be, as she clearly recognised Maisie. In his most polite, lowkey manner, he asked if she was Cora Angelakis, to which the woman nodded trance-like. Sox went on to ask if she had a brother named Manolis, to which she nodded again, imperceptibly this time.

In his most reverent tone, he explained that he suspected Maisie was her brother's child, from the north west of England, born in 1960. Sox leapt up as he saw Cora crumple into her friend's arms, and gently cradled her as she drifted to the ground.

Chapter 26

Maisie and Sox spent several days travelling to, and from Spili, to spend time with Cora after that first surprising meeting. Manolis had died, some eight years ago in England, and Cora showed sensitivity towards Maisie, who soon realised any detail about the Petrakis family history was difficult for Cora to recount. The realisation that Maisie was very likely to be Manolis' daughter, interested Cora, in meeting her long-lost niece.

A revelation occurred when Maisie first set eyes upon a photograph of her birth grandmother, Xanthe. Sox remarked upon the incredible likeness between the women. It appeared unmistakable that Maisie was genetically linked to this family. Sox had suggested a DNA test if Cora wished, and Maisie reassured there was no ulterior motive for her search, other than to confirm her Greek heritage. Cora offered Maisie and Sox the inevitable Greek hospitality, whenever they visited. However she graciously declined invitations to join them to dine at The Pallas, which somewhat irritated Maisie. There was an invisible barrier there.

Over time, Cora eventually recounted what she knew of her father murdering her mother's lover. She remained distant, almost aloof when she spoke of it. Cora did say she and Manolis never saw him again after he went to prison when they were children; Xanthe wouldn't allow it. Cora recalled an occasion she had seen her father as an adult. 'I saw him once, he was quite old by then, and living in a hostel. It's really hard to look at the quiet man who is your father, and come to terms with the fact he killed someone.'

Cora was more comfortable talking about, Manolis and Xanthe.

'My mother stayed in England, but I knew Crete was my home as soon as I returned to live here. England was not a happy place for our family. My mother eventually settled with her partner who was,' she shrugged, 'okay, much older. He had money, so she lived comfortably, but I don't think she ever loved him. Manolis kept in touch with our father, and they visited together until my father's death, but I'm not sure it was healthy for Manolis. Eight years, Manolis has been gone now, he died not long after his seventieth birthday. He would've loved seeing you.' Cora seemed compelled to offer the truth, 'but he would never have been a steady father for you. He could never live with this ... this, family curse over our heads, it was unbearable for him.'

Maisie sensed Cora was drowning in painful memories, and changed the subject. 'Your husband seemed such a lovely man. During our searches, we read about him, and he was loved by many people.'

'He was the best.' Cora's eyes twinkled. 'I'll get our wedding photos,' she delved into the cupboard where she found the old family pictures, and the two women talked about life, about having children and losing those you dearly love. There was a distant respect between the two women. Sox took the hint, as they indulged looking through the albums, he went next door to ask the neighbour if he'd like a drive along the coastline.

Maisie had seen a few photographs of her birth father, Manolis, mostly in black and white, though there was one of him in his forties in colour. He was indeed a rather handsome man. Maisie had recently lost her beloved mother and husband, and meeting with Cora helped her to appreciate those relationships were more important, than being genetically linked to Manolis Petrakis or his family. She felt little emotion when looking at his image.

'No wonder Ellen fell for him,' she said wistfully.

'As soon as she became aware that a young woman had become pregnant and Manolis was probably the father, our mother moved us to another town.' Cora was wistful, 'we moved on quite a lot. I cannot remember the number of homes I lived in, or schools I attended. I never made any true friends as a child. I only married to get away from the misery of our house; Manolis drinking, and my mother, sad, always so sad. I was young, only seventeen, when my first marriage failed spectacularly after eight months, as I had no support. So, I lived alone once me and my husband separated. I built some friendships, but really wasn't interested in another relationship. I was in my thirties when I decided to return to Greece, and fortunately met my second husband; I was forty when I had my daughter.'

Cora turned, looking deeply into Maisie's eyes. 'Manolis would have known Ellen was pregnant. There was once, years later, he briefly mentioned that he wondered what may have happened. I do believe he was taken with her, but of course, he did nothing about it.' Cora sighed. 'No doubt he had the pick of women and girls wherever he went. He was charming, Maisie, really quite charming. Most of the time, my brother pleased himself. He had two failed marriages and ended up on his own, but with lots of different partners. I'm glad one of his son's did keep in touch with him.'

Cora paused. 'Maisie … I'm sorry to say Manolis wasn't a good father, the drinking …' She lowered her gaze. 'He died quite young, and never meant harm to anyone, and only harmed himself.'

'So, maybe I have lots of half siblings, the nieces and nephews you know about, and many you don't.'

Cora looked shocked. She hadn't considered the genetic relationships.

'Don't worry, I'm not going to demand their contact details. I've lived a lifetime without them already,' said Maisie truthfully. Cora seemed rather dismayed by Maisie's comment.

Maisie continued undaunted, 'do you remember the time he

spent with my mum Ellen, or was she just another one of his conquests? You know the expression, *another notch on the bedpost,* it sometimes feels like she was simply another triumph for him. But my mum, was worth so much more.'

'I do remember her a little; she was a kind, sweet girl, and very pretty.'

'So, he took advantage of her, I'd imagine.'

'You know the expression, *it takes two to tango,* don't you?' Cora was defensive.

'I have. But in these circumstances, he was an eighteen-year-old man, and yes, it does take two, but Ellen was only fifteen and fell madly in love with him. She wrote in her diaries that she dreamed of them getting married. She believed he would stand by her, but I guess your mother couldn't take another family scandal.'

The congenial atmosphere darkened. Cora stood and asked Maisie if she'd like a coffee, but looking at her watch, remarked that time was getting on and suggested Sox would be back soon.

Maisie was not going to be fobbed off; she had a right to understand her past. 'What was Xanthe like?'

'You have inherited her beauty, and should be grateful for this.' Cora was sharp, as if Maisie didn't deserve the beauty she'd been gifted.

'It is purely genetics, though isn't it? Maisie said, 'but I'm glad to be healthy at least.' Maisie sensed Cora's subtle hostility, but she didn't care.

Cora did soften a little. 'My mother enjoyed her beauty, I think. She was a good mother, me and Manolis wanted for nothing. As a small child, I have memories of her playing with us; she sang to us, cared for us when we were ill, and made sure we had all we needed. After the … incident, she changed, everything changed for us all. She had to go out and find work. It wasn't easy in those days to make a living with two children and no family to help.'

'Why didn't she return to Crete?'

'Shame.'

'Shame for what her husband did, or for what *she* did?' asked Maisie.

'Who knows?' Cora shrugged. 'She was … em … she became tough-hearted at times. Not with me and Manolis, but I believe she used her looks to attract men who would help her with money. She had affairs and so on. We moved around a lot.'

Maisie recognised the difficulty Xanthe must have experienced as a migrant single mother in mid-1940s Britain, and the coercive abuse she would have been subject to. She owed it to Cora to express some empathy. 'It must have been incredibly difficult for her. Maybe if she'd returned to Greece, she could have been happy.'

'I doubt that Maisie,' said Cora, 'she was forever seen as the problem. It was her who made Nikolaos kill. You know how it is, always the woman's fault. She would never have been accepted back into the community. Nikolaos' parents, never forgave her. They would say it was she, *who put the knife in his hand*, and called her awful names, but it was their son who did the crime, not her. Yes she was wrong to do what she did, but who knows what troubles there may have been in the marriage. He clearly saw red and couldn't deal with his anger.'

Cora was exasperated, and with despair, held out her arms with a questioning gesture. 'I mean, who does that? My mother was shunned with the reputation of a scarlet woman. She had to get on with it.' 'Do you remember Nikolaos?' Maisie asked.

Cora smiled. 'Only a little. He had soft eyes and a calming voice. He was loving; there were cuddles, and he would tuck us in at night when he was home early and tell us stories. He worked hard, I'm told, and moved to England for a better standard of living for his family. I try to think of this, and not some insane man stabbing another human being five times in his back.' She put her head in her hands. 'When I imagine the blood, the screaming … although I haven't thought of it for years and years. I left England with unhappy memories and try to forget the places I lived, and every other bad thing about that place. I won't go back … ever.'

Cora looked tired. Maisie recognised it was time to go; she didn't want Cora to have to relive any more trauma. She achieved what she wanted to know, she reached for her shawl, and her phone to summon Sox.

Cora said, 'Manolis adored his father. A lot of his problems as an adult, and as a dad came from our father being suddenly taken away. Ellen was better off not being with him.'

Maisie stood, Cora reacted, and Maisie could tell she was relieved when she heard Sox's vehicle pulling up outside. They parted company and half-heartedly mentioned meeting up. There was a generous hug, but Maisie knew it was a final hug, and they wouldn't meet again. All they saw in each other was pain and sorrow from the actions of other people.

Maisie picked up the small bundle of photos Cora had sorted out, thanked her, and left.

Chapter 27

Maisie was waiting outside The Pallas. She had watered the plants and placed them in positions to show the best view leading up to the restaurant. Her love of outdoor spaces, flowers and being near water, stemmed from her time with her foster family. In her mind, she would repeat, *blooms for the Blossoms*, reflecting on everything she was taught about gardening from the audacious Lizzie Blossom. It was four in the afternoon, and her beloved sisters would be arriving soon. Their flight was on time, and Sox had gone to pick them up at the airport. Maisie wouldn't have fit into the car, so she waited patiently. Mixed feelings of loving excitement washed over her, with a yearning to belong to her sisterhood again.

Maisie couldn't resist feelings of their potential judgement, anticipating she was absolutely crazy living in this little one-horse town of a Cretan tourist resort. She thought her two younger sisters, Alice and Grace, would accept her new lifestyle as a wonderful adventure and would engage with Greek culture. And though Neve was her younger sister by almost ten years, Maisie wondered if she'd somehow be demeaned for leaving the family and distancing herself; how is she going to keep in touch with them in a fruitful way. It was Jen who worried her most. Living in this dusty, hot, some may say almost rudimentary place. She envisaged Jen looking with disdain whilst trying to maintain a positive expression on her face, no matter how fake. It worried Maisie.

With the help of Sox's son, Stefanos, Maisie had gone all out to decorate and upgrade those little jobs that required attention at the restaurant. Sox had closed the restaurant to the public for a private gathering that evening with their families.

'I mustn't dwell on it,' Maisie said, not realising she's spoken aloud.

Stefanos, popped his head up from behind the bar where he was fixing the slow leak under the sink unit with a questioning look. 'It's ok, just thinking aloud.'

'Do not worry, Maisie, your sisters will have the best time here in Crete.' He offered up the same engaging grin of his father, appreciating her nervousness.

Maisie thought if they wanted to judge her, or Sox for that matter, that was up to them. She chuckled at the thought of Sox's open dialogue and wondered how they'd cope with his direct approach. She really hoped the trips and events she had planned would go well. Maisie had organised a mystery trip with each sister on separate occasions, so she could spend time individually with them. Often, the nuances of the five sisters chattering together left little room for indulgent conversations.

The hum of a vehicle approached, then stopped, and the Clarke sisters arrived in a tumble of arms and legs, climbing out of the car, wearing huge sunglasses. They resembled a human spider with compound eyes and eight limbs, scampering toward Maisie.

'Maisie!' Grace was the first to run up and grab her in a warm embrace.

The tears flowed. Maisie couldn't hold them back.

'Little Gracie, my baby sister.' Maisie cupped Grace's face in her hands. 'I've missed you, I've missed you all so much.'

Opening her arms wide, the other three sisters converged on Maisie, with hugs, kisses, and a babble of tales of how hot it was; and of the four-hour flight with the numerous bottles of fizz they'd consumed since arriving at Manchester airport earlier that day. They gabbled continuously about the purchases in duty free and, whether they'd brought enough clothing for the week, and how they'd cope in the July heat.

The Pallas staff were superb. They took orders for drinks and laid out tasty morsels of aperitifs of vine leaves; Greek salad, mini mixed pitta with light bites of souvlaki and calamari, with plenty of cold iced water to replenish their hydration. Neve, Jen, Alice, and Grace were immediately taken with Sox and his son, who entertained them with humorous tales of Lemonikis and drunk tourists from around the world who visited The Pallas. Maisie relaxed, sat back, and smiled at the warm feeling of being part of both families. Even Jen was grinning and engaging, but it could be the fizz, she thought.

Sox had rented a luxurious villa for the Clarkes, where he took them now to refresh and rest, to prepare for the evening of entertainment with his family and friends.

Neve

Two days after The Pallas celebration, and much lounging on the beach, Maisie and Neve set off to visit Archanes, where it all began for Maisie. Neve was the eldest Clarke sister, before Maisie arrived and usurped the position. She was a well-behaved girl who studied hard, with an exemplary record in education. Maisie was convinced Neve would be interested in her background, and with her stoic, calm demeanour, she would cope with the devastating back story if it emerged. Maisie, having found the confidence to drive around her vicinity, showed her around Archanes, stopping off for the stunning views from their elevated position. She told Neve about the history of this ancient village and pointed out the Turkish and Byzantine influences of the buildings.

Maisie got the distinct impression Neve was becoming bored, but maybe she was simply tired out with the journey, and the heat. They passed by the old couple's house, where she and Sox originally gleaned details of the Petrakis family, eventually leading to Cora. But Maisie didn't stop; she hoped they wouldn't spot her driving by. Neve wasn't interested in conversations with locals, which Maisie interpreted, now that her spoken language skills were coming along a treat, as she and Sox conversed as best they could in Greek. She noticed Neve's tiresome glance when she addressed or greeted anyone in Greek.

They shared a mezzo lunch at the charming cafe with its abundant floral display. She watched Neve pushing the food around her plate and got the impression she'd have preferred afternoon tea in an English restaurant. She'd get along well with Fran's partner, Liam, Maisie thought disappointedly to herself. Maisie was confused. She thought Neve would compliment her on her ability to assimilate with her new surroundings and communicate in a foreign tongue, but it did not seem to impress her at all.

Maisie made a decision not to introduce her sisters to Cora. They had seen the photos, and Maisie offered her own selective narrative of her life history. She didn't want to recount all of the horrific details about murder, alcoholism and, for want of a better expression, her natal grandmother being a bit of a slapper. No, Maisie would keep the two parts of her family separate, and she reaffirmed this in her mind from Neve's now dismissive attitude to Maisie's birth heritage. She had always had a sense of being part of numerous families and didn't want them to merge. Some parts made her proud, other aspects were humiliating.

After they had seen the ruins of the Minoan palace, Maisie got a sense Neve was at the end of her tether, stopping, rubbing her feet, and looking decidedly sweaty, even though Maisie chose all of the sheltered routes. She had supplied small electric fans, ensured they wore sun hats and sun protection. Maisie carried a backpack with a small ice bag full of grapes, offering little freezing bursts of sweet juicy nutrition, and bottles of cool water to keep them going, which she encouraged her to periodically sip. Though Neve complained it would only make her need a pee, and there may not be any decent toilets. Neve was feigning interest by this stage.

Funnily enough, Neve hadn't indicated any discomfort when

they all took a group trip to Knossos, led by Sox, which was a much more rigorous and demanding event.

Similarly, Neve appeared disinterested in the pastel coloured buildings they drove by, or the quaint cobbled streets. Neve had switched off. Maybe it was too much, Maisie thought, and to be honest, it was *her* story; why should anyone else be as interested. Neve seemed completely relieved to be heading back to The Pallas and became animated once she was in the company of their sisters. She said little about the Archanes trip, and Maisie noticed Sox acknowledged Neve's reticence to discuss anything.

Maisie spotted Sox glancing over to her, their eyes met, and she turned away. He said in Neve's direction, 'maybe you need to go have a siesta; it gets very hot here.' Maisie knew he was giving Neve excuses for her lack of enthusiasm. She saw his subtle shrug and heard his sigh as he walked toward the bar to get on with preparing for the evening.

Maisie, too, was surprised at Neve's reaction to the trip. She told Sox about the day, believing she had got it wrong and maybe should organise another trip.

Sox dissuaded her from that. 'I believe there is something else. I have a sense she only feels safe when everyone is together, and she can keep an eye on everything.'

'I know I'm the oldest, but because of the circumstances, Neve does act more like the matriarch and fair play to her. I was off and married with a baby while she was kind of in charge of the younger girls, especially when Grace came along, she was only a teenager, so she took on a lot of responsibility at a young age when mum worked. I'll try and suss out if there's anything untoward going on, if she's concerned about anything, perhaps. She doesn't seem well in herself.'

Jen

Maisie and Jen were deposited in Heraklion town centre, the next day, and as Sox drove away, he shouted in Greek, then English, 'and don't get too drunk like you did last time, falling all over the place!' With huge guffaws, and head lolling back, off he drove, not giving Maisie time to retort. Jen couldn't stop giggling at his outrageous comments. Maisie noticed she really enjoyed Sox's company and his extrovert ways. She watched Jen often agreeing with Sox about his philosophy in life, and this pleasantly surprised her. Jen engaged with every bit of Greek culture, and was thrilled about their Heraklion shopping tour with lunch and a spa visit.

Maisie had organised this trip, given Jen's lifelong dedication to fashion, cosmetics, and looking good. Even as a young girl and into adulthood, Jen was meticulous about her appearance and enjoyed glamorous occasions. No surprise, she went into modelling and became the owner of an exclusive women's clothes boutique.

'I'd really like to understand more about the history too, Maisie, it's ever-so interesting. I've been on so many wonderful holidays to far off places, but you know, I've never really taken much notice of the history and culture. Me and the hubby have always been ensconced within tourist complexes or villas on the beach. I've never really *seen* anywhere,' she gushed, spreading her hands out wide.

'Okay,' said Maisie, 'we'll mix some history with shopping, sipping fizz, and generally chilling out Cretan style."

'Sounds perfect,' said Jen. 'Which way first?'

'Let's go to Susanna's, where Fran worked, to start the trip off with a pop. The two sisters, yes, you could tell they were sisters, both tall and lean, one with sultry Mediterranean looks, the other an English-rose, set off towards the bar. Jen engaged enthusiastically with Sox's brother, the owner of Susanna's, who she had met at The Pallas. He, with a more outrageous personality than Sox, had Jen up on her feet, showing her the finer moves of Greek dancing. When he offered another speciality cocktail, Maisie wondered if they'd get any shopping done at all, as it was only half past one in the afternoon.

Maisie reflected that Jen would probably have loved the trip around Archanes, meeting the locals, trying out the food, and showing interest. She wondered if she had got this the wrong way around; maybe Neve would've been happier shopping, and indulging in a relaxing spa day.

After a few hours of drifting in and out of many boutiques, and fashion stores, the women were invited into the rear of one store for the owners to show off their latest delivery of gorgeous gowns. They tried on several outfits and Jen bought a few. After a couple of glasses of Ouzo, and a few snacks provided by the shop-owner, they tottered on to the next store, slipping and tripping on the uneven flagged pathway.

Jen mentioned to Maisie that she'd maybe look into importing some of the Greek styles into her own exclusive boutique back home. Maisie was delighted. 'Let's drop these off at Sox's cousin's salon,' she said, lifting the abundant bags full of purchases.

Jen laughed, 'I'll have to buy another suitcase at this rate, and pay for excess baggage.'

They arrived at the salon, feeling overheated, with throbbing feet, despite wearing the ultra-comfortable walking sandals. They stepped into an oasis of tranquility. The double glass doors silently glided open, revealing a calm reception area, where the scent of comforting neroli and refreshing fresh citrus hit their senses.

'I could do with a scrub up,' remarked Jen. She gazed upward at the cleverly designed undulating ceiling, in light blue with intermittent spotlights, that offered the illusion of a sparkling sea. The elegant modernised versions of several Greek godlike statues adorned the arched enclosures, with only a splash of colour on each marble-white figurine. One held a plate of bright oranges; one had dark green vines adorning its body; one was holding a basket of vivid yellow lemons; another offered an urn complete with the darkest purple grapes. The central statue was reaching downwards to a grey blue dolphin's head popping up from the sea.

'That is a simple but effective look,' Jen admired.

'Maybe you can use the design influence for the boutique?' Maisie suggested.

'I'm thinking for my house,' Jen enthused.

As they dropped into the hip-hugging bucket seats, with bags strewn about them, Sox's cousin, Chrissy, appeared, greeted them warmly, and asked if they'd like their treatments on the veranda overlooking the ocean. The spa was designed with some open cubicles on the second floor, where the whole glass wall overlooked the sea. Privacy was ensured as no-one could look into the cubicles at the elevated position, and the draped pale blue rippled curtains gave an opaque view of the sea whilst getting treatments. They were led from the main area to their own personal cubicle, and greeted by their therapist.

Maisie spoke with the staff; they all knew who she was by now, and they giggled when she tried out her new-found language skills, making inappropriate pronunciations of some words. Maisie realised Sox, initially, and unbeknown to her, had slipped in a few rude phrases and expletives in his teachings.

Maisie indulged in a special top to toe treatment to release her headache and ease her sore feet. She was relaxing when there was an imperceptible tap on the door; one of the young therapists gently spoke to her colleague, Maisie's therapist. She was trying to get the message across that her sister, in the next cubicle, was upset. Two Greek words Maisie knew very well, represented, *sister*, and, *sad*. She took the soft, sumptuous white towelling robe offered, the scent of which always reminded her of baby talcum powder, from the young girl, and headed towards the treatment room. She found Jen, sitting in the relaxation chair with tears rolling down her pink cheeks, incongruent with the huge smile on her face.

'Please tell her I'm okay,' as she gestured gently towards the young girl who was stunned with disbelief in case she had done something wrong, or hurt her client in some way.

'I don't know what it is Maisie. The fizz, sun, cocktails, Greek mythology, you and Sox, and shopping has left me feeling so emotional. Honestly, these are happy tears, please tell her,' Jen implored.

Maisie understood the overwhelming sense of joy that invades your spirit and gently bubbles from your toes, up to the pit of your stomach, through your heart centre, until it reaches your brain, and your head almost explodes from this state of exhilaration. Though she never in a million years believed she would see that in her sister Jen.

Maisie turned to the young woman and tried to calmly convey what Jen was saying. When she translated, *'happy'* and, *'tears'* as best she could, the young woman seemed satisfied.

Jen beckoned the young woman over, held her hand, and with her other hand on her heart, said, *'efharisto para poli.'* A phrase she had learnt and embraced, thank you so much.

'Honestly Maisie, this feeling of … of peace … and … and of inner strength, hopefulness and love, as she was massaging my back, it crept over me. I tried to stop it welling up inside, I didn't want to upset or frighten her, but I couldn't stop it with all my might. When I began sniffling, she must have sensed my body starting to shake, and I put my hand up, then the floodgates opened. Bless her heart, she dashed away to get you. It was so spontaneous, and the relief of letting go was glorious.'

Maisie poured them both a large glass of water, adding chunks of ice, bitter lime, and sweet lemon slices. She handed one to Jen. 'I know that feeling; it comes upon me sometimes when I'm lying on the beach, or swimming in the ocean, especially when were out on Sox's boat and the sun warms your face and body. It's like a feeling of tranquility and absolute freedom.' She looked at Jen. 'It overwhelms your being, doesn't it.

'I'm so glad you get it, Maisie; I thought I was going out of my mind.' Jen raised her hand, and with a serious look on her face, insisted, 'it was *definitely* nothing whatsoever to do with drinking a bottle of fizz, three potent cocktails, and numerous ouzos, of course.'

Water sprayed out of Maisie's mouth as she laughed; she swept it off her robe before it became absorbed in the sumptuous fabric.

Maisie opened the drapes so they got an unobstructed view of the sea; she was enthralled in the open lightness of the moment that she was sharing with her sister.

After some quiet contemplation, they moved to the dressing area and indulged in beautifying themselves with gorgeous scented creams, potions, and lotions. They dressed, in new outfits, of course, complete with the softest leather open-toed pumps and glittering wraps around their tanned shoulders.

Maisie took a call from Sox, saying, no, she had no idea when they would be back, and gave him a potted account of the day, reassuring him they'd get a taxi back if he was busy in The Pallas later, and couldn't provide a lift. He was satisfied with the reply.

The women ate at a lovely little bistro, one which many locals used off the main tourist track, and settled in for a traditional meal, with a verbal contract between themselves to only share one bottle of wine.

'Sox cares so much about you. Such a lovely chap; I'm glad you have met him. It's been so awful for you since Jimmy died.'

Maisie agreed, and the women had a heartfelt conversation about, mainly their love lives and despair, with humour too. Jen talking openly about the disappointment and devastation in her previous marriage.

'I am so incredibly happy for you. Look at you! Almost sixty, having the best adventure, living on an island, speaking the language, and you look fab-u-lous! I am secretly envious of you, and I can say that now, honestly. I couldn't have done when that toe-rag left me; I felt wretched.'

'I take that as a huge compliment, and back at you, Jen. Most people think we are full siblings, being the most alike. I love that.' Maisie had a satisfied smile on her face, then faked annoyance. 'Erm, quiet about the age, by the way, but what better time in your life to have an adventure?'

'Very true.' Softly, Jen said, 'I always felt a failure. You all managed to have great marriages. I know Alice and her husband went through a rotten patch, but they got their acts together and couldn't be happier now. Joined at the hip those two.'

'You … a failure?' Maisie was astonished. 'I would never have thought that.'

'I hide it well, don't I? Behind the facade of being a successful business woman, in with the right crowd, you may say.' said Jen with an accompanying eye roll. 'Mum knew. She was the one person who I could truly be open and honest with. Goodness knows how many times, she held me, rocked me like a baby, stroking my hair, and cried with me, telling me it would be okay.'

Tears sprang into both women's eyes. 'I really do miss her.' Jen's eyes glistened.

'I miss her terribly too. You'll always have me, honey, your oldest sister. I'm here for you anytime; I can be on a plane back to you in no time.'

The sisters held hands over the dining table; Maisie had never felt this close to Jen. Of all the sisters, she was the most unlikely confidante. The waiter, sauntered over, asked if he could fill up their wine glasses, and as the sisters eyes met, they burst into giggles as he smirked, tipped his head to one side, and began pouring.

Instinctively, they clinked glasses, still holding hands.

'To Ellen, the best mum anyone could ever have,' said Jen.

Maisie nodded in agreement, however did think, Jen and their sisters would never understand the concept of having more than one mother, and having to select which one you judged was best.

The day following Jen and Maisie's spa day, it happened that Maisie and Neve were having lunch together at The Pallas in a quiet corner. The other sisters, with Stefanos, had decided to hire pedalos, then go paragliding, which Neve decided was far too energetic for her.

'Same for me, Neve,' said Maisie, 'not a chance I could be bothered larking about on those things, but they'll have fun with Stefanos.' Maisie noticed, or rather sensed, a level of anxiety in

Neve as they watched the noisy troupe making their way to the beach. 'He's a brilliant swimmer, a really strong lad, they won't get into any trouble with Stefanos around.' Did she sense a slight easing perhaps in Neve's shoulders? Maisie made them a cool frappe with lots of ice and a shot of amaretto. 'Are you worried about them, Neve, please tell me?'

'A little.'

'It's natural. You're in a strange, unfamiliar environment. If it hadn't been for Fran, and Sox guiding me through island life, I'd have been terrified and back on the next plane home. I'd never in a million years come out here alone, or gone anywhere on my own after Jimmy died. It annoys me, really, because most of the time, everything turns out okay. But it's awful feeling as though there's danger around every corner.'

'You must have got the shock of your life when Jimmy died, so suddenly. Don't know how you coped.' Neve picked up her drink and sipped as Maisie observed her.

'Do you think something bad is going to happen, Neve? Please tell me; you don't have to deal with *everything* alone. What's going on?'

A torrent flooded from Neve. 'I just don't know, Maisie, since mum died and this fucking menopause, I don't know my arse from my elbow. I'm starting to doubt my ability at work. I'm sitting at my desk, as I have for years, trying to concentrate on some project; someone pops into the office to ask me a question as per normal, and all that's going through my head on a loop is that daft song from the eighties, *hot dog, jumping frog, Albuquerque!*

'I worry like hell about the kids, waking up in the night and checking their online activity to gauge how long it's been since they were active. I mean, what if I have a heart attack or something, I'm putting on so much weight, constantly getting headaches. Every time I have a twinge, I believe I've got cancer, a tumour, an aneurism, or something horrific; then what would happen to my children?' Maisie rested her hand on Neve's, who had turned her head away from the main area of the bar.

Maisie nodded to Sox. He nodded back and went to the back of the restaurant. There was a small paved area that was only used for staff to sit at the table and have a cigarette or coffee break. He wiped down the area and returned to pick up their drinks. Maisie led Neve to the rear of The Pallas, and they sat in private. Briefly, Sox mentioned he wouldn't let the staff out there.

Before they had even sat, Neve blurted out, 'I'm so fucking tired all of the time.' Her eyes were drawn and baggy. 'I'm not sleeping; I ache all over from morning 'til night. Absolutely everything is a massive effort. I haven't been out with the lunch bunch for months; I keep avoiding it. I've stopped all of my exercise classes. I'm forever scanning the internet for ridiculously expensive miracle wrinkle creams, and eternal youth serums, and it can all go and fuck off! None of it works; it's just exploiting people feeling bad about themselves.

'I can't be bothered with Barry; he's irritating me all of the time; I'm having a go at him for nothing. We sit in separate rooms in the evenings, and I'm sleeping in the other bedroom because of the night sweats. I know he wants to help, but doesn't know what the hell to say. Thought I'd get some new undies to cheer things up, but my arse really did look big in them, and the gusset was the size of a postage stamp. I feel disgusting, fat, bloated, and my hair has decided to frizz up like … like fucking Fozzie Bear or something.

'He's a muppet, isn't he?' asked Maisie, 'Fozzie Bear, I mean, not Barry.'

'Exactly! A fucking muppet is exactly what I am!' The giggle began at the end of the sentence, which Maisie joined in with.

Trying to straighten her face, Maisie said, 'Neve, you definitely aren't a muppet. Maybe; a peri-menopausal, mother, wife, friend, sister, successful career woman, and bereaved daughter, who's lost the plot a bit, but no, definitely not a muppet.'

Neve softened. 'I really can't stand myself, or what I've become, and my life is such a mess; I'm no good to anyone. I should've been looking forward to this holiday with all my sisters, but, and I'll be honest Maisie, if anyone had given me an excuse to stay at home, off work for a week by myself, I'd gladly have missed the whole thing. It seemed insurmountable, too much effort. Everything is out of control. Nothing is good. I can't ... feel ... any happiness.'

Maisie was heartbroken to see her sister so sad. What do you think is out of control?' asked Maisie. Neve was always pragmatic, rational, and, yes, in control. She appeared to be in contemplation, but didn't reply.

Maisie continued. 'I remember mum telling me around my fiftieth birthday, each decade brings its own set of challenges, and you'll feel it. The things you did in your thirties and forties you'll find harder in your fifties and sixties. It's the time in our lives when we have the most pressure; adult children still at home, or worryingly they're attempting to become independent, grandchildren may come along, caring for elderly relatives, feeling exhausted with the fucking menopause, and taking more responsibility at work until we can afford to retire.' Maisie paused, 'she was a wise old thing, mum, wasn't she?'

'She was,' said Neve wistfully, 'I've been thinking of reducing my hours at work, not that I don't love it, I still do, but don't have the enthusiasm ... or the energy. My body is fighting me, these horrible peri-menopausal random periods where I'm soaked through in meetings, making excuses to go to the loo all the time. I'm concentrating on that, instead of focussing on my work, and the bloody headaches, hot flushes, and sleepless nights to top it off is all bloody unbearable.'

Maisie nodded with full appreciation of the situation from only a few years ago herself. 'Have a chat when you get back to work; if you're okay financially, go for reduced hours. Why don't you and Barry come over here for a break, just chill out, not to do anything in particular, but relax ... be here.'

Neve looked into Maisie's eyes. 'I want everything to be alright again, and for everyone to be okay, and safe.'

'It's part of the grieving process, Neve, wanting life to be how it was before mum died, and when it's taken from you … well, you lose your stability and confidence.' Maisie changed tac. 'You do know your kids will be on the phone the second anything goes wrong.'

'I know, little sodding snowflakes, they have it all on a plate, don't they?' Neve smirked.

'Exactly, allow them to grow up. They won't make huge mistakes; they'll make some, of course, but nothing drastic, I'm sure. They're bright and sensible.'

Neve smiled at the thought of her children, 'they are wonderful, my proudest achievement, but I'm losing them.'

'No, I'll stop you there, not losing them at all; you've helped them to become wonderful adults, they'll be fine, and you can enjoy them as grown-ups.'

'What about this, though?' Neve held her arms out, looking down at her body, 'this frumpy, lumpy dough ball?'

'Only you see it. No-one else, of any relevance, is taking any notice. But … if you're feeling it, let's do something about it. A special spa day, and a bit of shopping, new comfy chique clothes no one will have back home, you'll feel like a new wo—'

'Jen said you had a fabulous day.' Neve interrupted Maisie's flow, 'I'm sorry I was a grumpy old bag when we went to Archanes Maisie, really sorry. I *am* interested in your past; I care a lot about you and about it all. It's part of mum's history too, part of *our* family history.'

Maisie nodded, 'I know,' enjoying the inclusivity. Then enthusiastically, 'look, we've still got time to have a spa session, no time like the present.' Maisie rang the salon and arranged for two sessions if they had space. Neve looked on expectantly, and as Maisie nodded, affirming the booking, she was relieved.

'When?'

'They have space now.'

'Oh bugger, I need to take a shower and get myself ready, I can't go looking like—'

'Come on! That's the whole point of giving yourself up to someone else to put your pieces back together.' Maisie stood. 'Sox … *agápi mou!*' Maisie had more frequently taken to using, *my love,* when she addressed Sox.

A concerned face appeared.

'Endaksi, spa time.' Maisie knew Sox would ferry the sisters there to chill out. He shouted instructions to a couple of members of staff, and the three walked to the car. Maisie hoped there may be a glimmer of the exhilaration for Neve that Jen experienced. She couldn't promise anything, but could maybe help to start the process of putting some pieces back together.

Alice

'Aaand we're off!' Alice had arrived at The Pallas to meet Maisie for their trip to the, Kourlou Winery for a vineyard tour and wine-tasting. This was going to be an energetic trip, lots of walking, and experiencing grape picking in the vineyard, finishing off with a delicious meal and wines. Alice had what could only be described as an easily distracted personality, often described as ditsy, dizzy, or scatter-brained. Her dad named her fondly, Dilly-Dally-Alli; there were no surprises when she was assessed as having dyslexia, also a propensity for attention deficit disorder. Even Alice would refer to her, *monkey-mind,* jumping around all over the place when she needed to focus; however, she was the most loving, kind, and compassionate person Maisie had ever known.

Alice jumped energetically into the passenger front seat of the car. Sox was driving, so he could describe landmarks on the way. Maisie was happy to recline in the rear seat and absorb the views. This journey was a little too far for Maisie to tackle, and she wasn't as confident as driving to Archanes, where she had been a number of times.

Alice was constantly thanking them. Money had been tight at

times; she and her husband weren't in the Neve-and-Jen-category of earnings, and had spent a lot of time, energy, and money on their three children and two dogs. She missed Harley, a female golden retriever, and Davison, a black Labrador nick-named Davy, even more than her children, Maisie thought, constantly ringing home and showing off pictures of the two.

'Not another message. You're supposed to be on holiday,' chastised Maisie.

'I know, but Debbie gets herself in a right tizzy. She's fretting about a late delivery of orange juice to the home. Worried there won't be enough for breakfast for the residents.'

'Couldn't she send someone out for juice to a store, to tide them over. You don't even work at the elderly home now, what is she thinking calling you?'

'She lacks initiative and relies on ringing me all of the time … even though I'm no longer her manager.'

'Exactly. Okay, when she was your deputy manager, but now she's got your job, surely she can make decisions about orange juice.'

'You'd think so. To be fair, no one wants anyone over the age of eighty suffering from constipation; they'll need a double dose of lactulose.' Alice clarified it was a laxative to Sox.

Sox burst out laughing. 'It could go the other way.' He blew a raspberry making a loud farting noise, and swept his hand downwards to his bottom.

He and Alice did engage in some basic toilet humour. Maisie noted he loved Alice's self-deprecating comments, always pointing out her flaws and laughing; *a dose of the squirtles,* as she'd say, rubbing her stomach, or pointing out her sunburnt bright red peeling nose, a big rash, swollen ankles from bites, and dodgy tan lines where she hadn't applied her sun cream properly.

Maisie often wondered how Alice successfully brought up three children, with her impulsive disorganised personality, and working full time shifts. Managing an elderly care home was stressful, as it, *'became political, all about finances and not the people,'* so Alice took a job working with severely disabled children in a small specialised residential care home.

'Wouldn't be at all surprised if we bump into someone you know, Alice. I wondered if you'd know half the people on the plane, or met someone from school in the airport. I've never known anyone like you, who can't go to a pub, shopping, or on holiday, and you know about half the people there.'

Alice laughed. 'It's my magnetism and sparkling wit, you know. I just happen to be a very friendly, helpful person.'

'You can be over generous at times.'

'I know, I won't make that mistake again.' knowing exactly what Maisie was referring to.

'Do you ever see anything of that conniving toe rag?'

'No. No-one knows where she went, off to fleece other poor souls. I couldn't believe what she did; she seemed so genuine.'

Sox looked on with a questioning expression. Alice turned to Maisie in the rear seat and said, 'I don't mind if you tell Sox.' Alice patted his shoulder. 'He's one of the good guys, I can tell.' She winked at Sox as he gave her a nod.

Maisie recounted the situation where one of Alice's neighbour's and her so-called friend, whom she'd known for three years, scammed money out of Alice and her husband, feigning she couldn't afford to pay her bills, or for her children's school uniforms. She often borrowed food when she knew Alice had been shopping.

Alice interjected, 'it was only a few tins of beans, cereal, or a bag of pasta or frozen chips for her children. I bought in extra, you know, in case she needed anything. I knew she'd be around for something, and I really didn't mind,' Alice turned away and gazed out of the window, 'at first.'

Maisie continued. 'It came to a head when the woman asked Alice to help her with rent money. She told tales of her ex being mean with money. Alice and her husband agreed to loan her two months' rent, amounting to some two thousand pounds, until she got sorted. Then one day, she disappeared. Alice's husband had come in from work to find their next-door neighbour had packed up and gone.'

Alice took up the story. 'Yep, she did a moonlight flit, and it came to light that she had been giving others the same sob story. Said she felt humiliated and asked me not to mention the loan we had offered, but was saying the same to everyone. She must have raked in thousands of pounds. A few of us got together to try and trace her as she had run up debts amounting to ten grand. Obviously her phone was dead, and no-one knew where she went. She's one manipulative woman, great actress, that's for sure.

'Her landlord was also struggling to trace her, and reported her to the police as she'd given false documentation. He confirmed she was not going to be evicted, as she had claimed, despite having rent arrears. Nothing came of the investigations; the police explained it seems she must have obtained a first-level document like a stolen driver's license or fake passport, then applied for bank accounts in that name, Tara Firth; once the false document was accepted, she was on a roll with a new identity. A professional scammer, and she did just enough with her play acting to keep us all on board.'

Alice looked away; it was clear the humiliation of being taken for a fool still hurt.

Sox said, 'Alice, you believed someone was in trouble, someone with children. You worried that they may be hungry or cold; it was the human thing to do. You were right to do it at the time. It is sad that liars and cheats walk in this life alongside us all.' Sox continued to explain how a few times people had taken advantage of his generous hospitality, not paid their bill at the restaurant, and took the opportunity to sneak away. Maisie noticed Alice appeared to be grateful for Sox's testimony that she wasn't a complete idiot.

Alice relaxed and gazed out over the hillside. 'Can't thank you enough for treating me, for treating all of us. It's so wonderful, thank you both, I'm so happy, but I am missing Harley and Davy.'

'Not your husband or your children?' queried Maisie.

Alice laughed. Maisie adored her generous, free-spirited sister. If she had a fault, it was to become over-emotional, getting too involved, trying to support others, and neglecting time for herself. Maisie studied her sister's profile, enjoying her laughter at Sox's humour. Her delicate features and her rose-gold pixie haircut were lit up by the sun. She'd lost count of how many hair colours Alice had; Maisie loved her quirky boho dress sense too; the nose stud, the tattoos, particularly the seahorses and seashells on her ankle. Everything about her was, *'our Dilly-Dally Alli'* as dad would say.

Sox dropped them off at Kourlou vineyard, where the tour began. Maisie and Alice were in a small group of friendly, chatty people, and they gelled really well with the help of their guide, who led them around the wine cellars, explaining the intricate process involved.

Alice was a skilled communicator who made everyone feel at ease with her light-hearted quips, and polite demeanour. Alice asked technical questions, showing real interest in the winemaking process. The group found it humorous from Alice's obvious dislike of a couple of the wines at the tasting. Retsina wasn't to her liking. Even the erudite guide couldn't resist a miniscule, wry smile when he overheard her mocking connoisseur comment, after swishing the wine in her mouth. 'Hm yes, a hint of pine-tree and tyre-rubber there.'

He explained Retsina was an acquired taste, and passed Alice what he described as, 'a dry, crisp and noble Cabernet Sauvignon,' then patiently awaited her judgement.

'Now that's gorgeous, bet it costs a bomb.'

'A beautiful wine is like a beautiful woman, and should be admired and savoured,' he said

'True.' Alice nodded.

Maisie couldn't help but notice the guide was quite taken with

Alice. She looked stunning with her golden tan, light capri pants, and floral print gypsy top that skimmed her petite figure perfectly; her dainty feet with brightly painted toenails peeped out from her walking sandals.

The group were ushered outside after the tasting to behold the sight of regimented lines of vines sweeping downwards in a gentle slope of the hillside. The smell was delicious; a sweet but earthy aroma filled their nostrils. It was really hot, with only a gentle breeze.

The winery guide left them at this point with a grin, a wave, and a hearty, 'good luck!'

'Oh, so you're not joining the workers then?' remarked Alice.

'This is my work.' He grinned as he gestured towards the building, and walked away laughing to himself.

Maisie dipped out of the grape-picking session after a short while, as did a few other members of the group, to sit on picnic chairs, in the shade of the truck with its tarpaulin awning. They drank copious amounts of water with the wine on offer. Alice kept going until the end of the session, with her competitive spirit and natural athleticism. She showed curiosity about the process of picking the fruits at exactly the correct ripeness and filled many baskets with glistening grapes.

The meal provided was fabulous, accompanied with Alice's choice of the noble Cab Sav.

As they sat watching the sunset, Maisie took Alice's hand. 'Thank you for being you.'

Alice offered a delightful questioning frown.

Maisie continued, 'that's all, just thank you Alice, I'm so proud of you.'

Alice squeezed Maisie's hand. 'Not sure what for, and as for you … you've been there for all of us, can't imagine life without you. And thank you for this trip, Maisie.'

Maisie felt her hand being squeezed again as Alice said, 'Mum would've loved this.' Alice looked into Maisie's eyes, 'it's been one of the best days of my life … it really has.'

The sunset's golden-red rays lit up their faces. The sound of gentle chatter, and the heady scent of the landscape, was the perfect backdrop for Maisie and Alice to relish their sisterly love and respect for each other.

GRACE

Maisie hadn't told each sister where they would be going, so when the transport arrived to take Grace to the Traditional Crete Cooking Class the next day, she was thrilled. Grace was the baby of the sisters, similar in age to Maisie's own daughter Kate, so she had been a mother-figure to Grace, not a sister. Nothing really bothered Grace, she was easygoing, but her grief when Ellen died was insurmountable, being so young when she lost her lovely mum. Grace always had an interest in food and was an excellent host when the sisters met up at her home.

There were two couples already sitting in the comfortable airconditioned mini-bus, and after the driver's introduction and polite, *kalimera*, they set off, picking up another eight people en route. Grace asked a few people if they enjoyed cooking, and hardly waited for their replies before she offered up her suggestions about how she would cook certain meals. Offering advice like, *'oh, well, I've found if you do it this way,'* or similar. Maisie was surprised and could sense some of the guests found it a little overbearing, as they wanted to enjoy the journey, rather than listen to advice about what temperature you need a souffle or meringue to stop it collapsing. Maybe it was simply Grace's enthusiasm.

They travelled along the breath-taking countryside of Heraklion and turned off onto a bumpy, off the beaten track through Cretan villages. The journey was only some thirty minutes from Heraklion city, and the village location looked out over herb-scented hilltops with the sea in the distance.

The group were introduced to two Cretan cooks at the village, who offered their culinary credentials, along with typical welcoming and relaxed Greek hospitality. With hundred-year-old recipes that had been passed down through generations, Maisie thought about Xenia again; although it was a paid event, the sense of welcome and giving of food and comfort was evident. She had discussed this with Sox; he was eloquent in his interpretation of Greek mythology and mainly of the good in people. Maisie realised in that moment as she saw his face in her mind's eye, she admitted, she had inadvertently allowed herself to fall in love with him.

Individually, the group were asked to introduce themselves briefly, only their name if they preferred, and add anything they'd particularly like to learn. At this point, Maisie was astonished when it was Grace's turn, and she asked, 'has anyone heard of Bake Off?' Some nodded, affirming they had; others looked mystified; it was a mixed international group of British, Italian, Polish, and American.

Grace talked for over five minutes about the time she reached the final phase of the famous British tv competition in 2011, announcing the various things she created, using her hands to illustrate, and speaking of the intricacies of the bakes, plus how well she got along with the presenters, and professional celebrity chefs judging the competition.

It became embarrassing, particularly because half of the people, had no clue what she was on about. Even the lovely and patient host, Rhea, seemed disconcerted with her fixed fake grin, waiting for an opportunity for a polite interjection. Eventually, she took her chance. 'That is so interesting,' she halted Grace's flow, moving on to the next person … Maisie briefly introduced herself and that she hoped to take a few tips to help out at the restaurant where she worked.

The group proceeded on a tour of the village, which had been renovated from humble ruins, into a purpose-built tourist attraction. The talk about Cretan culture, from a culinary history perspective and the influences, was interesting, then they were guided to an area with several cooking stations to try out various food prep and recipes.

Grace was in her element, bustling around, often repeating, 'I was a Bake-off finalist, don't forget,' with a laugh and a flourish. It was cringeworthy to Maisie when she was offering suggestions to other guests about, *'you could try this,'* or, *'there's maybe a better way,'* to do something. It was the oddest behaviour Maisie had seen from her, Little Gracie, and it was not endearing; she was turning out to be a right royal pain in the arse with her attention-seeking behaviour. Maisie acknowledged the guests were trying to avoid them, but Rhea, was skilled in dampening down the narcissism as soon as Grace began.

That said, Grace was fun to be around, her enthusiasm and jokes worked well, and at one point she had everyone singing *'That's Amoré'*, and those that recognised the song, joined in with the lyrics;

When the moon hits your eye like a big pizza pie, that's amoré. When the world seems to shine like you had too much wine ... that's amoré.

One older American chap continued the song with aplomb. Grace stood and beckoned him, gesturing they should waltz, resulting in a round of applause as he bowed, and she curtseyed when the rendition ended. Maisie sensed, Grace's compulsion to join in was, because she was miffed the attention had completely changed direction away from her. The dance and the adulation seemed to satisfy her need for attention.

The group sat around a candle-lit vine-strewn dining area, enjoying the variety of meals they'd made. They enjoyed appetiser mezes of *Dakos*, Cretan rusks topped with tomato and feta cheese, and *Dolmadakia*, stuffed vine leaves. Then followed the main dishes of Souvlaki grilled over charcoal ovens, and a herby lamb Kleftiko with artichokes. This was followed by sumptuous *Zoumero*, originating from the western Chania region, which means juicy, and aptly described the rich, decadent, moist chocolate cake; served with velvety home-made ice cream, fresh fruit, and chocolate syrup drizzled over it.

Then, as if they weren't full enough, *Xerotigana*, were placed on the table, fried dough strips wound into neat spirals with honey and nuts, all washed down with local wines. The atmosphere was fun and relaxed, with lots of chatter, oohs, and aahs, with many a chef's kiss gesture as they ate.

The group were driven away, and after the initial chatter of how much everyone had enjoyed the day, with a final rendition of, '*That's Amore,*' a few people nodded off, or at the very least were satiated and sozzled, slumped in their seats. Grace seemed exhausted; Maisie put her arm around her beloved little sister's shoulders, as she softened with fatigue. Maisie wondered if she had always had to compete with her elder sisters. Their mum Ellen would have been so busy, that she probably felt left out, so the dancing and singing when she was a little girl that elicited delightful reactions was her way of saying, look over here, look at me!

Maisie tucked Grace further under her arm, her head resting on Maisie's shoulder, her eyes closed; Maisie could feel Grace's warm breath on her neck as she snoozed. She lightly swept strands of Grace's hair off her face, which had been wafted by the air con, then kissed Grace's forehead. Maisie turned and gazed out over the dramatic mountain path, but with the hum of the vehicle and the low, hot sun rays shining through the window, she closed her eyes and thought of Sox; she couldn't wait to see him, and couldn't imagine her life without him now.

Chapter 28

A resounding send off for Neve, Jen, Alice, and Grace, with Sox's family and friends at The Pallas took place. The decision to have the raucous goodbye celebration on the penultimate night, was a sound one. The following morning consisted of, getting everything packed up and dealing-with-hangovers-day. They had a restful last day on the island, with lunch on the beach, a gentle swim, and a final meal at The Pallas.

Neve admonished her sisters if they seemed to be drinking too much, repeating, 'don't come to me when you're all suffering in the airport, or on the flight.' Though, she ensured she was well-equipped with loads of headache pills and anti-acid tablets in her bag.

After fond farewells the following morning, with copious hugs and tears, even Sox had watery eyes, the sisters left in a pre-booked cab, for which they got a good deal as it was Sox's friend's company. Maisie didn't want their goodbye to be a rushed, frantic event in airport departures. She watched the cab until they were out of sight, and couldn't hear their voices, or see their arms waving. She cried into Sox's shoulder, and they headed for a walk along the beach.

Alice announced she was popping into the shop to buy some snacks and bottled water for the flight, 'I'm not paying those prices on the plane; anyone want anything?'

'I'll come with you.' Grace leapt up. The extended flight delay in Heraklion airport was tedious. 'I can't stand another two hours of sitting here, bored out of my skull.'

Neve and Jen were on their phones relaying messages about the delay to those collecting them from Manchester airport.

Alice and Grace were wandering around the shops with a bag full of treats for the flight when Alice stopped in her tracks. 'Bloody hell!'

Grace was a few steps ahead; she stopped and turned. 'Are you alright, you look like you've seen a ghost.'

'Not a ghost ... a bloody ghoul. Alice turned to head back to the seated area they had commandeered, with Grace tottering behind.

'You'll never believe this!' she exclaimed to Neve and Jen. 'I've just seen Tara Firth. At least I think I have.'

'No. Really?' exclaimed Neve. The three sisters were craning their necks in all directions.

Jen stood. 'Where is she?'

Alice thought Jen was going to storm off, spoiling for a fight, to search for the woman who had made Alice's life a misery a few years ago when she unabashedly scammed her, and several neighbours out of thousands.

Alice's face was steadfast. 'There she is, over there with some old bugger.' She grimaced. 'Look.' Alice indicated the direction with her elbow as her arms were firmly crossed over her chest.

'Jesus, she's had some work done,' said Jen, 'and badly too. Look at the stretched papery skin, rigid eyebrows, dodgy lips, and she's definitely had a tit lift, maybe an arse lift too.'

'Arse lift? What the hell is that?' asked Neve.

'You know, a Kardashian thing, enlarge and firm up the arse, makes your waist look thinner,' replied Jen.

'Uurrgh.' Neve crinkled her nose.

'Voldemort!' announced Grace.

The sisters stopped, turned, and stared at Grace, waiting for an explanation.

'I think women like that, look like snakes,' said Grace thoughtfully, 'you know their skin seems somehow to be thin and stretched, and their nostrils have been pulled back and widened.' Grace put her hands on either side of her face and stretched her cheeks backwards. 'Like this, you know, Harry Potter, like Voldemort, he who cannot be named.'

'She's definitely a snake, alright,' said Alice, 'and look at him, old bloody Biggles.' Alice made the gesture of linking fingers, turning her palms, placing them under her chin, and creating goggle-like holes with her forefinger and thumb. 'Chocks away chaps,' she said.

'Looks like a complete twat if you ask me.' said Neve. Something about her menopause conversation with Maisie had opened Neve's mental filter. It was incredibly liberating saying aloud now, what she was actually thinking.

The women burst into fits of giggles, then calmly but intensely chatted, making suggestions to help Alice decide whether to, and how to, confront Tara. Alice was fidgeting, pushing her hands down her thighs; her hackles rising, she was incensed. 'I've got to say something. I'll regret it if I don't.'

Jen and Grace shadowed Alice, walking in Tara's direction. Alice turned and looked toward her elder sister, who nodded. Neve stayed behind to keep their seats in the departure area secure.

As Alice approached Tara a few steps ahead of her two sisters, Jen said with venom, 'no-one messes with the Clarke sisters, no-one.'

Grace added, 'we're right here, Alice, right behind you.'

The two sisters stopped as if they were casually making conversation.

Alice walked ahead, straight toward Tara, and said, 'well I never, it's Tara, isn't it? Tara Firth, you used to live in my street in Swinton.' Feigning a wide smile with gritted teeth, Alice continued, 'fancy meeting you here. It must be four years since you moved, quite suddenly too as I recall. How on earth are you doing?' Still smiling.

Tara looked into Alice's face; she feigned a nonchalant, quizzical look as if she was confused at who this person was. 'Sorry, I'm not sure I—'

'Don't tell me you've forgotten me … your old neighbour? How are those lovely kids of yours, what was it now?' Alice clicked her fingers, 'Carter, and Kiara, if those *are* their real names? Always thought Kiara reminded me of an orange juice drink you'd get at the cinema,' she said thoughtfully, hand resting on her chin. Alice was doing everything within her power not to reveal her angst.

By this time, Tara's male friend was looking on with detached amusement. He was in a smart navy blazer, had a mop of white unruly hair, huge sideburns, a reddish-purple nose with open pores, and the distinctly dishevelled look of a former military man turned drinker. There was little curiosity about who this woman was, talking with his wife.

Tara turned to him, 'Giles honey, I'll catch up with my old neighbour here, and will join you soon. It'll be boring listening to us.' She shoved him away, and he wandered back to the bar. With a wave of her hand, Tara turned to Alice, and lied, 'I really didn't recognise you at first.' She walked to a quiet area near the huge windows overlooking the runways, away from the airport shopping hub.

Alice matched her stride for stride. 'I wouldn't think of running either; I still hold the hundred metres sprint record from school. Over twenty odd years and it hasn't been broken yet.'

'Are you hurrying for your flight or anything?' Tara asked, or hoped, straining to see if she was out of the wing commander's vision.

'Nope, got all the time in the world, our flight is delayed,' replied Alice, calmly.

'Look, I can't have any hassle, my husband, he's a councillor, he's well known, and a scandal would be—'

'If you think I'm remotely bothered about you, your situation, and sugar daddy Giles over there, you are quite mistaken. You scammed me and my neighbours out of thousands, all hard-working folk, but you took the money and ran, didn't you? You literally ran away and left one hell of a mess. What kind of sick example is that to set for your children.'

'My children are fine, actually,' said Tara, glancing over to the bar.

'I bet they are. Best schools, designer clothes, and what are you driving these days, a Jag?'

'Look, what the hell do you want from me … money?' Aggression was showing on Tara's face, replacing her previous serene, superior look.

At first, Alice said, 'no, you can stick it! Although, hang on, lots of people gave up their hard-earned cash for you, and they all deserve their money back. There are two ways we can do this. I can contact you in England … at least, my solicitor can. Or, I'll report you to that police officer over there. I'd imagine he'd be under an obligation to take a statement linked to a scam in 2015. Let me see your passport please.'

Tara looked around, reluctant to delve into her bag.

'Biggles over there is more interested in his drink than his arm candy for the moment. Tara, look, my sisters are all here.' Alice pointed toward them; there was a glimmer of recognition on Tara's face. 'Don't disappear; they'll follow and find you. They're not shy of making a fuss.'

Tara hesitated, but couldn't take the risk of Giles getting wind of a big problem. She opened her passport briefly, enough time for Alice to take a shot with her mobile, now quite adept at using all of its features since learning about the torch function in the loft. She read aloud, 'Sandra Joan Smith, hmm average, dropped the, *Tara Firth,* pseudonym eh?'

'It's Sandy, if you must know.'

'Ookaay, Sandee' drawled Alice, looking at the date of birth. 'Hard paper round? All that surgery,' Alice looked up, circled her own face with her forefinger, 'you've got to keep getting it done you know, love.'

Sandy was furious but couldn't say a thing.

'And your address?' asked Alice. Sandy wouldn't speak, arms folded, looking out of the window with her back to Alice, who took a photo of the address tag dangling from Sandy's hand luggage.

'Just in case you're thinking of changing your documents again. Well, Tara … Sandra … Sandy, or whoever the hell you are, this has been lovely. You'll be hearing from a representative from me and my neighbours.' Alice paused, and said with meaning. 'Fraud is a really serious crime; it hurts people … really hurts good people.'

With that, Alice walked away, shaking, back to the sanctuary of her sisters. Conversation with her sisters during the flight, was whether to inform the authorities, at least Tara's former landlord, or not to tell. Alice concluded, if she did report it, her neighbours might stand a chance of getting their money back. But if she didn't, Tara Firth / Sandra Smith would wonder if, or when, something may happen, like a police officer turning up at her door, or a solicitor letter dropping on her doormat. In some ways, that may be a better punishment.

At Manchester airport, the sisters were weary, yet tranquil after their wonderful experiences with their sister Maisie, and Sox. They trudged through customs, then slouched at baggage reclaim; it was all so tedious. They agreed to meet the following day for a fizz, cake, and a catch up at Jen's house and would skype Maisie.

As they waited, Jen said, 'Maisie seems so happy. She looks as though she belongs there, doesn't she?'

Grace replied, 'yes, she does. I think we've lost her to the Greek Islands and to Sox, can't blame her.'

The sisters took a moment with their own private memories of conversations with Sox, some humorous, some profound, but all positive.

'He'll look after her. I know he will,' said Alice.

Neve added, 'I'll miss her, so we'll simply have to visit every year.'

'Why not twice a year,' said Jen.

Jen felt her elbow being nudged, by Alice. 'Jen, doesn't that bloke over there look like, *Twat-in-a-hat*?'

'I think you're right. Look at the state of him, who wears a cap inside an airport in summer, bet he's losing his hair.' Jen said with glee at the sight of her ex-husband.

Jen's former husband had been bequeathed the, *Twat-in-a-hat* moniker because, in recent times, he'd taken to wearing a flat cap, à la famous, former English footballer David Beckham.

'Christ, he still thinks he's Beckham, except DB looks rather sexy and dapper in those country-gent type photos. It's not so suave a look in the butchers on the main road in Chorley, is it?' Jen eye-rolled. 'I dodged a bullet there girls, didn't I? But at least the genes are offering our kids lucrative careers.' Jen's son was already forging a sound career as a youth coach for one of the top clubs in England, and her daughter was modelling in London.

'He's still good looking, even at his age. He always was a handsome guy,' observed Grace. 'Still … I'm sure he looks like every other bloke when he's straining for a shit.'

The sisters were in fits of exhaustive, suppressed laughter whilst watching the palaver unfold.

'Goodness, are those his kids … and his WAG! She looks about nineteen,' said Jen, still gleeful at the sight of her harassed ex, struggling to hang on to a wayward toddler, frustrated at trying to assemble a pushchair off the baggage carousel at the same time, as his wife fussed over a tiny baby in a papoose.

'Jeez, mid-fifties with his third, maybe even fourth wife, who looks young enough to be his daughter, and two tiny kids,' Jen sighed. 'The price you pay for keeping young, ay? Bet he's absolutely knackered.'

'It feels good to be rid of people who you had a toxic relationship with doesn't it,' said Alice.

'They get what they deserve in life,' said Jen.

Jen turned to her younger sister; they smiled at each other, cementing that clear understanding, and acknowledgement of vindication after the pain of humiliation. They spontaneously high-fived each other.

Chapter 29

Maisie received the skype call from her sisters, all gathered with their glasses of fizz, as was she. They gushed about the weird coincidence of meeting Alice's ex-neighbour, *Sandy the Scammer*, at the airport.

'Told you Alice, you always meet someone you know, even criminals, no matter where you go,' confirmed Maisie.

They chatted about seeing Jen's ex, *Twat-in-a-hat*, on arrival at Manchester airport, and he didn't seem to be having an easy life. It was delightful speaking with her sisters and they all promised to keep in touch and try to hook up online regularly. However, as life gets in the way, the calls faded after the initial whirlwind of her sisters' visit, and memories faded too. Texts still arrived with updates, but it wasn't the same. Sitting on the beach, feeling quite alone, Maisie received a simple text message from Fran, to arrange a time to call her later, which she did.

Maisie was now living together permanently with Sox, five kilometres from The Pallas, and they had become an established couple. Later she was lounging by the small pool in their neat, compact villa and rang Fran at the agreed time.

'I'm coming back.' Was the first statement Fran made. Her voice sounded feeble, as if she had aged.

'What?' Maisie was taken aback.

'I'm coming back to Crete. Is it okay if I stay with you and Sox until I get sorted?'

'Of course, what's happened ... oh Fran, are you okay, sweetheart?'

'It's been a really difficult time, Nansie.' Fran paused. 'I'll tell you all about it when I see you. I've extended my time off to a career break, and I'm taking some savings from what I had for the wedding and the house and everything ...' her voice cracked, then there was silence.

Maisie heard her daughter Kate's voice. 'Hey Mum, you okay?' she asked.

'I'm fine, how's my poor granddaughter, what's wrong?'

Kate sighed. 'She's okay. Seemed fine at first with Liam, they were happy. But, I can only say this from my observations, she began to put in some different boundaries, you know, suggesting things they should be doing together. Like, maybe travelling, living a little before they settle down, and she wanted to buy a house somewhere on the coast, not locally around here. Liam ... I think, found it all a bit much. His girlfriend had changed; she had returned a different person, not willing to just jog along in their same old ways. They had a massive argument about it one night, and he stormed off. They met up a few times, but it appears to have reached a stalemate, neither wanting to concede to the other's wishes. Anyway, I've been trying to be a bit of an arbitrator, seeing both sides, and I realise he's completely out of his comfort zone with her; he doesn't know what to do.'

'And Fran?'

'She seems so confused, Mum, off centre. She's been doing the routine stuff okay, work, meals, everything, but her spark is missing. She's definitely lost her mojo, and doesn't know where to put herself. So, the engagement, the wedding, everything is all off. That's all she said. I've tried to ask more questions, but she's clammed up, won't even say if it's been a mutual decision or not. I am worried that she is simply running away from her responsibility after the freedom of being in Crete. Although, I do understand why she wants a few more years of fun and travel, and not being tied down, like you and I were.'

'It definitely could be that,' suggested Maisie. 'We had a chat about Liam and the marriage one day, and maybe I questioned her motivation to get married so young. I'm desperately sorry if I've had a part in all this,' said Maisie.

'Don't think so, Mum, Fran is her own person and would only do what she feels is right. But my god, it's been awful seeing her like this. We try to cheer her up, but. To be honest, it's just as well they have split up now rather than it happen later on. Liam doesn't really want to keep in touch, which I understand, but it's tough. He's been part of the family for over four years now, and we miss him. Paul is past himself, he thinks Fran has gone off the rails, but I keep telling him to pipe down and let her sort herself out. And … be there for her, but he's struggling too, seeing her upset. I get the feeling something happened over there, maybe with someone, and it's knocked her off kilter.'

Maisie was unsure whether to say anything about Jonah. 'I don't think she was specifically with anyone, if that's what you mean. There was a lovely young German man who she went swimming with, but I've no evidence there was a relationship or anything between them. And … she was in touch with a lot of lovely young people, and made some great friendships, so maybe she's missing all that.'

'I guess so. If I know my daughter, I think she's had doubts about getting married but wanted to stay loyal to Liam. She experienced a new life, and maybe she did meet someone. I wouldn't blame her for that; she's only turned twenty, and it's so young to be settling down, don't I know it. But I did think Fran and Liam were well-suited, inseparable in fact, but … just shows you.'

Maisie said, 'I think you're absolutely right. She's a lovely, beautiful girl not only on the outside but inside too, and would want to do the right thing.'

'You're making me cry. Yes, she is a beautiful person, it's so awful seeing your daughter like this. Maybe if she goes back and stays with you and Sox for a while, she'll sort herself out.'

'Let me know when she's arranged travel plans, and we'll meet her at the airport.'

'Mum, you have no idea how glad I am Fran has someone to look out for her. I'll definitely be over in a month's time, I've requested annual leave, and I'll be damned if they try to change it again this time.

Looking forward to meeting Sox too. Heard a lot about him.'
'As long as you're okay with that, because of, well … your dad.'
'Of course I'm okay with it.' Kate reassured her mum.

A week later, Fran arrived looking pale, thin, and subdued through the airport arrival gate. Maisie and Sox greeted her with tempered but warm enthusiasm and settled her in at the villa. Fran did not want her old job back at Susanna's; she'd been in contact with Aussie Ash and was planning a trip to Chania to pick grapes for the autumn season.

Maisie and Fran had a few superficial conversations about Liam and the whole situation, but it was clear Fran did not want any in-depth discussions. She often turned the conversation around to Sox and her Nansie, and questioned how they were getting along, and how The Pallas was doing, asking whether Nansie would stay in Crete.

Fran was intrigued to hear about Cora, her great aunt by birth, and the details about her genetic grandfather Manolis. Maisie showed her the photographs Cora had given, and Fran also agreed from the look of things, Maisie could not be anything other than the beautiful Xanthe's granddaughter.

The women had a coffee, and Sox left for work at The Pallas; he'd prepared a comforting dinner of beef Stifado. Fran was guarded, she seemed to not want to open up about anything emotional.

Maisie suggested, 'before we eat, would you like to go for a little drive, a breath of evening air might be nice?'

Fran agreed. They got into Maisie's car, a small run-around Sox had acquired from somewhere, so Maisie had the freedom to go about wherever she liked.

'Driving around the island now Nansie, impressive?'

'I don't go far, just to a few beauty spots, shopping, and I like to pop down to the Pallas and help Sox out when it's busy. I know the perfect place we can go, one of our favourite picnic spots, it won't be too busy at this time.'

Maisie wore a pair of blue capri jeans, and vest top, Fran in a lightweight summer dress. The women set off and Maisie skillfully drove for twenty minutes to the coastline along rough terrain, to one of her favourite secluded areas. She parked the car on an elevated section above a cove, with nothing to spoil the view. The curve of the coast and the solitary Island of Dia, looking like a giant lizard floating in the sea, was visible in the distance.

The late summer breeze was cooling the air as they alighted, so Maisie took a couple of cotton cardigans from the back seat, and a turquoise beach throw adorned with mermaids. Fran was amused when Maisie spread the throw on the warm bonnet of the car, and sat on it. She turned and encouraged Fran to put on a cardigan, and join her.

Sitting side-by-side, they could only hear the sound of the sea rolling back and forth, and the faint murmur of human voices somewhere below. The setting sun threw an orange cast over the sand as the sky turned violet. A lone boat was sailing out to sea, and Maisie was about to suggest Fran joined her and Sox on one of his sunset boat trips to Dia Island, when Fran broke the silence.

'Oh, Lucy had a baby girl, Edie. Old fashioned name but I love it.'

'Your mum told me the lovely news, everything okay?'

'Yes she's gorgeous, I had a cuddle, she smelled of vanilla cupcakes.'

'Nothing nicer than a freshly baked new-born, but she won't smell like that all of the time. How's Lucy, no more cankles?'

Fran smiled and shook her head. 'Lucy wanted the nursery sea themed, and Greg has created a lovely, *Little Mermaid*, mural.'

The two women looked at each other, recalling the little girl's accident in the pool at the Anemios Apartments.

'I definitely won't be buying Edie an Ariel swimsuit that's for damn sure.' Fran grimaced.

She hesitated, then said, 'it felt so familiar being back with Liam. You know what he's like … easy as an old shoe, as dad would say. So … yea, it was comforting, and fun being back home with our friends, at first.' Fran was thoughtful. 'Maybe wanderlust has taken hold of me, I dunno. I'd suggest far-flung places to explore on holiday before we got married, maybe visiting Ash down under, but he found it really difficult to change his ways.'

Another pause. 'I realised we took a lot about each other for granted, but, it was mostly him taking me for granted. He liked it just the way it was, the routine, he'd stay over, his footy kit always ready for the weekend match, the lads' nights out, and me waiting in case he was available.'

Fran's face crumpled as she gazed over the view. 'Breaking up, it's all so bloody awful'

Maisie stroked Fran's golden mane; her hair had grown exponentially. She rested her arm gently around Fran's shoulders, recognising nothing she could say would help. After several minutes of tears, in the peaceful glow of evening, Maisie asked, 'are you hungry? Let's go back home and eat.'

Fran was more composed now, and nodded. She looked out toward the horizon. 'It's so beautiful here.'

The two arrived back at the villa, following a peaceful twilight drive, and soon Maisie was stirring the delicious Stifado stew Sox had left them, and poured wine. She served the aromatic dish between two large bowls, with servings of rice and vegetables on the poolside table. Fran said, 'this is so delicious,' between slurps.

'I know, I'm going to have to watch my figure, the way he presents me with all these goodies.'

The women continued chatting as they ate.

With disdain in her voice, Fran said, 'I still never got Liam to a Greek or Lebanese restaurant, and it was things like that which made me realise nothing would ever change, and I couldn't live like that, not after ...'

'Dare I say, Jonah? Sorry if I shouldn't bring him into it,' said Maisie.

'No, you're absolutely right. Nothing happened between us.' Fran was quick to point out.

'Even if it had, it's no-one's business but yours ... and his.'

'But, I regretted nothing happened, Nansie, really regretted it.' Fran's eyes spilled with tears again as Maisie moved toward her. Fran looked away; she didn't want the truth, the fact that would prove she had missed a golden opportunity with someone she truly connected with.

After a few more drinks and as the moonlight glinted upon the ripples of the pool, Fran explained more personal details. A little sheepish, she said, 'Liam was quite taken aback by my ... erm, creativity in the bedroom.' A wry smile spread across her lips, 'I'll say no more, but I think I shocked him with my suggestions, and the thing is, he ... was reticent, kind of mocked me, seemed suspicious as if someone influenced me, and ... I dunno, he looked embarrassed. You'd think any young bloke would be up for some night-time antics, but not Liam; just keep it routine, no frills.

'All of it made me wonder if this was it, and even if it was, what was wrong with that? We were great together, but ... the thought of the big white wedding and stuff wasn't doing it for me any longer, and made me anxious. All he cared about was organising his stag do with the lads.' 'Sounds like you've given Liam a bit of a surprise, coming home and wanting different things in life. He may have been intimidated, that he couldn't live up to your expectations, and fulfil your dreams of travel, your sexual desires, and wanting to live away.

Fran looked puzzled.

'Your mum told me you'd talked with him about living near the coast.'

Fran nodded in recognition. 'I never intended to make him feel any of that, but we couldn't agree on anything, there was no compromise.'

'You might get back together when your both a little older,' suggested Maisie, 'a break may finally help realise you're right for each other? I'm so sorry if I've been the cause of disrupting your life; I really am. I shouldn't have interfered at all.'

'It wasn't just what you said at the spa. It was mostly Jonah. I am at home with him; I don't know why. We're worlds apart, don't speak the same language, from different backgrounds; I mean, what do we have in common?' Fran paused. 'And … I now feel, it … it's like … I'm not finished with the world yet.'

Maisie looked at her granddaughter's rigid, tense profile, up-lit by moonbeams reflecting off the surface of the pool onto her youthful face. 'Look at me and Sox; you would never have thought that wily old goat would be the right man for me after Jimmy McLaine, would you?' Fran shook her head. 'Absolutely not, but you both seem content.'

'So why couldn't it work with you and Jonah. Ask yourself, is it worth giving it a try?'

Maisie stood to get more drinks, she looked at her watch and said, 'it's only nine o'clock in Köln. Do you still have his number? Jonah may love to hear from the girl he met in Crete. I'll be about twenty minutes cleaning up the kitchen.' Before she made her way to the kitchen, Maisie popped her head around the shutter door to the pool, looked at Fran, and said quietly, 'do it, you won't regret it.'

Fran got her phone and tapped the keys. Within a few minutes, Maisie could hear her voice in conversation.

After half an hour, Maisie swept out onto the poolside and placed drinks down as Fran was saying goodnight to Jonah. She timed it perfectly, and uttered a long, slow, questioning 'Sssoo …?'

'After I'm done grape picking with Ash, I've been invited to Germany as Jonah is about to begin his final year at Uni.' Fran stopped, 'I'll have to check how long I can stay in Europe; I think the rules may have changed. You know Aussies have unlimited travel, daft isn't it when they live so far away, and we are European neighbours.' Following her incessant chatter, Fran was gazing into the pool.

'Was it good to chat with Jonah?' Maisie's voice was soft.

Fran took a huge drink, got up from her chair, did a happy-dance, and jumped in the pool, laughing with glee as she soaked her grandmother, who also burst out laughing with water dripping down her face and half the pool diluting her wine.

Chapter 30

Five days later, Fran was gone, off on another adventure with her Antipodean ally, Ash. Maisie and Sox offered tremendous hugs and kisses, then waved her off on the bus to meet Ash in Heraklion. Weighed down by her rucksack, Fran still refused a lift.

Maisie was bereft one evening looking at several old photos, she never went anywhere without. An early photo was of her with her adoptive parents, the Thomsons, holding a little white bundle. They were meaningless to her, yet these were the strangers who fed her, bathed her, clothed her, and changed her nappies in the early part of her life. There had never been any contact after she was returned into care. She had little memory of her adoptive mother as she gazed into the photograph, hoping for some spark of connection, even comfort. Her adoptive name, *Marie Thomson*, was written on the reverse of the photo; she couldn't identify with the name at all. Maisie had read the letter, signed by, *Mr Thomson*, who wrote to the adoption service saying how he couldn't cope after the death of, *Mrs Thomson,* and no-one in the family had volunteered to care for Marie.

Maisie sat swirling the ice-cubes in her drink, recalling how she tore up the letter into tiny pieces, and another photo of her with, *Mr Thomson*. He meant nothing to her, though the photo with her adoptive mother did show some tenderness, or was it only in her imagination?

'No-one volunteered,' she said, of the handwritten rejection, 'so I was handed back, always going to be second best for you, Mr fucking Thomson, wasn't I?'

Maisie kept a number of photographs of the Blossoms, her foster family, during her years with them. There were a couple of the professional photos showing her looking a million dollars in expensive couture outfits, which Lizzie had organised to send to model and movie agents. Maisie thought her eyes looked vacant, and her smile false. There were some of the family, with Lizzie Blossom, always resplendent, sitting proudly, yet formally, in the drawing room with her three sons, and Maisie, with the wonderful Bertie Blossom. Lizzie decided to revert her name to be 'known as' Maisie Blossom, instead of the adopted name Marie, which Lizzie thought was too common. It wasn't a bad move thought Maisie, who completed the legal procedure to revert to her birth name, Maisie Florence Simpson when she returned to live with Ellen, extinguishing her adoptive name forever. However, most of their friends and family referred to her as Maisie Clarke, a Clarke sister, until she married.

Maisie stroked the image of Bertie's face and said softly, 'I'm so glad I called to see you, when I did; I think you were waiting for me to say goodbye, weren't you?' Tears trickled down her face as she gazed into the handsome face of the upright military man, standing at the helm of his family. She understood Bertie; Maisie had a sense of his post-war trauma, she read the signs, a sad stare, a slight twitch of his lips; she knew when to grasp his hand or bring a book for him to read to her, and he would emerge from his dark reverie. Maisie recalled his softness and his patience with her. But now Bertie was gone.

Maisie looked through several photos with her sisters, one taken not long after she joined Ellen and the family as a seventeen-year-old. She reflected that she looked like a child, even though she felt quite grown-up. There were many photos of their, big zero birthday celebrations over the years, having a raucous time. She took out her mobile and scrolled through the images from their recent trip. Her sisters were gone too, they had returned home to their lives and families, after a fleeting visit, it was now a mere memory. Fran had also left for her new adventure.

'I suppose everyone leaves you at some point,' said Maisie as she held a wedding photo with Jimmy. 'Why did you leave me so soon. Why Jimmy?' The pain was real, 'you couldn't have hung on for me, could you?' A deep visceral feeling of guilt and hurt overtook Maisie, realising it would have been their wedding anniversary yesterday. She sobbed into physical helplessness.

Sox was at work; there was no comfort here. This was a feeling of loss even Sox couldn't assuage; she was glad he was not present as the pouring out of grief completely encompassed her. The emotional waves eventually diminished, and Maisie was exhausted. She needed a drink to soothe, to take away some of the familiar deadening pain in her chest and stomach. It had been some time since she had cried so much, alcohol would lessen the aching melancholy. It had worked in the past.

Maisie looked at a couple of photos Cora had given her, of her birth father, Manolis, and grandmother Xanthe. Although she was welcomed into Cora's life, she didn't truly belong to that family apart from genetics; even culturally, there were anomalies. Maisie wondered whether Cora was faking it, being forced into a relationship with someone who only reminded her of a devastating past. Manny was a drinker, a cheating liar by all accounts, and Xanthe's part in Nikolaos resorting to killing a man, couldn't be dismissed.

Glancing at the picture of Xanthe, her stunning grandmother, she said, 'you buggered off as quickly as you could at the thought of your pathetic son becoming a father. Another dirty secret for the tainted Petrakis family.' Her grandmother rejected her before she was even born, her alcoholic father couldn't have cared less it seemed, and her grandfather was a murderer; it was all so sad and seedy in this moment.

Maisie considered there may be something not quite right with her own DNA. Worthlessness, and people simply having to tolerate her, invaded Maisie's psyche. There was guilt that she may have inadvertently infected her own daughter Kate with the negative effect of her paternity; when Kate had post-natal depression; possibly that was the bad genes, too. Maybe she should return home to her daughter Kate; at least she had a flesh and blood claim upon that family. But then, she wondered if Manchester really was home for her now Jimmy was gone?

She poured a large drink, and took it to bed. She raised her glass and made a toast. 'To Maisie Florence Simpson. Or is it Marie Thomson, or Maisie Blossom, or Maisie Clarke, or Maisie McLaine, widowed, and now … Margarita!' The last name she said with a flourish. 'Who the bloody hell are you?' She took another large sip.

There was a huge influx of tourists this week, and she knew Sox wouldn't be around until the early hours, and thankfully wouldn't witness her descent into desolation. He sometimes slept on the sofa, and even at the bar when it was extremely busy. Perhaps she was a simple convenience for him, maybe he was tempted by other openly available women. He had spoken of many lovers since his wife died. Maisie concluded he'd be fine without her, and would he even be bothered if she returned to England? She was an alien on a strange planet. What was she doing here? She was a half-tourist, an imposter with no right to claim this as her homeland, but couldn't say if she would feel at home again in Manchester either.

Maisie lay in bed, and after two and a half hours of wakefulness, she took a sleeping pill. She'd hung onto them like a comfort blanket for those nights when her equilibrium tipped after Jimmy died. She'd taken one on the overnight train when she and Fran left Florence, but it made her feel nauseous the next day, and she recalled being sharp with Fran which upset her.

The following morning, as Maisie predicted, Sox hadn't returned home. Maybe he had slept on the sofa, then set off early for the breakfast tourist contingent. Or had he spent the night with someone. She couldn't help the doubts and anxieties about everything; weary and groggy, she dozed on and off in fitful naps.

It was mid-afternoon, and she decided she needed a dose of sea air. She packed her beach bag and, in flowing summer dress, and sandals, got into her car to drive to the coast. There was never anyone on the dusty road, the brightness glared into her eyes, and she raised her hand to drop the sunglasses from her head, as she simultaneously turned the steering wheel around a sharp bend. A deafening horn ricocheted around her brain, as a large delivery truck approached head on; both swerved!

Maisie ended up veering, and skidding onto some scrubland adjacent to the track as she hit the brakes. The repeated horn blasts reverberated from the disappearing truck in the rear-view mirror. She vaguely heard the driver yelling and glimpsed his hand out of her driver's side wing mirror, giving her the bird before it disappeared from view.

All around was silent. She gathered herself now that the shaking had abated, and her alarmed brain was soothed by her calming brain. She was okay, but that could have been deathly, and it would have been her fault. Tears dripped down her face, thinking she could have ended her life, and that of the truck driver, maybe he was a father or husband; he was certainly someone's son. She'd be no better than her alcoholic father, and her murdering grandfather. As the car crawled along the remaining track down to the village, she took deep breaths.

She called in to see Sox, said nothing about the near miss; they had a brief embrace, he was distracted, and she clicked her tongue at the rammed restaurant. Sox's response was to say, 'it was great for business.'

Maisie said, 'I'll be here later to help with the evening rush.' But he hadn't heard and had already walked away, responding to the demands of the tourists.

Maisie wandered down a rocky beach path to the more secluded areas she and Fran discovered when they first arrived. She set up her little part of the beach, and walked into the sea. It was an unusually breezy mid-August day, and the water was cool and choppy. Ominous clouds loomed in the far distance. Ordinarily, the glittering benign gentle waves, and hot sunshine on her face, with fine sand between her toes, inspired calmness. Today, she felt ill at ease; even the sea wasn't welcoming her as she swam. The exhilaration she spoke about with Jen was absent.

A criss-cross of waves hit her face, as she swallowed mouthfuls of briny sea. Treading water, she turned to head back to the shore. The clouds were drifting across the sunlight, the azure water around her darkened to navy blue, and she couldn't see or feel the sea bed. Maisie sensed there was something lurking in the waters below. She treadwater and twisted around as fast as she could against the strong resistance of the tide. Malevolent creatures would grab her and drag her under, the ones she and Bertie would fight; he could protect her then, but can't now; he's gone. Maybe this was her destiny, to drown in the Aegean.

With every scrap of her weakened strength, she tried to swim, but her arms weren't working properly; they were made of lead and she was swimming slow-motion in treacle. She gasped at each laboured breath. It was utterly draining, swimming ashore against the rapidly undulating waves pulling her back. She eventually dragged herself onto the sand, completely exhausted; the muscles in her legs were quivering, as she collapsed onto the sand.

A concerned older couple were looking over at her, but she forced a smile and waved a dismissive hand. Maisie packed up her things and walked to her car. She spotted Sox dashing around making space in the overcrowded Pallas; as many tourists were leaving the beach, heading for shelter in anticipation of the oncoming storm. Maisie was groggy, and couldn't be bothered being sociable, so headed directly for the car.

Arriving back at the villa, she prepared a few morsels of food; she'd lost her appetite; she felt nauseous, as her stomach kept churning; the swim had unnerved her. She spotted the array of photographs from the previous evening on the poolside table.

Maisie glanced up at the gloomy sky; no abundant twinkling stars; they were covered by ominous, black, bubbling clouds. She picked up the photograph of herself, aged about six, with Ellen, though she didn't know at the time, she was her birth mother, and couldn't distinctly recall it being taken. The Blossoms had agreed to meet with Ellen once, arranged by the social worker, so Ellen could see she was okay.

'Why didn't you take me home with you, Mum, you could have if you had really wanted to fight for me? You told me often enough how much you wanted me, how much you wished you'd kept me.' Maisie looked skywards, and her next question drifted into the ether, as tears rolled down her cheeks. 'Why didn't you come back for me?'

Maisie delved into the dark inner thought that, at least she hadn't ended up as a bloody mess on the floor of a back street abortion hovel, and Ellen hadn't died from infection.

It had been a tough day; Maisie sat out by the pool, as the wind swirled her hair. With vehemence, she said aloud. 'I wonder how many mothers and fathers you have to go through, before one of them actually chooses to keep you.' She thought about a comment Sox made when they first got together. He said she appeared to be floating in the wind, like a piece of paper, whichever way it blew her. No direction. He had questioned whether she may settle down in Crete, but now she knew she didn't belong here. This island had rejected her.

Maisie went into the kitchen, noticing the detritus of the previous evening's drinks that she hadn't cleared away; dismissing the mess, she poured another drink. It was soothing, as she sipped, a woozy light-headedness offered solace. She went to cut slices from the half lemon languishing on the chopping board with the large kitchen knife nearby. She'd clear it all up later. She held the lemon on the chopping board, but sliced into the side of her left forefinger instead of the fruit, which stung like hell. As she jerked her hand away, she caught the side of her forehead on the corner of the open kitchen cupboard door above her. It really smarted.

'For fucks sake, you idiot!' she shouted, so cross with herself, cross with her finger … cross with everything.

She was bleeding profusely as a red rivulet ran onto the draining board and into the sink. A small chunk of flesh was hanging off her finger. She flung the bloodied half lemon in the bin beside the sink unit and slammed the knife into the sink. She held reams of paper towel under the cold tap, wrapped it around her hand, and, briefly held a piece to the side of her head and saw a tiny bit of blood where she'd grazed her scalp near her hairline. She decided it would stop bleeding soon. It felt tender, and she winced at the slightest touch.

Maisie lifted the paper towel, and peeped at the damage to her hand. Her finger was still producing bright red liquid from the five centimetre, deep sever in the flesh. It just would not stop. Wearily, she took the first aid kit from a cupboard and manipulated some dressing around it, then tightened a wet tea towel around her hand, in case there was any leakage. Dazed and queasy, Maisie took herself off to bed. She swallowed a sleeping pill in anticipation of the sleepless night she would inevitably have, washed down with a drink from the bedside table. Her temple was really tender, and the injury to her hand throbbed beneath the dressing wad. She took some painkillers to try and ease the pulsating ache. Maisie had a moment of lucidity recognising similar feelings from the reactive depression after Jimmy died, but it was different this time; she was unnerved; frightened. She wasn't at home in her safe place, but adrift, and alone on a foreign island.

Her brain was fogged, she must try to sleep, but couldn't face the dream that sometimes crept into her mind from the orphanage. The dark man-monster. He was too close. His breath was fiery. His hands were cold as ice. It wasn't a dream. Maisie winced, and pulled her knees in toward her, sitting bolt upright, glancing side to side; she saw shadows fleeting across the window. Bats! She stumbled toward the window, making sure it was firmly locked. She caught sight of her beach bag; those sea creatures had terrified her, and the bats, all telling her to leave. She didn't belong here. She didn't belong anywhere. She was damaged goods, alone, unclaimed, unwanted. Her soul was lost.

It had been a crazy night at The Pallas. The storm had brought so many people into the restaurant. Sox and his son Stefanos had extended the awnings from the canopy above the restaurant to cram as many people in whilst the big rains splattered down, and the wind howled. He was exhausted and nearly fell asleep at the wheel on his return home. He crept into the villa, and sneaked a peek into the darkened bedroom; seeing Maisie flat out asleep on her stomach, he quietly trudged to the sofa and in the darkness of the early hours, was virtually asleep before his head met the cushion. His last thought before dropping off was relief that his son told him to take the day off, as he had recruited a number of extra workers to help out in the morning. Sox fell into a glorious, golden slumber.

He was awakened by shafts of piercing sun blazing into the room. He blinked, had a generous yawn, and felt the physical stirrings that only Maisie could satisfy. He got up slowly and wandered into the kitchen to make a coffee, serene in the knowledge he didn't have to rush into work. He was taken aback at the state of the kitchen. There were several empty glasses and cups and some dried-up snacks on a plate. This was unusual; Maisie was rather meticulous about keeping the place neat, as she did at the restaurant. He leant toward the open cupboard above the chopping board and noticed a smudge of blood. Blood had also run down the draining board, then pooled and dried in the sink. There was a lot of blood. There was also a knife.

'Margarita!' He hurried to the bedroom. 'Margarita!' She didn't rouse; she was in exactly the same position, on her stomach, as when he saw her last night. He dashed to the bed and turned her over, gently shaking her, pleading with her to wake up. He checked she was breathing; why wasn't she waking up? He was in a panic. He grabbed his phone from the front room and rang the emergency services; a frantic call ensued, with Sox imploring them to get there now, and asking what he should do. They advised him to keep checking her vital signs and if she deteriorated, begin cardio resuscitation until they arrived.

Sox cradled Maisie's limp body; he gently stroked her pale grey skin, kissed her cool, clammy forehead, and wept, constantly checking her pulse and breathing.

His phone was in his pocket. He needed Fran by his side, but the call went straight to voicemail in an instant, but as Sox spoke, the line went dead. Tears streamed as he whispered into his phone, 'Fran, help me. Please hear me, Fran, please.'

CHAPTER 31

Chania

One hundred kilometres away, Fran and Aussie Ash were sitting in the front of a battered, ancient truck on their way to the district of Chania, to seek fruit-picking work. One of Ash's colleagues in the bar had given her a tip. A distant relative of theirs was a farmer, who ran a vineyard, and he was looking for seasonal workers to pick grapes. Ash showed Fran a scrap of paper with Greek writing on it, and the only discernible words she could establish was *Michalis,* the farmer, and *Epakorenou,* the name of the farm, with some numbers beneath, which Ash presumed was a form of regional code location.

'It may as well be hieroglyphs.' Fran shrugged. 'So, in effect, we're searching the largest Greek island ... for a tiny remote mountain village ... where your bar mate's grandad's distant cousin, Michael, has a farm ... and he *may* need some workers.'

'Sounds about right.' Ash nodded with confidence, 'I know the Greek spelling of the village, but can't pronounce it. No worries, we can look out for signposts.'

Fran sighed, shaking her head and smiled.

The women secured transport, having shown the address to a diminutive, wizened old man with limited English language, who indicated he knew the address. Ash had picked up decent Greek language skills, and negotiated a cheap price for the journey.

'You sure about this?' queried Fran as they dumped their rucksacks in the rear of the open truck, and slid along the two seats beside him in front.

'Yea, sure, all good.' That wonderful grin and innocent dimples were convincing. 'Be fine, ol' geezer here will get us there okay.'

The truck set off travelling deeper into the countryside, jiggling and bumping along, following craggy tracks, climbing higher, and passing small basic Cretan villages dotted along the route. After forty minutes, they reached what appeared to be a derelict building, atop the mountainous area. The ol' geezer pulled up at the rickety stone shack, which turned out to be a taverna. He encouraged the women to go in, which they did; both were desperate for the toilet.

'Well, this is charming,' said Ash as she looked around, hands on hips, as if admiring the bare stone walls, cracked wooden tables, and spindly stools. 'I need a pee, I'm busting.' She wandered through to the back of the building, and, on her return, said, 'that's the first time I've squatted and peed between two bricks with a herd of goats staring at me.'

'Oh god, is that the toilet?' asked Fran.

'Yup.' With a grimace, 'word of advice mate … breathe through your mouth and don't look down.' Ash took a drink of the clear liquid that had been offered, and winced like she was sucking a sour lime.

'It's mighty strong.' Ash coughed and spluttered to the merriment of several toothless, walnut-skinned old chaps looking on. The atmosphere was amiable.

'This stuff is Raki,' said Ash.

'Is it really? Sox told me about it, said it was ninety percent alcohol, the Greek version of Irish potcheen, you know, potato wine.'

'Good ol' moonshine, ay?' said Ash, downing the small glass.

Twenty-five minutes went by, and the women were getting twitchy; they needed to be on their way, trying to encourage ol' geezer to leave. He was very reluctant, and his cronies kept yelling and waving, encouraging them to stay. Fran and Ash swapped anxious looks; they had no idea where they were, and worried the situation may get rather tricky, if the crinkly drinkers became insistent on their company.

Eventually, ol' geezer agreed to leave with the women.

'He's as pissed as a fart,' said Fran, 'look at him, he can hardly walk, never mind drive.'

Ol' geezer was singing raucously as he stumbled into the driver's seat, he cranked the gears with an ear-splitting metallic crunch. Fran was sitting next to him, and when ol' geezer decided to pat her thigh with a leering look on his face; she slapped his hand away and yelled at him. He simply laughed and nearly drove them off the track, precariously close to the edge of a steep drop.

Fran and Ash conversed freely, as ol' geezer didn't understand a word of English, and they hatched a plan. Ash told him to stop the truck, gesturing that she needed the toilet. He brought the vehicle to a screeching juddering halt, and they all nearly head-butted the windscreen.

Both women jumped out of the truck; Ash went around to the driver's side and dragged him out of the seat. Ash was a fit woman, more than capable of wrestling a drunken old man to the ground, and there was little resistance. Fran helped Ash manhandle him into the rear of the truck. Ash then leapt into the driver's seat, and quickly figured out how to get the old banger going in seconds, and they sped along a rough track. They could hear him yelling as the vehicle bumped up and down and side to side. The contents of the truck, including their rucksacks, were sliding around banging into him; after several minutes, it went very quiet.

'Jeez, hope we haven't killed the ol' fucka!' said Ash, then burst out laughing.

They continued to drive along the track, which slowly began to descend. After a further half an hour, Ash recognised a sign for the village near to Michalis farm, and swerved perilously onto another track, miraculously finding their destination. They leapt out of the van, and opened the tailgate to find ol' geezer asleep, snoring for all he was worth in a contorted position, wrapped in some oily tarpaulin. Fran grabbed their rucksacks, checked the old man wasn't dying, and they scarpered.

Laughing, Ash said, 'I didn't even pay the old goat.'

They showed the address to the proprietor of a solitary taverna on the main street, and were directed to a house ten minutes from the centre of the village. It was getting dark as they approached the modest dwelling. There were a number of people milling around outside the place, including some women in long black clothing wearing veils. 'Is that traditional dress they're wearing?' Fran was puzzled.

It dawned upon Fran and Ash as they were approaching a house where a wake was taking place.

'Oh shit,' said Ash, 'what do we do now?'

A young woman approached them, and Ash showed her the note with an explanation of why they were there. She was kind to them, explained Michalis had died a week ago, and directed them to the rear of the house, where a garden shed became their room for the night. Even in the throes of mourning, Xenia dictated the travellers were offered much needed sustenance. Two plates brimming with food were ravenously eaten on the front porch of the house, before Fran and Ash settled for the night in sleeping bags, amongst tools and a friendly family of a mother hen and her chicks in the shed.

The following morning, one of Michalis' family, suggested the woman travelled to the next town square, where they would be able to tout for work in the many farms and vineyards in the area. It appeared to be the central hub for seasonal workers to gather, where farmers would engage a team of workers, and pile them into trucks to take them to their farms. It was about a forty-minute walk away, so they were told. Fran and Ash set off, wandering along a wide, lonely countryside road in the early afternoon searing heat. A swirling breeze whipped up sandy dry dust from the road.

The silence was broken by aggressive shouting ahead. Ash stopped abruptly, noticing a man beating up another man further up the road. 'Oh Christ, this could be a bit tricky.' It looked like a fiercely violent altercation, as the men punched and kicked out at each other. There was not another soul about, anywhere.

With a brush of her hand and in her innocence, Fran decreed it was okay, 'just ignore them,' and continued along the road, dismissively adding, 'we've had enough drama. We need to get to this town square to hook up with the transportation for the vineyards. If we're late and we miss the connection, we're out of work, and out of money.'

Ash became tetchy, turned and walked swiftly back along the road in the opposite direction to the altercation. Fran caught up with her, encouraging her to continue in the direction of the meeting point. Ash insisted they detoured from the main road, transfixed on the violence playing out; whilst Fran thought it foolish to stray off track, she accepted her friend's anxieties. She figured they could arc around the hill to avoid the fight.

There were no mobile number contacts, as arrangements were simply word of mouth, and the transport would leave without them. Fran scooped her mobile out of her shorts pocket, desperate to connect to GPS to establish if they were heading in the right direction. She looked at it disdainfully, and said, 'battery nearly out, and no signal at all … nothing.' She sighed.

Fran and Ash wandered up a leafy, bushy hill, in stark contrast to the desert-like road, completely ignorant of where it would lead. It was a voyage of discovery, a mystery tour. On approaching the brow of the hill, the bushes became sparse. Fran noticed a solitary man gesticulating wildly, and, fearing they were approaching yet another bizarre situation, stopped in her tracks. He was signalling toward the open sky, his face and head covered in some sort of mesh. His pale, billowing scarecrow clothing fluttered around his limbs.

Ash wasn't alarmed, she could instantly recognise real aggression; a former lover had demonstrated that enough in that relationship. Ash confided the sickening details of her former partner's controlling, aggressive behaviour as Fran held her tightly when they spooned in Ash's bed one night after work.

Both young women, heavily fatigued, gazed at the man's rhythmic, begging gestures, reaching skywards.

'Is he some kind of nutcase or what?' asked Ash watching him curiously.

'Dunno,' said Fran transfixed, 'but … we really are fucking lost, fuck knows where we are, or who the fuck he is, and what the fucking fuck he's doing, and we're probably going to miss the fucking trucks!'

Fran was tired, hungry and so thirsty, they'd walked for miles and drank most of their precious water. They were totally off-track, and needed to recalibrate. She checked, no mobile battery.

The man spotted them. Ash suddenly became aware of her surroundings as the man purposefully stomped toward them, and spoke in a frantic fashion, gesturing toward the sky. Fran realised he was a beekeeper; the gauze head covering and full-length protective clothing gave it away. She recalled her Nansie taking her to an interactive farm as a child, where she learnt about bee populations and the environmental dangers they faced.

'Ash,' she demanded of her friend, 'listen to him … what is he saying?' Fran held her hands openly toward the despondent man, demonstrating they wanted to help him.

The beekeeper softened, but kept his vigilant stare upwards. His tears were clearly visible through the mesh, coursing down his dark brown, deeply-lined, yet youthful face. It softened their hearts.

'His bees haven't returned … at least, that's the best translation I can come up with,' said Ash.

The two young women and the beekeeper scanned the skies for many minutes, in silence, with only the faintest breeze blowing across the hill.

He kept repeating a phrase in Greek, to their abject ignorance, then he spoke in vague English, pointing both arms inward. 'Me, you, nothing …' with arms outstretched. 'No bees … no honey … no food …' he dropped his head, 'no life.' He cupped his hands around both ears, eyes closed, listening intently.

Gazing upwards, Fran watched the billowing clouds change from the shape of an old boot, into a playful puppy, then a narwhal, which morphed into a floating angel. In this enlightening moment, time stood still, Fran appreciated the selfless gifts that nature brings to the world, and the fragility of her place in the universe, as she had done lying on a starlit beach months ago. She immediately thought of Jonah and his determination to conserve the oceans; she could also see her Nansie's calm face in her mind's eye, on that day they went out sailing with Sox. Such a beautiful face, yet she didn't know at this point, that she may never see that face again.

'Oh, look!' Fran's reverie was interrupted by Ash yelling. A low droning, flittering swarm swept up the undulating hill toward them. The beekeeper was leaping with joy as the dark murmuration emerged from below the hilltop horizon. He fell to his knees in the soft earth, hands clasped, offering gratitude for the return of his buzzing saviours. He ran after them; clothes flapping, and gauze headwear flailing behind him. There was no farewell as the two girls; one with long plaited golden hair, the other with abundant dark curls, stood in contemplation, holding hands in bright sunlight.

Fran wondered at the beauty of Mother Nature, at her most powerful, concocting natural alchemy in a world that allowed humans to live. These shared moments would never be forgotten by Fran and Ash, as they reflected upon, *'the ol' geezer, the wake, and the nutty beekeeper,'* for the rest of their friendship.

The two young women made it to their designated pick-up spot and teamed up with a few others. Their team consisted of an English boy named Roland, who looked as though mummy had packed his pristine rucksack, Fran wondered how long he'd last with the backbreaking work. Two Croatian students, Milenko, or Milo, and his good friend Andre, made up their team. They set off in the back of the truck, winding and bumping their way to a remote vineyard for a month of hard graft.

During one back-breaking picking session, Fran explained to Ash that Donna, who they had known in Heraklion, had returned to England having been assaulted one night by a punter.

'Ah no,' said Ash, 'that's terrible.'

'Yea, she took a thumping, but the cops were pretty good. They came to our bar and asked a lot of questions. They did a full report, and she told me she went through the whole sexual offences process, must've been awful. Hopefully, they'll get DNA. She was going to slink back to the UK alone, but we got wind of it and made her last few nights okay … safe, you know … and saw her to the airport.'

'Some men can be cruel bastards.' Ash was referring to her former partner's behaviour. 'Don't really trust 'em.' There was a pause. 'You know, I'll probably settle down with a woman, I think. Not you, though. I've told you, you're not pretty enough for my tastes.' Her gorgeous, dimpled smile shone out from the bunch of wild hair.

Fran winked. 'You wish.'

Theirs was a deep loving, enduring friendship. Fran had changed. Her life at home seemed superficial; here she was, working hard in searing heat, eating mostly bread, cheese and grapes, washed down with tepid water. Occasionally she worried about her future, she had a good job to return to, but her motivation was to learn more about nature, and she'd thought about re-training. Jonah and protecting the environment had become her raison d'être.

Chapter 32

The insipid coffee from a machine in the hospital foyer spluttered, staccato-like into the white plastic ringed cup. Sox picked up the bendy, flimsy receptacle and drew it to his lips. He walked toward the waiting area of the emergency department of Heraklion University General Hospital at Stavrakia. His brown wrinkled hand holding up his weary, fuzzy head, full of questions.

He tried to make sense of the last few hours. Why had he fallen asleep on the sofa? He should've gone into the bedroom and checked on his Margarita, but he'd never had to check on her before, she was always so calm, so capable. She had a lovely time with her sisters recently. What could have caused her to become so ill? Why did she need sleeping pills? *Zopiclone*, he'd never heard of them but found the blister pack by her bedside. She'd been drinking too; she must know not to mix alcohol with pills. Why?

He conjured up too many hypotheses. Had Maisie stumbled and banged her head, then gone to bed feeling dizzy and fainted, but was actually concussed? Was it the sight of blood from the cut? The wound having been so deep it required stitches, the medics had advised.

Sox tried to piece through what happened and recalled his actions and the words he'd conveyed to the paramedics.

'I found her in bed, she wouldn't wake. Her skin was grey, she was hardly breathing. Her hand was wrapped in a cloth, and she had a cut on her head.'

He disregarded any inner dialogue Maisie had harmed herself intentionally; she couldn't have; they were happy. He tried to make her happy, always. The mere suggestions this was, a cry for help, as the saying goes, was alien to him. Maisie had everything to live for; they were good together, she loved her family, and they loved her. Was it being here in Crete and the effect of learning more about her birth family that affected her?

Only Sox really understood her feelings about her birth father, and her birth grandparents, and whilst Cora had been kind and tried to show some compassion, the relationship was never going to work. The sad news of her foster dad Bertie Blossom's death had been difficult too; he sounded as though he'd been a good man. There were times Sox would've liked to shake his hand, and that of Jimmy, her husband; both clearly had a bond with Maisie and looked out for her.

Sox pictured Maisie in his mind's eye; several recent scenarios flashed into his brain; her face soaking up the sun when they were on the boat, her smile from behind the bar at The Pallas, to him and the punters; she was always so friendly. The joy and laughter with her sisters and with Fran. Oh no, Fran, Sox still hadn't been able to make contact. He had texted Neve to tell her Maisie had to go into hospital for treatment. This was all his fault; he should have taken better care of her; he should have been there for her. Others in the waiting room would've witnessed this strong man quietly crumpling into tears with his head in his hands and an abandoned coffee at his feet.

Sox was alerted by a physician. The young doctor was a picture of efficiency, his hair neatly cut, wearing glasses, and with a neutral expression, he encouraged Sox into a consulting room. He explained, 'the mixture of sleeping pills and alcohol had caused the patient to black out, and she was still unconscious.' He advised the patient's breathing and cardiovascular systems were stable and they were trying to negate the effects of the chemical mixture, but would not attempt to reverse sedation yet, as this procedure can affect heart function, or prompt a seizure. The doctor continued to offer medical information, which Sox was struggling to understand.

The doctor concluded in a rather matter-of-fact way, 'observation and care was the least invasive treatment plan, in the hope the patient would regain consciousness in her own time.'

More compassionately, he asked, 'have you noticed any change in Mrs McLaine's behaviour recently? Anything she may have been worried about?'

Sox replied, 'no. Her sisters visited recently, and she has seemed fine, she was healthy. She had suffered from depression after her husband died a few years ago.' Sox looked up despairingly, 'I can't accept this has been deliberate.'

'It may not have been, but most people know that sleeping pills and alcohol aren't a good mix, so it's more likely to have been an error.'

'Could she have taken too many pills on purpose?' asked Sox directly.

'It doesn't appear so. However, if she hasn't been sleeping well, and began taking them again without medical supervision, it could have induced other symptoms quite rapidly.'

'Other symptoms?'

'Despondency, headaches, feeling dizzy, unsteady, nausea, numbness, tingling, aches and cramps.' The doctor advised, 'sleeping pills, when a person is not used to them, or takes them not as prescribed, can induce nightmares, and even hallucinations in extreme cases.'

Sox was astounded; this was all new to him. After his wife died, he experienced insurmountable grief and took solace in alcohol, until he realised he had to care for his sons or he'd lose them too. But drugs, prescribed drugs at that, were a mystery.

There was a tense silence, Sox's shoulders dropped, and he hung his head. 'Will she wake up?'

'We really can't tell yet,' replied the doctor.

'So ... is she in a coma?'

'That is the situation. It is complicated by low blood sugar from the alcohol, blood loss from the cut finger, and the head trauma, even though these were mild injuries. We don't know if there will be any residual long-term effects.' He said Sox could go in and see her. He spoke encouragingly but moderated his language; it was good she was breathing on her own and monitored results of her vital signs were stable so far.

'Whilst the patient is still vulnerable,' he reassured Sox, 'we will be constantly treating her condition.

'Will she be able to hear me?'

The doctor smiled. 'That is something we never know. I haven't known a patient who can recall if they heard conversations. However, some clinical trials suggest the brain may be able to receive sounds, even if the patient cannot respond. It's reported some patients speak of lingering dreams.'

Sox entered the small clinically white room, and noticed the cobalt blue curtain drawn around Maisie's pristine white bed. There was a chair beside her; Sox couldn't take his eyes off her beautiful face; she looked so much younger and completely peaceful. Her tanned face was at ease, and there was a small dressing on the injury at the side of her forehead.

A nurse explained the monitoring equipment attached to Maisie for heart rate, blood pressure, oxygen levels and intravenous lines for fluids and medication. There was a thin feeding tube in her nose, and he realised drains were in place to release fluids from her body by the side of the bed. The nurse explained the various bleeps from the machines, saying they were normal and someone would come if alarms triggered at the nurses station.

Sox was dumbfounded. How was he here? Why was he here? How did things end up like this? He sat in the chair, the nurse left, and it was eerily quiet, apart from noises from the machines. He watched the regular rise and fall of Maisie's chest and took her hand.

'Margarita, it's me, Sox. I'm sorry, so sorry, my love. I should have been there for you. I should have known you were suffering, my darling.' Sox's tears flowed. He tried to talk in a normal fashion; after all, if Maisie could hear him, she wouldn't want to hear him distressed. He couldn't believe he may never hear her voice again, see her swim, dance, and laugh. He recalled his favourite memories over the last several months they had been together; recounting the times they went out on the boat, and the recent trip her sisters made. He tried to speak in a positive way, telling her about some funny instances at the restaurant.

Sox stayed with Maisie for over three hours, breaking out of the room, only to call Neve and update the situation. He arranged, in fact, insisted, that the doctor should speak with Maisie's daughter Kate to fully inform her of the situation. Before the day was out, Kate was on a plane to Heraklion. She told Sox, she had no success in contacting Fran; however, her husband would keep trying.

In his quiet reverie, as he held Maisie's hand, Sox recalled a conversation he had with her. She said she had felt like a commodity, a transaction. She told Sox her mother Ellen, like all the pregnant women, worked in the laundry before and after they gave birth, which raised funds for the Catholic society. She understood the parents of the *fallen women*, as Maisie put it, who could afford to, would make donations to the home for their daughters and the babies to be housed. Her adopters also paid a fee to the adoption service for her, and the Blossoms were paid an allowance to look after her.

He said softly to her now, 'everyone paid a price, but you are paying the highest price, my darling Margarita.' Sox wept, his tears dripped down Maisie's hand, and off the end of her fingertips; his grief was insurmountable; he couldn't lose another woman he loved.

Sox thought of Fran, dear sweet Fran, who was on this island and had no idea her Nansie may never regain consciousness. He tried Fran's number again, but there was no connection.

Several hours later, in the dead of night, Sox welcomed Kate at the airport, looking grave. Bleary-eyed, with her hair pulled back into her usual no-nonsense pony tail, Kate said, 'not how I'd hope to meet you Sox.' There were tears and hugs.

Sox drove immediately to the hospital. The conversation centred on the mystery of how Maisie ended up where she was. Kate informed Sox of Maisie's depression, and the incidence where she had similarly found her some years ago, but said she had seemed to come to terms with life, and was moving forward.

When they arrived, like Sox had done, Kate tentatively walked into the antiseptic-smelling ward room, as if not to wake her sleeping mother. She held Maisie's hand, with tears dripping off her chin at the bedside, but desperately trying to keep a level head. She told Maisie of all the things that were going on at home. It was devastating as the only response was the regular beeps emanating from Maisie's support machines.

One morning, it was Sox's shift at Maisie's bedside. He continued his narrative of what had been going on over the last day or so, and how they'd finally made contact with Fran, who was on her way to visit. Sox seemed to sense there was a change in Maisie; her face appeared to show a little stress for want of a better expression. The blank facade was now showing the lines on her forehead in more definition, and her mouth looked pursed somehow. It was an infinitesimal difference, or maybe he'd never noticed beforehand, and it was simply his imagination. He had been told there may be eyelid movement, but often, it didn't mean the patient would wake.

Sox let go of Maisie's hand to get out his phone and text Stefanos to ensure everything that was required at The Pallas was in place, and said he would be there later when Kate took over at the hospital. They had never once left Maisie's side unless the medics asked them to leave for turning and cleaning the patient, and various medical procedures they had to undertake.

Sox turned and looked at Maisie's face; her eyelids had raised to halfway open! She seemed to be looking into his eyes. Sox stared back into those deep brown eyes, and studied every centimetre of her face, trying to detect the most discernible of movements. He could have sworn he saw her mouth turn up slightly at the corners; then, she closed her eyes again. He didn't want to startle Maisie by shouting for a nurse, or leave her side to fetch someone.

He whispered, 'I love you Margarita. Come back to us please.' He wanted a nurse to come now, but didn't want to take his eyes of Maisie in case he missed something. He had to tell someone; he hadn't imagined it. He quickly ran to the door, whilst still looking toward the bed, and called, 'she opened her eyes! Nurse … nurse please come.' A few people were shocked at this large gentleman gesticulating wildly and shouting from the door of the ward.

By the time the nurse arrived, Sox was back at Maisie's bedside, not taking his eyes off her as he recounted what he had seen. The nurse checked all of the monitoring equipment and agreed there was a change in Maisie's appearance. The doctor was called, and arrangements were made for a brain scan to detect any cerebral changes. Sox was thrilled at this development, however recalled the hours just before his wife died; she had a few moments of lucidity, where she opened her eyes and looked into his with the hint of a smile. She was at peace; she was telling him goodbye. He discovered afterwards this often happens when a loved one is near death; they can experience a brief temporary phase of mental clarity. Sox hoped with all his heart this was not Maisie's final, fond farewell.

He held her hand and whispered close to her, 'I'm here, I'm here for you, Margarita, my beautiful pearl.'

Chapter 33

Maisie stirred, in between sleep and wakefulness. She relaxed each bone, muscle, tendon and fibre in her body, sinking into the soft, padded white chaise-long; it was like floating on a cloud. She looked down toward her feet, and wriggled her toes; the silver toe rings adorning her feet sparkled in the bright sunlight that was streaming through the open balcony doors. The heat of the day was beginning to rise. The featherlight filigree gold anklet caught her eye too, glinting with studded coloured gems around the edge. She regarded the coloured dots on the skin around her ankle, where the sun projected through the gems.

Maisie smoothed her white toga dress with her hands. She vaguely recalled buying it at the busy agora. She loved the bustling marketplace with stall-holders peddling their wares, but today, she enjoyed the peace of her white room. Her toga felt different somehow, like gossamer, draped around her body keeping her cool.

Glancing around the room, Maisie saw the four wide terracotta urns in each corner. They all held a two-metre sapling tree with reflective silver trunks. Their slender branches were bursting with small triangular shaped leaves; their canopies shimmered in the hazy heat. One tree had light golden yellow leaves; another had bright glossy green leaves, the next, burnt orange leaves, and the last, had dark bronze leaves. Maisie wondered, if she had been here for four seasons?

DESTINATION MAISIE

It was time to get up. She had only to think about sitting, and her upper body raised without effort. She thought about standing, and her body responded, floating upright. She glided toward the ornate mirror on the wall, silently with each step. It was like walking across a perfectly flat, smooth ice rink, yet it warmed the soles of her feet. She looked in the mirror, a thirty-year-old Maisie was reflected back. She was serene and content as she headed for the balcony.

The cobalt blue gauze-like drapes were fluttering in the breeze. The vista from the elevated balcony was magnificent. The azure sea rippling toward the distant horizon met the celestial blue, cloudless sky. All was calm. Drifting back toward her cloud-like seat, she enjoyed looking at the colourful mosaic floor. The repeating square swirling pattern of white, turquoise and dark sea-green glass tiles stretched out before her like waves. She lay down and closed her eyes, enjoying the warm breeze from the balcony, which lightly brushed her face. Her visitors would arrive soon.

The double doors opened gently, without a sound, and six women with a young girl silently entered the room. Maisie greeted them with telepathic words; she didn't need to speak; none of them did. All she had to do was think about what she wanted to say, and they intuitively understood. The women replied in the same way; Maisie absorbed all of their thoughts.

The oldest woman, who had a calm, serene expression on her face, sat next to Maisie. The young girl, not much more than a child, sat on her other side. Her peach-like skin was soft, quite dreamy, and her golden hair fell around her shoulders in tousled tresses.

The other women left the room and returned soon afterwards, holding trays of food; amphoras brimming with wine, a large empty bowl, water jugs and squares of muslin cloths. Platters of bright citrus fruits, purple and green grapes, olives, bowls of yoghurt, oils, and fresh bread were placed on a table.

Two of the women tipped drops of golden oil, and a dark

viscous fluid from ampules into the bowl, then poured in warm water from the jugs. They dipped muslin cloths into the water and began sweeping the calming elixir down Maisie's arms and legs, gently wiping her hands and feet. She turned so they could anoint her back and shoulders with the lightest of touches. It was refreshing, yet simultaneously calming. The bowl was removed, and the women sat around Maisie, continuing their telepathic conversations. The older woman leant over to Maisie, embraced her lovingly, kissed her forehead, and Maisie knew she wanted her to leave this white room.

Two men walked into the room, the older man, dressed in a long robe, replaced the older woman at Maisie's side. He held her hand, kissed her cheek and she knew he also wanted her to leave this place soon. But she didn't want to go anywhere, she was at peace. She realised her visitors had to leave, and the young girl did not want to go, and looked sad. Maisie embraced her and felt the warm, downy skin brush her cheek. The girl skipped out of the room, holding hands with the older woman.

Only the handsome bearded man remained. They smiled at each other; they did not need to speak; the telepathy was strong between them. As they touched and embraced, their bodies joined in familiar unison. Maisie wanted to stay here forever, in her content, peaceful blue and white world where there was no pain, but somehow knew she had to go back to the noisy place, with its sharp edges.

The man knew it too. He gently stroked her face, telling her it was time to come back. He held her hand, and this time she heard his voice in an echoing whisper, 'I'm here, I'm here for you, Margarita, my beautiful pearl.'

Chapter 34

The following week was hopeful, and rewarding as Maisie showed more signs of consciousness. The medics were pleased with her progress, as her responses were judged against the scale of coma recovery. Maisie had blinked a few times and opened her eyes, looking around without much recognition. There appeared to be a vacant, but definite smile when Kate's face was close to hers, and when she heard her voice. Gradual progress was being made, but Maisie, for the most part, was sleepy. There was mixed news from the brain scan; there were no indications of deterioration or swelling; and the patient may regain consciousness, however they could not determine if full functionality would be restored.

Conversations between Sox, and Kate were centred on their wishes she would return to full consciousness, or at least gain an ability to communicate. Their worst fears were if she acquired a condition similar to someone who had a severe stroke, with limited communication and physical ability. Maybe she would require permanent care. Sox vowed to spend the rest of his life caring for her, only if it was the wish of her family. However, if she should return to England, he would still want to be part of her life. There were some terribly difficult emotive conversations to be had during Kate's extended compassionate leave.

Fran arrived in Heraklion; finally, her mobile had sprung to life once she borrowed Roland's charger, and connected to the internet when she visited a local town in the area. She was distraught at the many text messages and voicemails left for her, asking to call back urgently. She was panicking, but managed to speak with her mum, who explained what had happened. Ash offered all the support and reassurance she could, saying she would stay with Fran until she got back to her mum, which she did.

Fran and Sox had a warm embrace, and he comforted her when she wept. Kate was at the hospital and would meet them there. Apart from being tense, Fran looked fit and healthy, her skin was glowing, and her hair was much shorter.

'Ash gave me a haircut,' she said noticing Sox's surprise. Fran dumped her rucksack on the floor, and took off her cargo jacket, revealing a grey T-shirt with a tree image, and the letters B.U.N.D. below in green, which Sox glanced at. Fran explained Jonah had worn similar, which she liked, so she ordered one before she left to go grape picking with Ash. It represented the German equivalent of, *Friends of the Earth*, and she repeated competently, 'Bund für Umwelt und Naturschutz Deutschland.'

Sox smiled. 'Jonah is a good guy.'

'I can't wait to see him again.' Fran's longing was visible.

Sox recounted all the details of how he found Maisie unconscious. Fran asked if her Nansie would be okay; however, Sox couldn't, with any truth, reply either way. They drove to the hospital where her mum Kate was waiting at the entrance. Excitedly, Kate spoke of the progress Maisie had made overnight, also to warn Fran not to expect too much. With her arm around her daughter's shoulders, they walked to the ward.

Before entering the room, Kate said, 'Mum has opened her eyes; she is looking around. She'll offer a, hello, which is only a small nod. You can tell she's comfortable, but she may not recognise you. It's strange because you expect her to be as she was … but she isn't. She often drifts off, but the doctor says it takes a long time for people to regain full consciousness and strength, so don't worry if she falls asleep.'

'Can't she speak or even feed herself?' asked Fran. She didn't see Sox and Kate glance at each other.

Not yet, love, but it can take a long while for things to function properly again,' reassured Kate.

Fran entered the pristine room, though it's clinical bareness was brightened up now with pictures of family, of Sox's boat and The Pallas Taverna, plus a print of their local beach. There were some trinkets, and a little jewellery on the cabinet, and her favourite ABBA songs played from a playlist. Everything possible was utilised to help trigger any deep-rooted memory to prompt cognition. Fran tried to be as normal as possible. Maisie stared blankly at her, and lifted her fingers.

'That's her signal to hold her hand,' said Sox, beaming at the miraculous development Maisie had achieved these last few days. Fran held her hand and began to talk, stuttering and embarrassed at first, forgetting not to ask questions, and blushed when she asked if Maisie remembered Jonah or Ash, to a non-response.

Sox filled the gap, 'I'm sure she will recall events as time goes on.' At least, he hoped.

The indiscernible Maisie smile was on her lips when she heard Sox's deep resonating tones around the room.

Fran continued to tell a story. She told her Nansie about the farm, about the back-breaking work. Staying in the bunks at the back of the farmhouse, having to use the outside shower, nothing more than a bucket on a plinth you tipped over your head. She told Nansie about the journey with the ol' geezer, and about the wake, and the cute baby chicks, and how, during the night, living on the farm, some random donkey decided to bray and wake everyone up.

'What with the chirping, hee-hawing, and the bloody cock-a-doodle-doing at the crack of dawn, I haven't slept properly for weeks. One time, a huge rooster decided to leap in through the open window onto Ash's bunk; she freaked out until Milo, grabbed it by the legs, swung it around his head and flung it back out of the window, with an almighty skwark. No-one even mentioned it, we all just drifted back off to sleep,' recounted Fran, who grinned at the memories.

Kate and Sox enjoyed the new vibrant voice in the room, so they left Fran to entertain her grandma, for a coffee break. Before they left the room Fran said, 'Mum, I think she squeezed my hand!'

Fran spoke to her grandma of the beekeeper and explained how wonderful bees are; she reminded Nansie of when they went to the farm. Fran noticed Maisie's eyes dropping, and realised she had fallen asleep. The clicks and beeps of the monitoring machines continued as her grandma's chest rose and fell calmly. Fran joined her mum and Sox in the hospital canteen.

Sox said gently, 'she'll be tired from all of your exciting tales. Me and your mum have thoroughly enjoyed hearing about your adventures too.'

'I'll say, you've got me worn out,' added Kate. 'They'll be coming to bathe her shortly, so let's go for some food.'

Fran hugged her Mum; yes, she did look really fatigued; it can't be easy seeing her own mother lying half-awake in a hospital bed surrounded by machines.

Fran was added to the hospital visiting rota, and completed some shifts at The Pallas too, as the tourist season was slowing down by the end of September.

'Are you okay to stay with Nansie for a few hours today, Fran?' asked Kate. 'I need to talk with Sox about where we go with mum's care, you know, back home or here.'

Kate was devastated; she truly thought the last several days would have roused Maisie into some semblance of recognition or cognition; but apart from a little more physical progress, over three weeks in hospital, it didn't seem much. 'I have to return to work soon, I'll need an interview to ask if I can take extended leave on compassionate grounds, as I think it has to go to a panel or something. Anyway …' Kate trailed off.

'Yes, of course,' Fran said as she tucked into some nut and

honey drizzled pastries for breakfast with a strong coffee at The Pallas. Often Fran recognised the deep, distressing sadness inside, shared with her mum and Sox. They tried to be positive that her Nansie would fully recover, but no-one knew if she would. They had to consider she may never be herself again, and her life may be compromised forever.

Sox drove Fran to the hospital; it was routine when she went into Maisie's familiar room. Fran was used to breezing in now, settling in, holding her hand, and telling her all about what was going on, and the telephone conversations she had with Jonah.

'So, Nansie, Jonah is going to ring me while I'm here; I hope that's ok with you, because it's the only time he's free.' Remembering she wouldn't get an answer, she smiled directly at her and said, 'I'm sure you don't mind, it was your idea I call him in the first place.'

There were moments when there were glimmers of recognition. Fran had now indulged in her newly-found passion for all things natural, and went on a tirade of information to a sleepy Maisie.

'I watched a David Attenborough program at home. Remember I told you about the beekeeper?' Fran was used to not getting answers and continued on. 'Bees are really intelligent. Sorry if I'm repeating stories here; I hope you're not bored out of your brain. Anyway ... Mr Attenborough described how bees tell their colony where the best flowers are for nectar. A bee returns to the hive, climbs on top of another bee, and vibrates to get attention. When they have an audience, they do a, waggle dance. It's so cute.' Fran stood and waggled her hips.

Mr Attenborough explained, 'the waggle dance is the bee communicating directions in relation to the position of the sun. The longer the waggle dance, the further away the flowers.'

Fran was on a roll, highly animated. 'Also, Nansie, did you know trees can speak to each other, well, not exactly speak. They give off scents called tannins to other trees beside them, and communicate through fungus lines beneath the ground to tell them they have an infestation, so all the other trees can try and defend themselves by producing their own chemicals to ward them off. It's called the Wood Wide Web ... isn't that amazing?

'There's this too ... and this is brilliant, Nansie. Jonah told me, that many years ago in history, I think it was 1970, someone recorded the first whale song and made it into a record. You remember those old fashioned black discs you and grandad had, like CDs but massive ... erm, vinyl. Anyway, when people heard the whales singing, there was a lot of sympathy for them, which hadn't been realised beforehand, and it helped with the, *Save the Whale*, campaign. A fourteen-year-old girl in California started printing t-shirts, and the campaign took off.'

Fran let up. She was silent for a few moments. She sighed, wistfully announcing, 'nature is so amazing.'

Maisie was fortunately already semi-comatose, as Fran's nature commentary would've been enough to put her into one.

Fran's phone rang, which halted her musings. Maisie turned at the sound; she was responding to a few more noises. During the call, Fran noticed that Maisie had drifted off to sleep again, so she took the chair over to the window to chat with Jonah. Their telephone chats were loving, and full of intimacy. Now that Jonah knew Fran intended to take their relationship to another level, he would become quite animated and tell her of the romantic and physical things he would like them to do together.

Fran found it deliciously tempting, and she often imagined how it would be, as she self-satisfied and soothed herself at nights thinking about him; about his touch when they were swimming and the near miss on the beach; the anticipation was like a delicious torture. She took her phone off the speaker settings when the conversation became personal. She wasn't sure if her Nansie could listen, or understand what was said, but she wanted to make sure she didn't inadvertently overhear.

Once the conversation finished and Fran delighted at crossing another day off until they could meet up, she noticed Maisie was sleeping soundly, so she went off to get a coffee. Sox would be here soon to take over the next shift. Fran was back at the bedside looking at her phone to check what time Sox was due. They had a well-coordinated approach of sharing information, when she heard a faint, *'yassou.'* She looked up expecting to see one of the nurses popping their head around the door, as they often checked in. There was no-one there. In the pristine silence, Fran turned and Maisie was looking straight at her, and this time, there was a definite trace of a smile.

Fran leant over the side of the bed; she held Maisie's hand and said softly, 'Nansie, can you hear me? Did you speak?'

An imperceptible nod. Fran didn't want to alarm Maisie by yelling and didn't want to leave her side, or do the wrong thing, but she must tell someone.

Wait there Nansie. She ran to the door, and down the corridor, 'she's talking, my Nansie, she's talking. Can somebody come, please!'

A nurse arrived, and Fran was already back at Maisie's bedside; she turned and said to the nurse, 'she spoke, she said yassou, she's going to be alright.'

Maisie had closed her eyes again, and the nurse busied about with readings and instructed Fran to keep talking slowly and steadily.

'I heard you, Nansie, didn't I? I didn't imagine it, did I? Can you say it again … please?'

Fran's soft voice must have reached into Maisie's consciousness; she turned her head, still with eyes closed, and nodded. Fran turned to the nurse and said with joy, 'I told you she spoke, she can understand me, she's going to be alright.'

Fran called her mum, and they were on their way. By the time Kate and Sox arrived, Maisie was becoming more animated; when Fran asked if she knew her, Maisie gave a slight nod and said, 'Fran.' Fran and Kate burst into tears; she was coming back to them. Sox appeared to have a serious expression, as if he didn't dare believe it, only to be disappointed again.

Kate sat on the bed. 'Mum, do you know who I am?'

With a croaky, slow drawl, Maisie said, 'Kate.' She sighed, looked beyond Kate, and said with a breathy effort, 'Sox.' Then she drifted into dreamland. Six fluorescent yellow, and black bees floated into the room, and the little girl with the long golden hair held out her arms. The bees landed on her hand, and began a synchronised dance; which the girl mirrored, wiggling her hips. She swayed her arms, and tip-toed with grace like a ballerina. The dance finished, and the bees lifted from the girl's hand into the air and flew back out into the blue sky. Maisie felt a soft peach-like cheek against hers, and a gentle kiss.

Chapter 35

A month passed by, Fran had returned to her work on the farm with Ash, and Kate returned home, leaving her mother in the secure care of Sox and his wonderful, kind family; they did everything for her. Maisie had been discharged from hospital and received intensive physiotherapy and speech therapy, and her vocal ability was more or less restored. The odd random word, phrase, and expression, emerged in hybrid Anglo-Greek. Physically, she was weak, however was determined to complete her communication, and physical strengthening exercises with vigour and commitment.

Maisie also received mental health support and was monitored for depression and anxiety. She was offered medication and refused, suggesting she preferred to work things through for herself, rather than rely on chemical inducement, but would keep her options open. She had a clearer image of who she was now, and where she wanted to be; and that was in Crete, with Sox. They would plan a trip to Manchester when she was strong enough; Christmas was mooted.

Maisie indicated to Sox she worried about how much all of her care may cost, as there was not a comparable National Health Service in Crete. He waved his hand; it wasn't important to him. He was overjoyed his Margarita had returned to him and back at the villa. Stefanos was managing The Pallas, and Maisie had her first short trip on the boat, feeling at peace. She confirmed to

Sox she hadn't wanted to keep in touch with Cora, and had firmly wedged the stopper permanently back in that particular Pandora's Jar.

Maisie's humour returned, and they had many enjoyable evenings when she would get her English and Greek words mixed up, often losing her thread, using the wrong term for objects, transposing words like, *'donkey'* for, *'door key'* and once called her sunglasses, *'my dark-eye-covers,'* indicating circles around her eyes, much to Sox's amusement.

Every odd word she uttered for inanimate objects, was adopted, along with accompanying hand gestures until they became embedded as a new vocabulary. Sometimes Maisie became frustrated, when she realised her recall of words wasn't there; however, tried to make a joke of it. She was becoming physically stronger, though Sox wouldn't let her swim alone now, since she described the incident after she was affected by the sleeping pills. It was the last thing she recalled.

'I really did not realise the effects of the pills would be that strong.' She repeated her often-used apology, 'I'm so sorry, so sorry I scared everyone. It was never my intention to … to … do anything serious.'

Maisie often looked ashamed and dejected that her inadvertent actions had caused so much pain to those she loved. It frightened her at first to consider she may not be here at all, but in many ways, she felt calmer; she was here, and there was a reason for that. It was as if the experience grounded her into where she was, and, most of all, who she was. She began life sixty years ago as abandoned Maisie Florence Simpson and was now Maisie McLaine, living her life in her rightful place with the second man she had ever loved in her life.

One morning, almost two months since Maisie's hospitalisation, Sox prepared a last breakfast at The Pallas, before closing down for the winter. He and Maisie were well wrapped up, insulated from October's coolness. Maisie liked to visit the beach most days and had begun writing her memoirs; it was good therapy for her to consider the difficult and wonderful events that had happened to her, and the people she loved.

Sox interrupted her thoughts as they walked along the beach, 'by the way, we have a visitor.' He nodded behind them.

Maisie turned, 'oh?' There was Fran walking toward them. She broke into a run, arms wide open.

'Surprise, Nansie! Yassou, Sox!' She launched herself at them, and they enjoyed a communal hug.

Ash was on her way back to Australia; they had finished their work at the farm, and Fran would be leaving for Köln soon to meet with Jonah.

'You look so different,' said Maisie, 'I like your hair shorter, it's gorgeous. Ah, my baby, how are you humpty?'

Fran looked mystified. Sox guffawed, as Maisie shook her head and shrugged. 'Honey! I mean honey, not humpty, for goodness sake!' Maisie said in frustration.

Fran looked at Sox, 'oh … this … is … hilarious, does it happen often?'

He nodded gravely, 'yes, often.' Then broke into a huge grin. 'The first few letters are usually accurate, or you have the beginning of one word and the end of another. It's good for my English, like living with a live crossword puzzle.'

Maisie thumped his arm. 'He thinks it's hilarious.'

'It is good to laugh though, eh, Nansie?'

'Absolutely. Come on, let's get back to the restaurant and tell me about your adventures with Ash.'

Fran and Maisie were chatting in The Pallas. The shutters were half-closed in defence of the cold breeze, and chinks of light filtered through. It made for such a cosy scene, feeling surprisingly small, without the extensive outdoor seating in the high summer months. Chairs and tables were stacked away until heat and brightness necessitated a return to their prime position.

Sox had switched the fairy lights on, and a blow heater was

nicely warming up the place. He brought over two hot chocolate drinks, gave Maisie a peck on the top of her head, and headed for the office.

'Just finishing the paperwork for the season and sending it to the accountant.' He rubbed his hands together. 'We've had a good summer, Margarita.' Sox walked into the small office behind the bar, and soft acoustic guitar music emanated from the speaker system.

Maisie said, 'he's a great business man, he's got a stake in Susanna's bar, and his sister's beauty spa too, so he's thinking of giving over management here to Stefanos. Said he'd like to do boat trips next summer for small groups, fishing and snorkelling, not the drunken tourist shenanigans, but folk who really want to appreciate the history and culture of island life.'

Fran said, 'it's fantastic here, it really is. I never dreamed I'd settle in a place other than England, but I feel so different now. There's a big wide world out there. I've met so many great people, and I've learnt loads of Greek swear words too, always useful.'

She giggled, then said seriously. 'I've really had a taste of what it's like to be a migrant worker; in a bar, cleaning up after people, serving, washing glasses, and fruit picking on a farm, also struggling to be understood in a strange place with a different language. I've felt real hunger at times when me and Ash were travelling, as we didn't want to spend too much money, to make it last. It's taught me a life lesson, to have respect for every bar worker, server, and cleaner, I have met, and will meet in the future. I've been that girl, and I know disrespect when I see it.'

Maisie nodded. 'This trip has really opened your eyes, I guess.'

'As for you, Nansie. I now understand bravery.' Fran was contemplative.

'Bravery?'

'I think you were terrified, remember, in that hotel bedroom in Florence, and how the little beds reminded you of something from your past. Then we met, *Sister Act,* those nuns on the train. I can't bear to think of you as a little girl going through all sorts of changes, and never really knowing where you should fit in.'

'Those nuns could be cruel,' said Maisie quietly. There was a long pause in the conversation.

Fran continued, 'you gave me great advice about Liam too. You knew I'd be tied into a relationship and a life where I'd never be fulfilled, happy, and free. You were right about Jonah, and I was awful to you.'

'I had no right—'

'You were absolutely right.' Fran was steadfast. 'That took bravery too, to call it out.'

'Alcohol and stupidity more like it, I could've lost you forever.'

'That would never happen. I really tried with Liam, but ...' there was melancholy in Fran's expression.

'It's going okay with Jonah?' asked Maisie.

Fran replied, 'yea, he's into climate activism in an organised and non-violent way.' Fran paused, searching for the right expression, then decided on, 'and he's as hot as hell too, can't wait to be with him ... in three days' time.'

The two women smiled. Maisie said, 'so you're going to save the planet, and enjoy yourself while you do it.'

Fran nodded enthusiastically with thoughts of a thrilling life ahead. Maisie enjoyed the sheer exuberance of her granddaughter's demeanour. They sat in silence, sipping their hot, sweet drinks.

After several minutes, Fran asked, 'could you hear anything, Nansie, when you were in the hospital bed, when we were talking to you?'

'Sort of, but it was like dreaming. I remember vaguely being in a beautiful white room, dressed in a toga, looking at silver birch trees. My family visited, I think, but we were in ancient Greece, and there were dancing bees too. In my confusion, I guess lots of fantasy was mixed in with real life. I don't recall the medical intervention, thank goodness, but something may have been going on in here, I guess.' Maisie tapped her temple. 'I feel ... somehow, that

I'm a whole person now. I know about the missing pieces in my life jigsaw. I'm getting there, with the help of the old goat.' Her eyes flicked toward the office.

'You love him really.'

'Yes, I do, and to think I would never have met him if *you* hadn't dragged me out here.'

'Whaat?' Fran noticed Maisie's sheepish grin. 'You weren't much fun to begin with, if I'm honest. That night in the hotel in Florence, I was ready to give it all up.'

'Why, because you had to wash your granny's knickers in the sink?'

'Oh yeah, that was a joy.' Fran rolled her eyes.

'I'm pleased you persevered, honey.' Maisie reached over and patted Fran's forearm resting on the table, then held her hand.

'We've had quite the journey. Everything that happened, you guided us through it, and you're so young. You took the lead, and I stood back; I didn't realise until much later the strain you must have been under to get things right, but you never gave up on anything. I've met new people here, tried new things. I didn't have the confidence before, always had Jimmy, or mum by my side, but once they were gone, I was lost. You've really helped me to be more open and welcoming of people. I'm not scared anymore.'

Fran leaned across to hug Maisie. 'Well, I guess we achieved what we intended.'

'We certainly have.'

The two women looked with knowing expressions and carried on sipping their drinks. The sound of a vehicle engine slowed to silence, as a car pulled up outside.

Sox popped his head out of the office door, 'Fran!' He nodded toward the restaurant entrance.

The women leaned toward the door to get a better view. A tall, slim, tousled-haired young man, wearing jeans, and a grey sweatshirt with a tree and German writing on it, was sauntering toward them, with a smile on his face.

Fran nearly dropped her cup on the table, 'Jonah! What … what on earth are you doing here?' She ran up to him, and as they embraced, Maisie looked at Sox, who gave her a wink and the biggest grin he could muster. Maisie smiled. Maisie McLaine truly had reached her destination.

Acknowledgements

First of all my heartfelt gratitude to my sister Valerie, and my good friends June and Diane, I can't thank you enough for your love, insight and unwavering support, I would not be a writer without you. To my wonderful sons, Daniel and Joel, always an inspiration to me. Thank you both for supporting me in my endeavours to become a writer, you mean the world to me. I thank my patient husband John, for your encouragement, and creating that amazing spreadsheet which kept my writing on track. I am grateful to the team involved in preparing Destination Maisie for publication, with special thanks to Vidya, for her guidance, and professionalism.

I will take the opportunity to write a little about the initial concept of Destination Maisie, and with that, give grateful thanks to all the women and men in my family who exist now, and those who've gone before.

My Grandma, Mary Frances Holmes was born on 15th August 1911 in Queen Charlotte's Lying-in Hospital in Marylebone. Though I have fictionalised the description of the hospital, the following quote is from an archived record entitled, A History of Queen Charlotte's Hospital. It indicates the hospital assisted the, 'once fallen' which is interpreted as, a first pregnancy.

'To endeavour to rescue those who have once fallen, to aid them in obtaining situations, and to assist them in placing their children out to nurse.'

Mary Frances' mother, my great grandma, is noted as Helen Holmes on the birth certificate, but my diligent ancestral research discovered her name was in fact, Ellen. I wonder, was the family using a pseudonym purposefully? Maybe the registrar recorded 'Helen' mistakenly? Ellen could easily be misconstrued as Helen, with the dropped 'H' northern English pronunciation. I'll never know. Amazingly, I randomly chose the name Ellen for Maisie's mother in this story before I knew that detail … kismet! Ellen was a draper's assistant originally from Staffordshire, who at nineteen, gave birth to my grandma. Unmarried Ellen was expected to give up her baby daughter. The identity of my great-grandfather remains a mystery.

Little is known, or recalled from my grandma's early life, but that she was brought up in an orphanage by nuns. She chose Frances as her first name, not Mary, and described herself latterly as a lapsed catholic. I have used her words, *'those nuns could be cruel,'* which she once said to me, with pained expression. Frances did make her way to Manchester, aged seventeen to live with her mum, Ellen, who had four more daughters by then. Fictitious parallels at play here, but I do wonder how a teenage Frances made her way from London to Manchester in the late 1920s. I wish I'd asked her.

I am sincerely happy Frances reached adulthood, with her four sisters, my great aunts; Kathleen, Jessie, Alma, and Nina. I have fond early memories of meeting them. Frances married Jim, they lived in Manchester, and had three children, one of whom is my mother Florence. This story celebrates mothers, daughters and sisters, and I have dedicated, Destination Maisie, to my loving and compassionate Mam, who was quite the fashionista in her day. I only wish she was here to read it.

With sadness I write that my great gran Ellen died at the age of forty-four from pulmonary tuberculosis, in a sanitorium in 1936. Her death was six days before Frances' twenty fifth birthday. At least they shared eight years together. Ellen's life, like many other, 'fallen women' I hope can be honoured and respected in the pages of this book. Without them, some of us wouldn't exist.

Finally to joyful matters. Last, and very much not least, to you lovely readers. I am eternally grateful and incredibly thrilled you chose to read this book. With all my heart, *thank you*! I do hope you have enjoyed Maisie's journey, as much as I enjoyed sending her on the way to finally reaching you, her true destination.

About the Author

Mel was born and bred in Newcastle, the second of four children, and hails from a large extended family. She is married with two adult sons. She spent most of her career in Children's Social Care. When she is not writing, you will find Mel socialising with friends and family on Newcastle's Quayside, taking walks along the stunning north-east coastline, and has been known to take a dip in the North Sea! Say hello to Mel and find details of her books on her website at; melfrances.co.uk.

THE LETTER FROM ITALY – *A Broken Bond in a Broken World.* Hannah and Verna were the best of friends, but their friendship fractures when one accuses the other's husband of infidelity. The timing couldn't be worse, he's stranded in Italy during the pandemic, but is he hiding secrets? Tensions rise, harsh words are spoken, and their friendship bond is broken, leaving them estranged and bitter. Then, a letter arrives, not just any letter, it's a revelation. As the truth unfolds, both women must confront the fragile nature of trust. How one moment can erase everything, and how one letter from abroad can tell a different story. Can they reconcile? Or is the damage too deep?

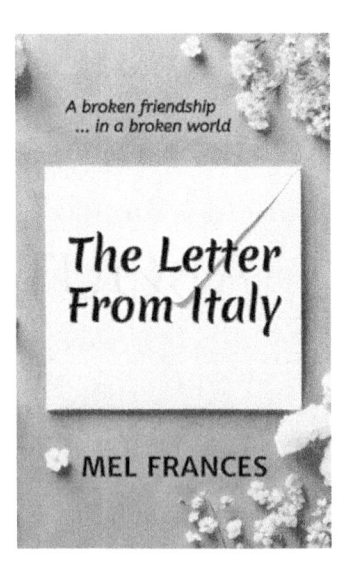

THE IMPROBABLE THREE – *One death, three strangers, and a secret.* Set in the heart of Newcastle City, journalist Maia Hewson navigates a new career, a tumultuous love-life, and a ten-year-old secret that threatens to unravel her world. When teenage sweetheart, Tom, meets a tragic end, Maia is drawn into the dangerous world of narcotics and child abuse. Together with two of Tom's friends from a children's home; the audacious Aimee, and Jordan, whose background led to addiction and homelessness, they discover a sinister figure with a twisted past stretching back decades to the 1990s. The improbable allies must gather evidence, but what will each of them risk to bring him to justice?

Printed in Great Britain
by Amazon